death & peaches

13 Sweet and Sour Short Stories

Jack Kardiac

Mills Creative Minds

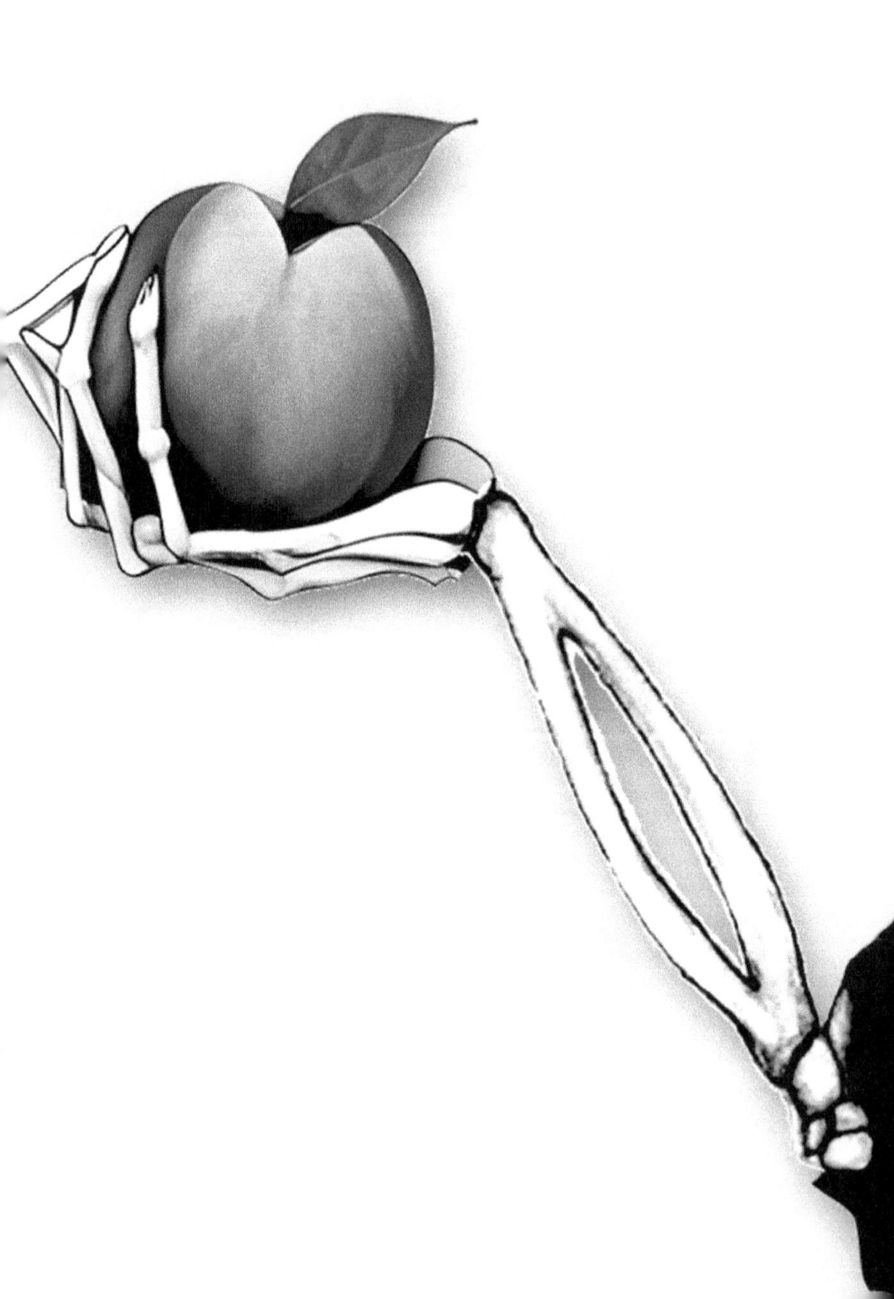

☠ + 🍑

Death & Peaches is dedicated to:

• My patient and adoring fans
(Well, patient, at least…)

• Bryce Nickisch
*You had no idea when you gave me a stack of your comic books
as a kid that I would be so heavily influenced. Thank you for
fueling the fire inside me with heroes and monsters,
superpowers, and ample examples of crisp, concise dialogue.
I'm forever in your debt.*

• Chase Claussen
*I've yet to meet such an obsessed, dedicated fan
stalking my every story, and I'm glad it's you.
Never change.*

• The letter K

contents

introduction

First, my apologies. I wrote this collection of short stories many, many years ago (I won't say how many because it's depressing). Suffice it to say, it shouldn't have taken this long to publish Death & Peaches, and I offer you, the reader, my sincere apology.

I won't try to explain it all away and justify the delay or any of that, but I am grateful for your patience. Good things come to those who wait? Sure, let's go with that.

Just like with Southwest Airlines, you have a lot of choices when it comes to entertaining yourself in your spare time. Please know that I'm forever thankful for your choosing to spend it with me. Now let's get to it!

- Jack Kardiac

Life's jagged paths of stones and weeds,
    And yet we trudge forth, through thick brambled reeds,
    Seeking a solace, relief, some peace
    From a life that is constant, that sorrows might cease.

Yet joys and wonders are oft found between,
    Smoothing a pathway through all unforeseen,
    Friends round tables, short stories spun,
    Meals of merry, united as one.

With humor and wisdom, we must thus employ
    To savor this life! Hands clasping to joy!
    And when the light fades with the sun's final set,
    We'll bury all worries (alongside regret).

So savor the flavor, these layers of life,
    The skin the sun kissed, the tartness of strife,
    Mingled in the mix of a dish served too cold,
    For Death, he befriends all souls... young and old.

Now go, live and love, for we must concede this:
    Life remains but a bowl of Death & Peaches.

- Anonymous

Death & Peaches

DRAG IN A BAG

JACK KARDIAC

drag in a bag

MR. WO'S breath was short and labored as he clutched the black satchel tighter in his left hand, carefully inserting the key into the worn lock with the other. He felt for the tactile *click*, testing the door once more to ensure it was secure. In the six years he had owned and operated his Asian collectibles shop, the Mei Long, he'd never once been burglarized. Tonight was not the night to become lax about it, not while he was still in what some would call the "sketchy" area of town.

He called it Chinatown, and he called it home. It was as close to an authentic Chinese atmosphere as could be expected in suburban Indiana, so he couldn't complain. Between him and the various salons, restaurants and pawn shops sporadically lining the streets, Wo was more than comfortable with what the area had to offer.

Returning the key to his pocket, Wo turned and scanned the street. Twilight was quickly fading into the night's darkening sky, the autumn air crisp and clear, alive with the faint hint of a cold snap to come. He smiled. Wo loved this time of year, this time of night. It made him feel alive inside.

Despite his youthful outlook, the cracking of his joints when he shuffled down the street quickly reminded him of his true age. He glanced once more at the velvet bag in his hand, cinching the red rope around the top a bit tighter. Sighing deeply, he left the alcove of his store entrance and walked down the sidewalk. Wo shifted his weight to one side as he moved forward to lessen the growing ache in his hip. It was definitely going to rain soon, he could feel it.

Less than twenty steps later he slowed as he approached the old man sitting at the bottom of some apartment steps. Dressed in a ragged, brown corduroy jacket with dirty, faded jeans, the man's dark glasses covered eyes that Wo knew were clouded over. At his feet lay a plastic container filled with mixed change and a few crumpled bills.

The sign at his feet was hand-written in large block letters:

IT'S A BEAUTIFUL DAY AND I CAN'T EVEN SEE IT.

Wo dug around in his pocket for change. "Evening, Lancelot," he said. "New sign?"

The man's real name was Lance Jones, but he'd insisted Wo call him Lancelot since they first met. He liked thinking of him as a knight, despite his blindness.

Lancelot craned his head toward Wo's voice and grinned warmly. "Well hey there, Mr. Wo! And a good evening to *you!*" he said. "Yes, indeed. Some lady walked by this morning and said she wanted to give me an 'upgrade.'"

"Oh yes?"

"Yeah, but turns out she just meant a new sign. Not exactly the kinda upgrade I was hoping for, you know what I'm sayin'?" He forced his mouth into an exaggerated frown and chuckled, shaking his head in mock disappointment.

Wo laughed. "Oh, you a nasty old man, aren't you?"

"Nah, I'm just joshin' wit ya," the man laughed, waving a hand in the air. "Lord knows I ain't ready to settle down, take myself off the market just yet."

"Of course not."

"She *did* do a great job on the sign, though. People been droppin' coins left an' right today. Even bills! It's crazy!"

"She tell you what it says?" Wo leaned closer and dropped a handful of coins into the container.

"She did. An' she's right. It *is* a beautiful day!" Lancelot held up a finger and pointed it in Wo's direction. "Now, don't you be giving me no yuan in there, man," he chided.

"You so racist," Wo said, a thin smile forming across his lips.

"Me so *practical*, you mean. You ever seen a blind man try to convert a bag of change at a bank? Man, it'd make you wanna cry your eyes out."

"I will keep that in mind. And no, you get no yuan from me today, Mr. Picky."

"No? Well, has anyone told you they loved you today? 'Cause I do."

Wo laughed, shaking his head. "Hey. I go around corner, make special delivery. Going to pick up some nachos on the way back. Want some?"

"From Nacho Wong's? Across from that peach diner?"

"Where else?"

"I'm in."

Nacho Wong was an experimental restaurant around the corner that opened up a little over six months earlier. Sporting a fusion menu that offered some of the finest, most creative Mexican and Asian combinations known to man, Mr. Wo had fully expected it to fail within the first month or two. Instead it had flourished, primarily due to the late hours and the constant infusion of college crowds who relished the idea of cheap, fun food.

"Okay, then," Wo said as he walked away. "See you in half hour, yes?"

"You know it. I'll be right here, enjoyin' the evening breeze at the end of this beautiful day that I can't see," Lancelot said, giving him a thumbs up.

Wo laughed. "Okay. See you later, sir."

"Later, gator."

Wo walked away remembering when they were younger what a tomcat Lance had been. His inability to see had no effect on his charm, and he'd always find and hit on the prettiest girl in whatever bar or venue they happened to be at that evening. Wo reasoned the man could probably still get women to fawn over him, if the guy ever bothered to go out.

But they weren't young and stupid anymore, and those days were far behind them. Now they considered themselves lucky if a day went by without worrying about their aching joints, or worse — *falling* and not being able to get up. Who would have thought they'd be afraid of gravity when they reached this age? It was crazy.

Wo had only walked ten feet down the sidewalk when he noticed a man exit the pawn shop ahead of him. Dressed in black slacks and a black, button-up long sleeve shirt, he walked over to the light pole and leaned against it, crossing his arms and glancing over at him. He flashed him a smile and nodded.

Wo frowned and stopped walking. He glanced back at Lancelot, then down at the satchel held tightly in his grip and back up again. The man continued to watch him, smiling, unmoving.

Some would say Wo was being paranoid, but he didn't care for this stranger's presence or persistent interest. Especially tonight, of all nights.

He checked the street for oncoming traffic. It was clear. One of the little-known perks of owning a business on a dead-end street — you avoided the constant noise and hustle of speeding cars or other vehicles. Nobody went down this street unless they either lived here or had to make a delivery.

Wo carefully stepped off the curb and was halfway across the street when he saw the four youths step out of the alley, heading in his direction. Three guys and a girl. The boy in front raised his hand, waving at him.

"Hey, man. Can you help us out?" he called, stepping ahead of the others.

He wore an oversized sweatshirt with a faded logo across the front, pants hanging low on his waist. His high-tops were loose, the shoestrings untied and flopping against his shoes with each step he took. A small hoop earring hung from his left ear, just over the tattoo of a semi-dressed woman writhing down the side of his neck.

Wo turned his head to look at the others, now

surrounding him. They appeared to be in their early twenties, although he guessed the girl looked as if she could still pass for eighteen. She wore a deep purple skirt, a blue mesh shirt over a sports bra and charcoal black, torn tights with tall black boots. Her jet-black hair had a stark blue streak cascading down one side, and under her multiple piercings and caked make-up she might have even been considered attractive. Wo didn't think she cared.

Beside her, the other boy, the largest one, had on a bright orange T-shirt with the word "CRUSH" emblazoned across his chest. His shaved head glistened in the fading sunset, and he clearly hadn't missed a meal in a few years. The man stared back at Wo with cold, dead eyes.

Wo recognized the third youth instantly.

Deng.

Deng used to drop by the shop when it first opened, fascinated by the various collectibles Wo specialized in. The only child in a troubled family, Deng had been grateful for a safe place to hang out after school, and Wo was more than glad to educate the young boy about their shared Chinese heritage.

Sadly, the boy stopped visiting after three months, and while Wo had been concerned for the child's welfare, he simply assumed that his family had moved away. Staring at the young man standing before him now, however, he wished he had been more vigilant about tracking him down.

Deng avoided eye contact with him, so it was clear to Mr. Wo that he recognized him, even after all these years. Perhaps he had even been the one to lead them here.

"Hey! Did you hear me, man?" the guy approaching him said. "We need your help." He trotted forward a few more steps until he had positioned himself between Wo and the sidewalk.

Wo fixed his eyes on him and froze, squeezing the bag tighter in his hand. He slowly moved it behind his back, out of their line of sight. He glanced back to where Lance sat on the steps, unmoving. While scrappy in his youth, he wouldn't be able to do a blessed thing. Wo was on his own.

The man in black still stood rooted to the pole up the street, watching the spectacle as if enjoying the drama unfolding before him. Wo stared at him, quietly resenting him for his ambivalence to the situation.

He pressed the velvet bag firmly against his leg, reasserting his grip against its subtle increasing weight. Wo locked eyes with the boy. "How may I help you?" he asked quietly.

"So, yeah," the boy said, smiling at him. "We...ah... we're lookin' for a good place to eat around here. Maybe some Chinese food or somethin'."

"And?"

"An' we were hoping you might be able to help us out. 'Cause... you know... you're Chinese an' all."

Wo studied the boy's face for a few seconds, calculating a response. "Yes," he finally said, nodding his head. "I can help. There are many places to eat. Won Ton Express right over there." He used his free hand to motion behind them where the bright green and yellow sign was unmistakable, even from their distance.

"Awesome. Thanks," the kid said, nodding his head. "So... ah... you have any money?"

"Money?"

"Yeah, money. See, we don't have any, an' we kinda need

it to eat, y'know?" He glanced at his friends and grinned, then looked back at Wo, extending his expectant hand.

"Are... are you *mugging* me?" Wo raised his eyebrows.

The boy laughed. "What?"

"I ask if you are mugging me."

"Naw, we ain't muggin' you. That would be... wrong..." He shook his head in mock disapproval. "Just asking if you could help us out, is all. All friends here, old man. We all friends."

Wo's frown deepened. He glanced around at the others again. The larger one nodded in agreement, even though his stony expression remained unchanged. The girl smiled. Deng looked away.

Sighing deeply, Wo switched the satchel to his right hand and dug his left into his pants pocket. He removed a handful of colorful bills and held them out. "Here," he said, offering them.

The kid glanced down and sneered. "What's this?"

"Money."

"That ain't money."

"Is too money. Is *yuan*."

"Is what?"

"Yuan. *Chinese money!* You eat at Chinese restaurant? Pay with Chinese money."

The kid frowned at him. He reached out, took the money and slipped it into his back pocket. "Thanks. But now that I think about it, we might be in the mood for somethin' more American. Like a burger." He looked over at the girl. "Whaddaya say, Sophie?"

"Rather eat a greasy burger than a bowl of fried rice," she said, looking up at the boy beside her. "Munch?"

The larger kid nodded his head in response. "Yeah, Cash," he mumbled, voice low. "Burgers an' fries sound nice."

"There, see what I mean?" said Cash, shrugging. "So thanks for the yuan, but we're kinda gonna need some cold, hard *American* cash if we're gonna eat at an American restaurant."

"Listen," Wo said. "I don't—"

"Hey!" a voice yelled from the sidewalk.

Lance stood on his apartment steps up the street. "Hey!" he yelled again, standing up and pointing a finger at them. "You kids! Ya'll leave him alone, you hear? I mean it!" His voice cracked with nervousness, and Mr. Wo could see his friend was shaking with fear.

"You shut your hole, old timer!" Cash yelled. "Or we'll shut it for you!"

"Why you little—!"

Lance reached down and fumbled around the ground for his cane, the fury building up inside him. He was blind, but he wasn't about to let some young punk disrespect him like that.

Mr. Wo frowned. Although he appreciated his friend's protest, he also knew it wasn't going to end well if Lancelot got involved. "Lance!" he called out. "It alright! I handle this, okay? Please. You stay there, okay?"

Lancelot stopped moving and frowned. "Mr. Wo, don't let these—"

"Everything okay! I promise!" Wo protested. "Please sit. I am okay. We just talking is all." He looked over at Cash and gestured up the street. "You no worry about him. He blind man. Harmless."

Wo's heart hammered in his chest. He didn't know what

he could even do if they went after Lance. In the past he could've tackled one or two of them, maybe gotten lucky and break a nose or something. Not tonight. Lance was his oldest friend, sure, but the guy was completely helpless in this situation, despite his ability to run his mouth.

Cash laughed. "Whatever. I don't care 'bout no blind dude with attitude. What I *care* about is *money*, so—"

"Yes, I think I have some... let me see..." Mr. Wo reached into his back pocket and removed a twenty-dollar bill, handing it over to Cash. He smiled and bowed, keeping his head low. "There. American money for American food. Now, eat and be blessed. Yes?" He turned to walk away when Munch grabbed him by the shirt, pulling him back.

"Munch," Deng said beside him, stepping closer. "Don't hurt him, man."

"Shut up, Deng."

"I'm just saying—"

"An' *I'm* just sayin' shut the hell up, *DENG*."

The younger boy lowered his eyes and Mr. Wo's heart sank, seeing his former friend treated with such disrespect. He took solace that Deng still cared about him, even if he was spending his time with these kids.

"Funny thing, man," Cash began. "Twenty dollars? That's not gonna cut it. Burgers are like, *super* expensive nowadays, you know? So I think we're gonna need more than... this."

"But... I can't. I have no more!"

"Then I think we might have a problem." Cash stepped closer to him. "Tell me something," he said, raising an eyebrow and pointing at Wo's hand. "If you don't got any more cash on hand, then... what's in the bag?"

The expression on Wo's face changed instantly. Up until this moment he had only been annoyed and slightly concerned about the situation slowly unfolding. At the mention of the bag, however, his eyes grew wide with alarm.

"No..." he whispered, his breath suddenly becoming more labored. He shook his head insistently. "You not want this. Come, I will take you to bank. Get more money for you there. Please..."

"Whoa, whoa, whoa... Hold on a sec. Are you offering to give us *more* money now?"

"Yes."

"*Instead* of what you got in the bag?" Cash said, eyes alight with excitement.

Wo nodded. "Yes. One hundred... no, two hundred dollar!"

"Two hundred dollars?!"

"Yes."

"You're going to just give us *two hundred dollars?*"

Wo nodded again. "Yes. But we must go now. Go to bank now, I get you money."

Cash frowned. He stared intently at Wo, then looked back at the bag. After a few seconds he smiled, his eyes wandering back up to the older man's face. "Wow. Well, that is a *very* kind offer, but I gotta say, man... you got me *real* curious now!"

"Me, too, baby," Sophie said. She shuffled from foot to foot with nervous energy. Wo watched her scratching at her arm frantically. It was easy to guess what they really needed the money for.

Cash held out his hand. "Come on, man. We just wanna see what's in the bag is all."

Mr. Wo raised the satchel to his chest, both hands wrapped around it tightly. "No! Don't do this," he protested, shaking his head. "Please! I beg you!"

Cash stared at him, unblinking. "Munch?"

Two massive, apelike arms wrapped around Mr. Wo from behind, swiftly constricting as he was lifted off his feet. Cash casually reached over and snatched the black bag, wresting it from the man's weakened grasp.

Mr. Wo cried out, reaching out for the bag before Munch dropped him back to the pavement in a heap.

"No!" he yelled. "Don't do this! Please!" He attempted to push himself up to his feet but Munch placed a firm hand on his shoulder, holding him down.

"Shut it!" Cash yelled, holding the bag out of his reach. "We just wanna see is all."

Wo glanced from the satchel to the sidewalk. Lance was sitting on his steps in frustration and defeat, no longer attempting to stop what was happening. Behind him, the man in black still stood against the pole, watching everything unfold with unnerving interest, the same fixed smile now transforming into a grin. Then he slowly raised his hand... and waved.

Wo couldn't believe what he was seeing. What kind of demented person would stand by as someone was being accosted? Much less *wave* at the victim? He looked away in disgust.

"Deng," he whispered, turning to the youth. "Run."

Deng stared down at him and turned his head toward Cash, pretending not to hear.

Cash held the bag up, shaking it. "Holy crap! I think I know what this is!" He rattled it again and grinned. "You hear that? This thing's full of some kinda coins! Gold!!"

Everyone stared back at him, saying nothing.

"What? You guys don't believe me?! Listen!"

He shook the bag more violently. Munch's face betrayed his disbelief, while both Deng and Sophie looked horrified.

Mr. Wo sank lower to the ground, shaking his head fervently as he whispered to himself, looking away from the bag.

"Hear that?" Cash said excitedly. "*Coins!*"

"S'not coins, Cash," Munch mumbled.

"What?"

"Said I don't think it's gold. I—"

"What? You deaf?" Cash snapped, holding the bag up higher. "Listen closer!" He shook the bag from side to side. Sophie's eyes grew wide, and she brought her hand up to her mouth, clearly distressed.

"Skittles," Munch said.

"What? Are you serious?"

"Yeah, man. Shake it again, you'll see."

Cash grabbed the bag with both hands and wiggled it in the air.

Munch nodded. "See? Skittles."

"You're an idiot," Cash said. "You're goin' deaf or something."

At this point Deng's face has lost almost all its color, and he looked from the bag down at Mr. Wo.

"*Lǐmiàn de lóng,*" Wo whispered to him.

Deng's eyes widened, shot over to the bag and returned to

Wo. He shook his head in disbelief, but Mr. Wo simply nodded.

"*Lóng!*" he hissed. "Run!!"

Deng ran.

"Hey! Where the hell you goin'?" Cash barked, watching the boy sprint down the street. He shook his head. *Stupid kid.* As if they wouldn't find him later. Cash had to admit, though, he'd never seen Deng move so fast. The coward was fast, he'd give him that.

"Give it to me," Sophie said quietly, holding out her hands.

"Huh?" Cash asked.

"Give me the bag!!" she yelled, lurching forward and snatching it out of Munch's hands. She backed away and cradled it carefully in her arms, angry tears streaming down her face, staring back at Cash and Munch.

"What is *wrong* with you people?!?" she hissed.

Cash and Munch exchanged glances.

"What's up with *you*?" Cash laughed.

"What's up with—" she began, then stopped herself. "What's up with *me*? How can you *say* that? You *know* that I've wanted a baby for years, and now... how could you be so cruel?!" She turned away from them and started fumbling with the red rope cinched across the top. "She can't breathe in there! Can't you hear her?!?"

Wo looked at Sophie and tears welled up in his eyes. Despite his first impression of her, it was clear she was just another lost girl, looking for someone to love.

Wo whimpered and started to cry, covering both eyes with his hands. He knelt down lower, pressing his head against the pavement. His body shook as he sobbed, shaking his head in dread of the events he knew were about to unfold.

The three teens stared down at him, bewildered.

"Think he's trippin'," Munch mumbled, shaking his head.

"A'ight. That's enough, Sophie," Cash said, holding out his hand. "Gimme the bag."

"No."

Cash looked over at her and took a step closer. "Sophie. Just stop it, k? Stop playin' games and gimme the bag. I promise, we'll split it three ways. You, me an' Munch."

Sophie's face contorted into a look of disgust, abhorred with what he was saying "You're sick! Get away from me!!" She turned to run just as Munch reached out and wrapped a meaty hand around her upper arm. She shrieked, struggling to pull free. He casually reached across with his other hand and pulled the bag away with little effort.

"*No!*" she screamed. "Stop! Stop it! Don't hurt her!!"

"Now *she's* tripping," Munch said as he handed the bag back to Cash. Sophie brought a hand up to scratch him with her nails, but Munch caught her arm. He calmly twisted both arms behind her back, clenching them together in one hand. "Open it up, already. I'm gettin' hungry."

"What? You still think it's candy?" Cash held up the bag and shook it hard.

Sophie wailed, shaking her head in defiance. "Stop it!" she yelled. "Let her out!"

Cash ignored her and started working on the knot. The bag was cinched tighter than he'd expected, and he dropped it to the ground and knelt down to release it.

Sophie screamed again and attempted to kick him, but Munch pulled her back. Her legs thrashed in the empty air before she finally gave up. She stared at the bag through blurry tears, reassuring the child inside that everything was going to be okay, that she didn't have to be afraid.

Munch stared at her, expressionless.

"Ha! Got it!" Cash said, pulling the rope free and dropping it to the ground. He looked up at Munch and smiled. "Ladies and gentlemen," he said, thrusting his hand into the bag. "Prepare to be amazed!

A second later his arm jerked lower inside the bag. Cash flinched, then yelped and yanked his hand back out. He stared at it, horrified at the sight.

His entire pinky finger was missing.

Bright red blood started to pour out from where it had once been, running down the side of his hand in rhythmic spurts.

Cash screamed, staring down at the bloody, gushing nub where his pinky used to be. Munch swore quietly and lowered Sophie to the ground, releasing her. She clamped a hand over her mouth and backed away from them, staring at the bag in confusion.

Deep growling filled the air, emanating from the satchel slumped over on the ground. Suddenly it stiffened and stood erect as a tongue of bright red flame shot upward out of its mouth, like an impossible firework display emerging from inside. Munch took a step back, shielding his eyes from the exploding light and heat.

Fire blasted into the sky above them before stopping abruptly, the flames now concealed within the dark, swirling clouds gathering overhead.

Thick, ashen smoke poured out from the mouth of the bag, blanketing the street's surface, obscuring it entirely. Wo remained hunched over on the ground, frozen, unmoving. He continued to cry quietly, his face firmly buried in his hands.

The temperature in the evening air dropped sharply, a light drizzle beginning to fall from the looming sky, dense with sudden storm clouds. The sound of falling rain was soon superseded by a faint, inexplicable sizzling. Munch looked up when he realized it wasn't coming from the drops falling on the sun-soaked pavement.

It was in the clouds above them.

The noise shifted in tone, the sizzling slowly transforming into something more distinct, something far more ominous.

Hissing.

Something hidden deep within the clouds was *hissing* at them from above.

Munch stepped forward and brought a boot down on the smoking satchel, stomping it repeatedly until the mist began to dissipate around it. He reached down and gingerly picked up the bag from the bottom, holding it upside down. He shook it hard, the folds of the material snapping in the air.

It was empty.

He held it out toward Cash with a quizzical look when they were blinded by a bright red flash from above. Munch dropped the bag and backed away, swearing and staring up at the clouds.

The hissing grew louder, and he squinted to see through the rain and the thick, smoky mist swirling over him. He was preparing to run when he saw another faint flash higher in the clouds.

"There!" he shouted, pointing to the sky. "I see something."

All three of them looked up in time to see two large, red orbs appear in the clouds, hovering high above them. The spheres pulsated for a second, growing in intensity for a moment before fading once again.

Then they blinked.

Munch felt his blood turn cold. He swore again and began backing away from the others. Recognition of what he was seeing slipped into his thoughts, and he shook his head as he watched the figure overhead silently uncoil itself before it slithered out of the sky, rapidly descending toward them.

Munch shrieked and turned to run. The dragon's massive jaws swooped downward toward him, clamping hard over his head and torso. A second later the two of them disappeared into the night sky, as if he'd never been there.

Cash and Sophie stared in silence as the thin, black and red scaled tail slithered away into the cover of the clouds. The two of them listened unwillingly to Munch's continued, muffled screams before they ended abruptly. The sizzling hisses resumed above them, and they glanced at each other, horrified and helpless.

"What..." Cash stammered. "What the hell was *that?!?*" He searched the sky for a few seconds before the pain drew his focus back to his missing finger. He started to scream again.

Sophie wrapped her arms tightly around herself and started to cry, shaking her head. She whispered every prayer she could think of, to every deity she had ever remembered learning about in school. On a normal night she would have had the presence of mind to recognize that such a scattered, shotgun prayer probably wouldn't do her any good. Tonight wasn't a normal night, and her mind was effectively fracturing at what she was witnessing.

She looked over at Wo, then Cash, clutching his bloody hand. Sophie shook her head. She stared into his eyes, now filled with pain and confusion and terror.

"We never should have opened it," she whispered to him.

Something inside of her mind urged her to run, to escape to safety, but she couldn't. Her legs were frozen, feet unwilling to move. Sophie sank to her knees, doubling over the street and throwing up everything she had inside her.

Cash was about to respond when he saw the serpentine shape of the dragon descending from the clouds further up the street. His muscles tightened as he watched the monster glide toward them, hovering over the smoky street, slithering silently behind Sophie.

For a split-second Cash considered shouting a warning. A word to help her escape the approaching attack. Instead, he grew rigid and stopped breathing, making every effort to remain as still and as silent as possible. Maybe, just maybe, he could survive this. He had seen someone do this in a movie, hadn't he? About monsters? Or was that T-rexes?

A second too late, Sophie saw the look in his eyes and spun around just as the creature's head craned sideways, engulfing her within its jaws.

Cash remained frozen, petrified. He refused his body's urgent surge to run. The gigantic reptilian body sped past him like a scaled freight train, the trailing tail narrowly missing him as it sliced through the air beside his ear like a bullet from Hell. He listened as Sophie's high-pitched wailing rose into the clouds until it, too, ended as abruptly as Munch had.

Cold drizzle pelted hard against Cash's face, but he refused to blink, terrified the monster would reemerge in a split-second of darkness. He swallowed, studying the sky and straining to hear. Aside from the soft, agonized moaning of Mr. Wo at his feet, he heard nothing from above.

He looked over at the old man. "Is this real?" he asked.

Wo said nothing.

"Is this... is this really happening?" Cash whispered, looking down at his bloody hand. Maybe he was just having a bad trip. Had he taken something and forgotten about it? He didn't remember, couldn't think straight anymore. He looked up and listened.

No hissing. No more sizzling.

Nothing.

Was it over?

Cash looked around him. The street was almost completely obscured with smoke and fog, yet he could just make out the alley they had cut through before approaching Mr. Wo. If he was fast, maybe he could make it back there. Maybe he had a chance! He knew for a fact there was a dumpster in there, a safe place he could hide in until morning. He could do this!

He stole a quick glance back at the sky. Seeing no sign of the telltale red glow, Cash sprinted toward the alley, nearly tripping over Mr. Wo in the process.

Regaining his balance, Cash stumbled over the curb and dove between the buildings, knocking over a trash can as he ran. He froze, plastering his body against the bricks as the can rattled around for a few seconds before coming to rest.

He stared at it, cursing himself silently, listening, waiting. After a few seconds, he peeked around the corner to scan the street. Aside from Mr. Wo's prone body, the crumpled satchel and the thick fog surrounding the area, it was empty. The sky, while dark and foreboding, contained no red glow, no violent flashes.

Cash exhaled deeply and turned back toward the alley. He took a step, stumbled and fell, instinctively reaching out to catch himself. His hands slapped hard on the pavement, the newly exposed, boney nub of his former pinky finger grinding painfully into the ground.

Cash screamed.

He scrambled to push himself back up to his feet, but he couldn't move his legs. His jeans had caught on something, holding him back. Reaching back to free himself, Cash's bloody hand grazed against the cold, smooth skin of the reptilian tail now wrapped snugly around his ankle.

He shrieked as the tail tightened and slowly dragged him out of the alley and into the street. Cash clawed for anything to grab hold of, his chin bouncing painfully off the ground as his body was raised higher into the air until he was suspended upside down a few feet above the ground.

"Help!" Cash yelled. "Someone help me! Please!"

Cash whimpered and stared at the street below him, then fell silent once more. Hovering directly in front of Mr. Wo was the most terrifying creature he had ever imagined. The rain did nothing to hide the pulsating red eyes, each one the size of a basketball, set deep inside a massive black head, riddled with dark red thorns. Thick tendrils of smoke escaped like sentient serpents from its nostrils, the jaws snapping open and shut repeatedly with loud *clacks*, reminding him of a broken Nutcracker puppet he'd played with as a child.

The body was entirely black, as if it had been dipped in

pitch. Inky darkness dripped off it onto the pavement in thick, slick puddles. It had no visible arms or legs, only a massive dragon's head connected to an enormous, serpentine body. Its tail slithered around him, crawling up and coiling itself around Cash's body before drawing him closer to the head.

The boy whimpered as he was spun around, the tail wrapping him tightly like chords of steel. Cash tried to yelp but his chest was too constricted, too squeezed to even breathe. His eyes began to burn as his ears popped with the pressure. Opening and closing his mouth like a fish out of water, he tried desperately to take a breath, to scream.

When it reached his neck, the tail flipped him upright and brought him closer until he and the dragon were face to face. Cash tried to look away but couldn't. He could only stare back at the eyes that now bore into his. His skin started to bubble and burn, as if subjected to the harsh, heated glare of two gigantic heat lamps.

The monster loosened its grip on him, allowing just enough space for him to draw a breath once more. Cash gulped in air, his rib cage screaming with every breath. He felt something push into his back, prodding him from behind. A second later when he heard the voice, his heart sank.

It was the sound of someone's soft, subdued crying.

Sophie's crying.

Somehow she was still alive, slowly suffocating inside the stomach of the beast.

Cash shook his head. He'd been wrong. He should have warned her. Should have stood up, waved his arms, sacrificed himself so she could get away.

He didn't.

And now they were both dead.

Cash started to cry. The serpentine coils contracted once more, squeezing him slowly. There was a quick spasm of movement behind him, a muffled moan before Sophie went silent.

He turned his head to look into the dragon's eyes, his blistering skin sizzling under its poisonous gaze. Cash shook his head, pleading. "Please," he whispered.

The dragon's head tilted slightly to the right, and for a moment Cash thought it not only understood him, but was sincerely considering his plea for mercy. It brought him closer to its grotesque face, exhaled two long puffs of smoke from its nostrils... and smiled.

Mr. Wo remained absolutely motionless.

He had fallen silent as soon as he felt the creature's presence above him. He'd heard the boy's cries for mercy, felt the tactile *clacks* of the shifting scales, listened to the few, wheezing gasps and then, mercifully... silence.

This was followed by the distinct sound of slurping as the creature noisily consumed its meal, jaws clacking and lips smacking, as if the more clamor it created the tastier the flavor became. Wo shivered. He breathed slowly, focusing on the steady, intentional rhythm of every inhale and exhale. His hands remained affixed over his eyes, palms wet from sweat and his flood of tears.

Silence.

He felt the hot gaze fall upon him, the fetid breath on the back of his neck, threatening to scald him. A large, black glob dropped to the ground beside him, seeping into the edge of his slacks and burning like acid. Still, he didn't move.

The monster chuffed at him, filling his nostrils with the sickening scent of blood and ash. Wo wanted to cough, but focused every ounce of his self-control to restrain the urge. Chest burning inside, he started counting in his head. Every time he got to twenty he started over again, repeating himself. All the while his body remained rigid, frozen on the pavement, eyes closed tightly as trickles of sweat ran down his spine.

A second later the smothering presence and pressure left, the very air itself suddenly becoming cleaner, clearer. Wo opened his mouth, quietly coughed twice, then inhaled deeply.

Keeping his eyes shut, he fumbled about on the ground, hands searching for the satchel and rope. He located the velvet rope first, and Wo carefully coiled it around his wrist as he groped around for the bag.

A few seconds later his hand brushed against the smooth, velvet skin. Wo's palm hovered over it, hesitating for a second when he felt something inside it shift beneath his touch. He inhaled deeply, reached out and gripped the lip of the bag, clenching it tightly.

He recoiled when he felt the creature shift inside. He sucked in a deep breath, clenching the bag tightly as the retreating reptile tail slid slowly, sensuously across the back of his hand. Wo shuddered and calmly shoved it back inside before squeezing the bag shut.

He wrapped the rope around it three times, carefully retying it with the intricate knot he had learned earlier that afternoon, applying the exact same method he had read about in the legends as a child.

He regretted buying the bag from the old woman who had walked into his shop an hour ago. Wo had heard the legends as a child, but he was skeptical of her insistence that the unimpressive bag contained *the* Dragon of Sheng-kai. He could never imagine dragons surviving for centuries in a satchel, so Wo had foolishly dismissed her repeated warnings, reasoning that she probably needed the money and, worst-case scenario, he could always use a new satchel.

Overpaying for a satchel was not the worst-case scenario.

This was the worst-case scenario.

The Dragon of Sheng-kai was the worst-case scenario, having been both summoned and satiated. For tonight.

Mr. Wo opened his eyes, sighing deeply.

The street was empty once more, the thick fog and dark clouds were gone, and he raised his head to stare at the clear sky, now replete with stars. He looked over at Lancelot, who remained seated on the steps where he had been a few minutes ago. The old man was shaking, and for the first time in his life, Wo was glad his friend was blind from birth, having been spared the wrath of a bloodthirsty beast. The man in black was nowhere to be seen.

Wo pushed himself to his feet and slowly walked toward Lance, holding the bag tightly in his hand. And with every step, he thought he could still hear an almost imperceptible growl emanating from somewhere deep within it.

Author's Note

I'd been looking forward to writing this story for almost two years before I finally got around to capturing it. It was inspired by the excellent flash fiction story, *Snake Eyes Allison*, written by David Cousland, which I read on the flash fiction webzine *Shotgun Honey*.

Ever since I experienced the beautiful brevity of that story, my mind started spinning about other scenarios where there might be a mysterious, forbidden bag... and what would happen if it fell into the wrong hands.

I approached this story differently than others by consciously trying to pack it as full of "dragon" keywords as possible. *Puff, Magic, Imagine Dragons...* everything I could think of (or Wikipedia suggested). My hope is the references were subtle enough that readers like you would only spot them if you were *actively* looking for them.

Either way, this story was just as much fun to write as I had anticipated, so hopefully you enjoyed reading it half as much as I loved spinning it.

LAST DANCE

LAST KARDIAC

last dance

WHEN THE BANSHEE scream of the train whistle
pierces my head like a bullet, I'm instantly woke an' mad as
hell.

I open one eye and immediately regret it. The hellfire
light spittin' out of the sun directly above blazes a path
through my socket and into my brain. I swear loudly, shutting
the lid tight.

Body's stiff, refusing to cooperate as I try to prop myself
up. So I lay there flat on my back, Lord knows where. A cold
breeze blows across my face an' my mouth tastes like dust and
death, dry as a bitch's teat. The distinctive odor of freshly
squeezed horse crap fills my nostrils, but that ain't nothin'
new.

Bleakwater. Always smells like horse crap in Bleakwater.
But how'd I get here?

Moaning from the ache in my head, I force my body to
roll over onto its side, resting my forehead in the damp dirt.

What in hell happened to me...?

Arm feels numb. I raise it just enough to drape over my eyes, providing me with some much-appreciated shade from the scorching sun. I compel my eye open again, but a mite slower this time, aiming for just a small slit to let in a few rays. Even with the shade, light lashes out and stabs me in the eye again, sending another jolt straight into my skull. The pain rattles around a spell before spillin' somewhere out the back, leaving me to my misery.

I moan again, rolling onto my arm until I'm face down in the dirt. Dust kicks up and tries to crawl up my nose as I struggle to catch my breath. Satisfied I have the strength, I push myself up until I'm sittin' cross-legged, Injun-style. Head still feels like it's gonna split wide, but the light outside my lids feels like it's fadin'. I crank my eye open.

The pain pulsates for a quick second and then peters out. My sight returns to normal, and I find myself staring across the street at some pale, snot-nosed kid. He's holdin' onto his mama's hand, and they're just standin' there, gawkin' in my direction.

"Hell *you* lookin' at?" I growl, barely making out the words through my parched throat. I try hocking up some spit to send their way, but my body's plumb dry. Ain't got nothin'.

Spot my hat lying in the dirt beside me. I retrieve it, slapping it against my thigh to knock the dust off the faded blackness. Satisfied, I place it on my head and grin. Truly, nothing makes a man feel alive again quite like puttin' on his hat after nappin' in the dirt.

I scan the street and I'm somewhat surprised to find it's full of people. Looks like most everyone in the stinkin' town is out, standin' around on either side of the street like they's waiting for some kinda parade to tromp on through.

Instead they're all just standing around... staring at me.

I glare at the lot of 'em for a few seconds, ready to tell 'em off before my vengeful headache resurfaces, forcing me to shut my eyes again. This keeps up, I'm gonna have to find Doc, see if he got some kinda concoction what could prop me back up.

Searching my memories, I try to recall how I got here, replaying the night's events to give me some kinda clue as to how I wound up sleeping off a bender flat on my back in the middle of town.

Lemme see... I came sometime aroun' dinner, ate at that crappy diner up the street. Worst beans and jerky I'd had in weeks. Meat all stringy and gamey. Tasted like two turds dipped in dingo puke, an' I weren't afraid to tell 'em as much. For all's I know, might'a actually *been* someone's dead dog, tasted so bad. Doubt that's what sent me downwind, though... stomach was just fine afterwards. Tongue was the only thing suffered for it.

Then went 'cross town, had me some quality time with that short-haired pixie, Trixie. Hung 'round the saloon afterwards another hour or so, until...

I frown.

Until when?

What'd I do after that?

I remember the bartender giving me some kinda drink, said it was new, fresh outta 'Frisco. "On the house," he'd said. I figured, *Free booze? Why not?* Downed it in one gulp, shot him a smile and slammed the glass back down.

An' then... that's it.

That's all I recall.

Now I'm out here, bakin' in the dirt like a cake of crusty

crap, town starin' me down like I oughta be 'shamed of myself.

Well, hell with *that*.

Jet Carson ain't felt shame in years, an' I ain't about to start today.

I reach out my right hand to push myself up to my feet, yowling when a stitch of pain shoots up my arm. Yanking it back, I glare down at it, half expecting to see a rusty nail shot straight through or something, hurt so much.

Instead I'm starin' at a dusty palm, nary a scratch on it. Squinting closer at it, I reach over and poke it with my other hand.

Nope. That don't feel right.

Hell happened here?

I flip it over and back to examine it once more. Looks fine. No cuts, no bruisin' or nothin'. Plain as can be. So why's it feel like I jammed it onto a cactus an' dipped it in a barrel o' kerosene? Thing's pulsatin' between sharp pains and feeling all cold and tingly, like it's tryin' to fall asleep on me.

This ain't good. That there's my shootin' hand. If something's happening inside it, I'm gonna have a real big problem, real soon. Man who can't shoot's as good as dead around here.

Gotta find that Doc, have a word with him.

Leaning over, I slap my lefty into the dirt and push myself up to my feet, steadying my head as I feel the blood rushin' out of it, sensation flowing down my body an' into my boots. World gets woozy for a sec, so I end up holdin' my arms out for balance like I'm some kinda fancy performer. Wouldn't that be a hoot? Ol' Jet up on stage some day?

Grinning, I stare up at the clock tower at the end of the

street. 12:10pm. Explains why I woke to that blasted whistle in my head. Train's fixin' to leave the station.

Around me people smarten up an' start acting more normal, shuffling about the street again, goin' about their own business. Think they could stand around an' gawk at Jet Carson like that and *not* wind up starin' down the barrel of a gun for it? Shoot. They got another think comin'.

Kid standin' over by his Momma, though, he don't seem to get it. Eyes all wide an' saucer-like, like he's 'bout to start bawlin'.

I frown and saunter toward him, glowering as he hides half his face behind his momma's arm who don't notice one bit, wrapped up in a conversation with some lady next to her.

When I'm about six feet away I shuffle to a stop, give him the meanest stink eye I can muster. He just stares back, frozen like a baby possum. Grinning, I look away up the street, like I ain't interested no more. Then, quick as a rabbit I jump back at him, arms up in front.

"Boo!" I shriek.

The kid squawks, drops his momma's hand and bolts down the alley, whoopin' and hollering as she starts chasin' after.

I grin, satisfied with my performance. Heck, if I my ugly mug can't scare the piss out of a snot-nosed kid, what kinda outlaw would I be?

Another stiff wind blows through town, an' I slap my good hand on my hat to keep it from blowing away. Air's surprisingly cool for midday, and I steal a glance over my shoulder at the horizon. Sure enough, some kinda storm's foaming just outta town, angry clouds puffing up, dark as pitch.

I turn and head for the saloon across the street. Ain't got a clue what happened to me, but I do know this: I need a damn drink. Swallowing feels more an' more like someone's scouring my throat with sandpaper.

When I step inside folk don't even look my way, but that ain't new. Kill enough people an' you tend to have that effect on town folk. Making eye contact around here can get you killed, if you're not careful. I make my way straight to the bar, not sayin' a word to nobody.

Bellying up between two geezers, I yell for the bartender at the other end. He looks over in my direction for a second an' then turns around to continue polishing glasses.

I feel the fire inside start to spark, a cool flicker that only fans the flame of my cold, dead heart.

Who does that joker think he is, ignoring me? I know he knows who I am. I'm Jasper "Jet" Carson, dammit!

I have half a mind to pull an' shoot him dead right there, but decide he's not worth the bullet. Plus, since my shootin' hand's all messed up, figure I should try a different tack.

I clear my throat loud as I can, despite being so parched. "Hey!" I yell. "Barman! What's a guy gotta do, get some drink around here?"

He looks my way again and frowns. Setting the glass on the shelf, he flips the towel over his shoulder and starts amblin' toward me.

That's more like it.

I look over at the guy beside me. Some crusty prospector with a wiry salt and pepper beard, starin' at his empty mug like he's about to burst into tears.

"Aw, cheer up, buddy," I say, leaning closer. "You'll find gold in them there hills someday." I flash him a toothy grin.

"An' then I'll rob ya an' take it for myself." Chuckling a bit, I lean back, satisfied with my joke.

He ignores me, stares down into nothing. The bartender comes to a stop in front of us and coughs. The guy looks up, nods and returns his gaze to the mug, lost in thought.

Whatever. *I* know I'm funny, even if this yahoo don't know it. More'n likely he's just too scared to laugh, is all.

"Whisky," I say to the bartender. "An' none of that 'Frisco crap from last night, either. You hear me? Stuff was like turpentine!" I don't wait for a response, just turn around and survey the room.

In the far corner I spot Duncan, the guy who fancies himself a piano player. He's banging out some kinda cheerful show tune, the shrill notes slicing through the air and roosting in my head, somehow aggrivatin' the ache inside. I make a mental note to have a chat with him after my drink.

Beside the piano stands one of Trixie's new painted lady friends. What was her name again? Sweetie? Sugar, something...? No, that ain't it.

Candy!

Yeah, that was it. Calls herself Candy, on account'a her white an' red striped stockings, like a freakin' Christmas cane. I gawk at her an' grin as I envision all the fun we could have upstairs later.

Rest of the room's filled with ongoing poker games and riff raff sitting around, killin' time. Buncha losers, the lot of 'em.

I spy a collection of wanted posters on a nearby post and sneer. Hopping off my stool, I walk over and stop, squinting to read the text. There's a rough sketch of a guy with a lazy eye, an' when I read the name I curse under my breath.

Beady "Buck" Nicker, leader of a rival posse who's been claiming my kills as his own. Been lookin' for him 'bout three weeks, now. I find him, I'll be puttin' a bullet in the back of his head, that's for damn sure.

Reward says $100, which is ridiculous. Only a fool outta his mind would pay hundred bucks to bring that loser to justice. If anyone's worth that kinda coin, it's me.

I reach out and grab the paper, tryin' to rip it off the post. Thing's slippery, an' I fail twice before finally gettin' a decent grip an' I pull it loose, watching it flutter to the ground. I'm about to return to the bar when I stop, noticing the poster stuck up behind Buck's. I grin, cause it's me.

WANTED:
Dead or Alive
Jasper "Jet" Carson

*For the murder of Malcom Tulis on July 17th, 1884,
in addition to public drunkenness, lewdness and
indecency. If you have any information please contact
Sheriff Glenn Latham at the Bleakwater County Jail.*

Reward $25

My eye rolls to the bottom of the page, an' that's when I start to cuss. $25? Buck Nicker's worth a hunnerd dollars, an' I'm only a measly twenty-five? *That's crazy talk!*

Pinching the top of the paper, I fix my grip and pull hard. It rips diagonally and slips outta my fingers, the other half hanging on the post. Gamers at a nearby table stop and turn to look in my direction, but I ignore them, shuffling back to the bar.

Shoot.

Twenty-five bucks!

All the crap I've done in my life, and I'm only worth twenty-five stinkin' dollars?! Guess I'd better start stepping up my game a bit, kill a few more folk 'fore I lose my tarnished reputation to Nicker.

They'll never take me alive, of course, not if I have any say in it. Ain't no way I'm gonna let my life get snuffed out at the end of a rope. That's a *coward's* way to die. Not mine. Jet Carson'll never hang. *Ever.*

I belly up to the bar where my whisky awaits me, and I smile. Then just as I reach for it the prospector next to me shoots a hand forward, snatches it and tosses it back.

"*What... the hell...*"

I turn and face him, eyes glancing from his solemn face down to the empty glass. "What'd you do that for, ya idjit?! You wanna die today? Is *that* it!?"

He gazes grimly at the glass in his hand, rotating it between his fingers and thumb, not saying a word.

That's when I lose it.

Clenching my left fist tight, I swing wide and smash it dead center into his nose. He careens off the barstool and clumsily crashes to the floor, bouncing twice before skidding to a stop.

"Think you can steal liquor from *me*? From *Jet Carson*?!"

The entire saloon falls silent. They stare at him as he raises his head off the floor, wide-eyed and terrified. Even Duncan stops his blasted piano playing and the women quit their gabbin' to glance down at the duffer.

He looks at the bar, searching the faces of the onlookers, unsure of what to do next.

I decide to make it real easy for him.

"You gonna die today, mister!" I holler, reaching for my gun. My palm hammers down to my holster to draw, radiating the worst pain I felt since I woke up. In all the commotion I plumb forgot my blasted hand was messed up. The stinging pulsates simultaneously between my hand an' my head, so strong I get unsteady for a second, dropping to one knee.

Prospector pushes himself to his feet and scrambles toward the exit as the bartender behind me hollers after him about his tab. I watch him dart between the crowd an' through the swinging doors, disappearing into the bright light of day.

"You'd better run, old timer!" I yell. "'Cause the next time Jet Carson sees you 'round town? You're a dead man. Y'hear me? *A dead man!*"

I force myself to my feet and face the bar again, furious he got away. Numbness returns to my hand, growing stronger as my headache fixes to resurrect itself with renewed intensity. My body shivers, an' I chalk it up to the soreness an' sufferin'.

"Get me a new whisky," I bark over the counter. "An' turn those fancy ceilin' fans off! I'm freezin' in here!" He doesn't act like he's listening, but I watch him wander to the other side of the bar toward the switches.

I stare down at the empty glass and curse again, wondering how an' old prospectin' coot could suddenly grow a pair o' balls big enough to swipe my booze. Am I that washed up? Has it been that long since I've caused a stink in this town, even drunk inbreds think they can disrespect me?

Am I really only worth twenty-five dollars?

No.

Hell, no.

I refuse to let this town put me in a cheap box like that. They want some kinda show? I'll give 'em a show, down in the middle o' main street, I will.

Right after I'm good an' soused.

I glare at the countertop, boring a hateful hole in it with my eyes when I notice the guy sitting on the other side of me, gawking in my direction.

"What, you wanna die today too?" I snarl.

His eyes grow large and he starts to blink rapidly, like he's having some kind of seizure. Shakes his head from side to side, never taking his eyes off mine.

I have a powerful urge to reach over and slap him, but can't help respectin' a man who stares death in the face and doesn't piss his pants.

Never taking his eyes off mine, he reaches over and pushes his shot glass full of drink across the counter until it comes to rest in front of me. Slowly retracting his arm, he lays it across his lap and nods once.

I glance at the glass, full to the brim with some kinda smoky brown liquid. Leaning toward it, I take a deep whiff. I frown, pulling back. Whatever it is, this stuff's strong.

"Now, you ain't tryin' to poison ol' Jet, are ya?"

He shakes his head.

"'Cause if I take a drink'a this stuff and start to cough

more'n once? You know right well I'll have more'n enough time to gut you like a fish 'fore you take two steps."

He nods his head vigorously, eyes roaming about the room before settling back on me again. I can see he's starting to sweat, and it doesn't take a genius to see he's been drinkin' all morning, based offa his pastiness. Truth is, I'm kinda surprised fella can even sit upright.

"Well, then," I say, tipping the brim of my hat toward him. "Much obliged, stranger."

I'm about to reach down and gulp the thing when my new friend turns his head toward the squeak of the swinging doors. His eyes widen and he turns back, refocusing on me.

I frown. "What?" I mutter.

He says nothing, but slowly tilts his head toward the doors.

I crane my neck around just enough to see what he's staring at. Cursing under my breath, I slowly turn back to the counter, my frown growing deeper.

Sheriff Glenn "Whistler" Latham just walked in.

I swallow hard and close my eyes, mulling over in my aching head what I'm gonna do. Hovering my hand over my holster, I open my eyes and stare at my reflection in the murky mirror behind the bar. The silver's starting to tarnish and my face looks downright ashy, but it's still clear enough I can make out Latham's silhouette behind me.

Whistling the same dang melody he always does, he an' his deputy amble over to an empty table in the back corner. I tip my head to the right, just enough to get a clear view out the corner of my eye, but the crowd's too thick. Can't see him clearly.

Which means he can't see me, neither.

Any other day I'd be glad to call him out into the street, put him down like the dog he is. But today, what with my blasted head and messed up hand, I reckon it's best I make a quiet getaway while I still can.

Pushing away from the bar, I slide past the drunk and sidle up to the leftmost wall, turning all nonchalant-like to scan the room again. Latham's still out of view somewhere in the opposite corner. I glance toward the exit. Nobody coming or goin' — I got a clear path. All's I gotta do is keep my head down, my mug covered, and I'm home free.

Tipping my black hat low so as to cover my face, I'm making my way when my stomach seizes inside me. Feels like a rattler injected it with some kinda poison spit. I clutch my belly with both hands, head suddenly feeling woozy, like I'm gonna pitch over an' pass out right there on the floor. Instead, I stumble to my right, fallin' into the side of the piano with a loud *clang*.

Duncan stops playin', looks my way and frowns. He leans over and eyes the side of the piano for a few seconds before divin' right back in where he left off, but even louder this time.

My vision starts to clear, but my body's breakin' out in a cold sweat. I shiver, an' once again curse the drafty saloon and the oncoming storm. Middle of summer an' I feel like I'm freezing where I stand. I shake my head. I gotta find that Doc, see if I got a case of the flu or something. Picked it up from Trixie, I reckon.

I smile at the memory.

Ah, whatever this is... it was worth it.

Duncan's about to finish his song, so I lean in real close toward him. "Hey. Song man," I whisper. "Need you to play somethin' slow and quiet, y'hear? I'm kinda tryin' to avoid unwanted attention, if you get my drift."

He nods along to the song and then comes to a stop, reaching up and flipping through the pages of his songbook. A second later he grins and starts playing again, but it ain't slow nor quiet. It's snappy. Loud and lively. I'm livid, feeling my face flush as I notice heads start turnin' in our direction at the new tune.

Is he deaf? What is this idiot doin'?!

Without thinking, I mash my fist down on the keys, the harsh notes jarring against his melodic pounding. Duncan squeals and jumps to his feet, his chair clattering to the ground. He stares at the piano, swallowing hard. I slowly remove my mitt from the keys as he continues to stare, growing pale. I lean in closer, tipping my hat low so as to hide my face from onlookers.

"Like I was sayin'," I mutter quietly. "I need you to play somethin' *quiet-like*, or you won't be playin' nothin' at all. Y'unnerstan'?"

He avoids all eye contact with me. Without a word, he slowly picks his stool off the floor and places it upright again, avoiding the stares around him as he sits down.

I smile. *'Bout time I got some respect around here.*

Taking a deep breath, he looks back at the sheet music, exhaling slowly. His brow is furrowed as he turns a few pages and selects a new song. It's steady and soothing, almost somber. I nod at him in approval.

Across the room Latham's still out of view, though I can hear his laughter even from where I stand. The whistling, the laughing... idiot's a regular yokel, like he's some kinda stupid salesman with a badge.

I steal a glance back at the bar. The drunkard's still staring at me from across the room, eyes wide. My glass is still full, untouched. I nod, an' he nods back, then looks back at the glass longingly.

Drunks.

It's a wonder they can ever see straight.

My head starts aching again, like someone's slowly pushing a red-hot poker through my eye. I instinctively reach up and rub it with my hand, flinching as the pain in both worsens at the touch.

Gotta find Doc. Get me some medicine to take out whatever this thing is floatin' through my body.

I reach up and rub the back of my head, wincing. Got some kinda bump or bruise back there. Knot's pretty hefty, like I must've smacked it on something hard when I conked out last night.

"Hey, Duncan," says a soft voice from behind me. "That's a real nice tune you're playin' there."

I turn my head and watch Candy walk past. She leans over the back of the piano, flashing Duncan her warmest smile and ample assets. He barely pays her any mind, simply nods and continues playing. I study her face. Up close, she's even more of a looker than I first thought. Hair the color of coppery fire and emerald eyes that gleam like they're holding a dragon hostage. She's every Irishman's dream.

My eyes take in every inch of her body as my own starts to respond in approval. Leaning in closer, I take in a deep whiff of her hair and pull back, somewhat surprised. Smells like somethin'... familiar. Christmas? No, peppermint.

Who would'a guessed Candy smells like candy canes? Now *that* takes some serious commitment and forethought.

No doubt about it, this here is my kinda woman. Smokin' hot an' spicy to boot.

I move closer and breathe her in, relishing the sharp scent as it swirls merrily through my nose. "Hey there," I say, making sure my voice sounds low an' macho. "Why you wastin' your time with music man here when you an' I could go upstairs... make a little music of our own? Have ourselves a little dance? What'd ya say to that?" I flash her my sexiest smile, hoping I remembered to brush my teeth last Tuesday.

She glances toward me, confused, then turns her head back around and makes eyes at Duncan again. Ignoring me.

The iceburg inside me starts to spread, my grin fading into a fierce frown.

"Hey now! Maybe you din't hear what I said, huh?" I reach behind her and grab me a handful, squeezing it nice an' proper.

Candy yelps and spins around, eyes ablaze with green fury. She raises her hand to slap me silly, meeting my eyes for a second and stopping herself.

"Whoa, there, missy!" I chide, stepping well out of reach. "You don't wanna be doin' that, now..." I raise my hands in mock surrender. "No need for violence... I was just hopin' you an' I could go an'... talk. You know, get to know each other better..."

Her eyes dart back and forth, like she's looking at something behind me, avoiding me. She glances over at the nearest gaming table, but nobody pays her a lick of attention.

Smart folk, not getting mixed up in my business.

Candy shakes her head, confused. Then I watch her eyes lock onto something over my shoulder at the bar. I frown, wondering what in the world could be so interesting, while at the same time thinking this might just be her way of distracting me 'fore she off and kicks me in the nether regions.

I take a step back until I'm confident I'm outta striking distance, turning slowly, keeping tabs on her in my peripheral vision. There's a bright flash outside, shortly followed by an instant crack of thunder. The saloon shakes, but nobody moves a muscle. I steal a glance out a side window, but still looks dry as hay outside. Storm's about to arrive soon enough, I reckon.

Looking back at the bar, I spy the cordial drunk, still staring at me. I nod, then scan the rest of the bar. Aside from the same yahoos I saw a few minutes ago, nothing's changed.

Then my eyes fall back on my friend, only this time I get the feeling something ain't quite right. Somethin' about what I'm seeing feels off. I study the counter more closely.

My shot glass of hooch has disappeared.

I'm about to lose it when I suddenly spot it...

...sitting in his hand.

Empty.

"What...the HELL?!?" I scream from across the room.

Guy turns white as a sheet. He drops the glass onto the floor an' I'm half surprised it doesn't shatter as it bounces twice before rolling to a stop against a nearby stool. I start toward him and the idiot starts shaking his head from side to side.

"Now, just hold on!" he protests. "I... you said I should drink it! You nodded!!" His face twists up like he's about to cry.

As I get closer I start flexing my good arm, clenching my first, preparing to give him something to cry about. Just before I reach him he turns away an' grunts, grabbing at his chest and keeling over on the counter, face first. His body goes limp and he slumps down, slowly sliding off the stool and onto the floor with a muted thud.

I stop walking and stare down at him, furiously curious.

Did this loser just die on me?

I lean over and take a closer look. His eyes are wide open, cloudy, unblinking. Plus, he don't appear to be breathing no more.

Dang it. This loser just up an' died on me.

Ain't nothin' going right for me today.

I step back into the dark corner to put some distance between him an' me, when I see something most peculiar. Aside from the drunk closest to him, nobody else in the joint seems to notice or give a flyin' fig that the guy just kicked the bucket.

I look across the room and realize why.

All eyes are on Latham an' his deputy, rising to their feet. A shadowy figure pushes through the swinging doors and Latham seems quick to follow. Immediately the entire saloon starts clearing out, people scramblin' every which way to either run outside or stand near a window to get a better look.

I look back at the body on the floor. He moans and starts to stir.

Well, well... look at who cheated death.

I look around the room and realize nobody's looking at us, all eyes outside. I take two steps forward and bury my boot into his gut. Twice.

He groans, then shrivels up and curls into a tight ball.

I kneel down and grab hold of his hair. "That's for drinkin' my booze!" I snarl, spittle falling out of the corner of my mouth. I slam his head back into the floor and pause to look up, but no one's watching.

"Be back for you in a few minutes, so don't go nowhere." I stand up and stare out at the street, watching Latham disappear into the crowd. "Somethin' else I gotta do now."

That's when it hits me, why the place cleared out like it did. Only one thing clears out a room of whorin', gamblin' drunks, and that's a showdown. An' if Whistler Latham's about to get shot to pot, I sure as hell wanna be there to watch it happen.

Or finish the job, if the other guy can't shoot worth spit.

I step outside onto the sidewalk, crowding over with rubberneckers and lookey-loo's. I glance up the street both ways to see which side Latham's on. His white hat bobs up and down to my right, just over the shifting heads of the mob. I glance left to get a look at the shooter, but it's too crowded.

"Move outta the blasted way!" I holler, waving my arm to the side.

Nobody moves an inch. There's too much noise and excitement, sheer chaos. I reach for my gun to help clear a path, but stop myself short. Slowly I ease my hand back, away from my holster. Taking a deep breath, I look back at Latham's hat. Suddenly it occurs to me I'm on the wrong side of this equation.

I don't wanna be a hothead, jumpin' in half-cocked and messing up this showdown before it even begins. Heck, I give it a few more minutes an' all my problems in this town might be comin' to a glorious end.

Permanently.

I back away from the crowd, hovering close to the wall as I make my way toward the general store next door so's I can get a better view of Latham eatin' lead. My hat stays low to keep from being recognized, but I avoid eyes, jus' to be safe. Don't need no spirited squealers recognizing me, ruining my good time.

I spot an opening in the crowd and sidestep through it, finding a nearby post to lean against. A large lady next to me complains about the blasted heat. Judging by the sheen of sweat she's producing. I'm guessing her body's in overdrive. Meanwhile, mine's slowly killin' me with whatever it is I caught.

My teeth start to ache, and I wrap my arms around me tighter to fight off the chills. A prickly numbness creeps up my arm, so I slap it against my leg a few times, enough to wake it up but not so much it smarts. Doesn't seem to make a difference so I end up shoving it under my armpit, careful not to brush the hand.

Another flash of lightning from on high. I shudder, looking around to see if anyone noticed my case of the jitters. Sky's grown a few shades darker than when I first woke, more the color of an oil fire than thunderclouds. A sharp crack fills the air, so loud I can feel it in my bones. Sounds like the sky itself is crackin' in two, and I cover my ears, wincing at the pain.

Head feels like it's gonna split again, blasted ache behind my eye sharper'n ever. The peal of thunder is lazy an' drawn out, lasting a lot longer than I think it should. I curse until it slowly fades into echoes across the valley.

I start to cough, covering my mouth with my denim sleeve. When it comes back with blood on it I know I'm in some serious trouble.

Holy hell, I really gotta find that Doc.

Latham stands in the middle of the street, feet spread wide an' gun held out ahead of him, facing away. A wisp of smoke spirals up from the muzzle and disappears in the wind.

I search him, lookin' him up and down, but he ain't bleeding.

Dang.

Looks like the lawman lives to see another day.

Until I face off with him. I smile.

"Is he dead?" the lady next to me says, craning her neck.

"I'd imagine so," a guy next to her laughs. "Looks like Doc's gonna go check, make it official." He cackles again for no good reason.

Doc.

The Doc's here!

I step into the street, keeping my hat tilted down, looking away from Latham in case he's starin' my way. Sure enough, I catch sight of Doc stepping off the sidewalk up the street, walking toward the body in the middle of Main Street.

Wrapping my jacket tighter around me to fight off the cold, I walk toward him briskly.

"Hey, Doc!" I yell over the noise and commotion. "Doc! Need you to help me out, here!"

He's kneeling over the body, holding the limp wrist in his hand. I walk up beside him, my body launching into another coughing fit that just about splits my head in two. When I'm done, I spit at the ground, getting it all out. I start to speak, but don't get a word out.

My spit's dark red. All of it.

This ain't good.

I take a deep breath, look back at Doc and start talking. "Look, Doc. I know you're busy an' all, but I'm in serious need'a some kinda medicine or something. I'm coming down with a cold or flu or *somethin'*. Freezing to death, here, an' my head hurts something fierce. Maybe there's somethin' you can..."

I hear my voice trail off as my eyes fall upon the hat lying in the dirt next to him.

It's *my* hat.

What the hell...?

I reach down and pick it up, dusting it off and placing it back on my head. Must've lost it in my coughing fit.

"Doc?" I say, "You hearin' me?"

I glance down in disgust at the loser on the ground. Guy's right eye is blasted clear through the back of his head, blood and brains and bone seeping out into the red dirt beneath him. Stupid idiot probably didn't know what hit him. Personally, I'm surprised Whistler was such a good shot. A real dead-eye, I think, chuckling at my clever pun.

Without a word, Doc stands up, turns around and starts walking up the street toward the sheriff.

"Doc?" I say, raising my voice a few notches. "Hey! Don't walk away from me when I'm talkin' to you! You hear me?!"

He ignores me, and I take a step toward him, reaching out to grab his arm.

"You know who I am, old man?!? I'm Jet Carson! *JET*

CARSON! An' I'm gonna..." I lower my arm and freeze, my eye drawn back to the ground.

"I'm gonna..."

I stare down at the boots on the body beneath me.

They're mine.

My body drops in temperature a few more degrees as the air seems to whirl and swirl around me. My eyes travel up the leg to the man's gun, resting beside his mangled hand. Misfire. Frowning, I raise my aching hand up, disgusted as I discern it's a perfectly bloody, mangled match for his.

No...

I remove my hat and bend down, taking a closer look at the face, and that's when I start to curse. I'm spewing every word I ever heard, an' then I make up a few more just to get it all out. I haul back and kick the body on the ground repeatedly, cursing him, his stinking shooting and the gun to boot.

The weight settles on my shoulders and I sink to my knees, pounding on his chest with what little strength I have left. Through my tears I see the saloon, the crowd returning to their swill. The drunk stands outside the doors, staring at me through ashen eyes. Even from here, I can tell his neck ain't settin' right on his shoulders. Broke.

The shrill sound of a whistle pierces my head like a bullet. I wince, covering my ears as I look up main street. Clock reads 12:10pm.

Again.

There's a sudden flash of lightning, followed by the nearby sound of an approaching horse. Before I even turn my head, I feel the presence.

His presence.

I try to fight it, but I can't resist. Against my will, I turn my head and look up into the blazing red eyes of a wild bronco, midnight blue and enormous. Above him sits a man in black.

The man in black.

He stares back at me, and he looks downright angry.

I ponder the notion of pushing away, making a run for it, but I don't. Fact is, I'm too cold and tired to do much of anything 'cept sit here. Figure I've kept him waiting long enough all these years. An' if I were an honest man, I'd admit it weren't like I didn't know he was coming for me one day.

I just didn't want it to be today.

Author's Note

I'll admit it: I'm not a huge fan of Westerns. Aside from watching a few episodes of *Deadwood, 3:10 to Yuma* and Sam Raimi's underrated *The Quick and the Dead*, my exposure to Ye Olde West is quite limited indeed. (I did seem to enjoy *Back to The Future III*, now that I recall...)

Anyhow, one day I decided I kind of wanted to try my hand at writing a Western short story, but the problem was I didn't know where to start. All I knew is I wanted it to be original, with a supernatural twist to it, so it wouldn't just be a "boring old Western."

When the kernel of the idea had simmered long enough to conjure up a dead Western (now with the added goodness of *ghosts* and *a time loop!*), I felt I was onto something. So after a year of taking notes, fleshing it out and having some fun, I dug in and started to write.

Granted, I haven't read enough Western short stories to know if this is *truly* an original take on a showdown, but it's original enough for my satisfaction and enjoyment. Hopefully yours too.

PEST CONTROL
JACK KARDIAC

SOMETHING SINISTER STUNG the dead center of
Mason's hairy calf two seconds after he'd begun urinating on
the ant mound.

"Ow! Dang it!!"

Mason stamped his foot on the ground to shake it off and
jumped aside to avoid another attack. He quickly resumed
his activity, liberally dowsing the top of the mound with
everything inside him.

When he was done, he leaned over and glared down at
the swarming soldiers below, swimming in the fragrant,
frenzied chaos. He made a deep, guttural sound, sucking his
phlegm into his mouth repeatedly before dropping an
extended, viscous dollop into the center of the mix.

"There," he growled. "Make your nest in someone else's
yard, losers." He spat again before pulling the front of his
Speedo back up.

"Ewwww!!!"

The high-pitched squeal was soon accompanied by a
second, equally aghast exclamation.

"Oh. My. God. What are you *doing?!?*"

Mason pulled his shoulders back slightly and sucked in his ample gut, attempting to make himself as presentable as possible. He reached up and stroked his bushy goatee, shielding his eyes from the sun as he looked over the top of his fence at the two girls who glared down at him from their second-floor balcony next door.

"Well, well..." he said, flashing them his sexiest smile. "If it ain't the Doublemint Twins, Candy and Cutie."

"It's Sandy and Mandy," one of them retorted.

He nodded. Mason thought it was Sandy who spoke, but if he was being honest, he could never be quite sure. He would also admit he couldn't care less.

"Whatever." He relaxed his shoulders and let his body resume its natural potato shape, with his paunch hanging out over his Speedo once more. "Now, what's your problem again?"

"You! *You're* the problem, you pervert! What are you doing over there? Are you *exposing* yourself?!"

"Heh. Don't you wish," he chuckled. Mason watched as their faces drew back in identical expressions of horror and disgust, then continued before they had a chance to respond. "For your information, girlies, I was simply dispatching a nasty nest of critters *in the privacy of my own yard*, thank you very much."

"By *peeing* on it?!?"

"You are correct," he said, nodding. "Dispatched them by using the natural resources God gave me." He flashed them a lurid smile and offered a half-hearted bow. "You may thank me later."

"Thank you?!"

"Sure," he said. "'Cause now they're all gonna die, instead of digging a nest over to *your* side of the fence."

"Whatever," the one on the right said. "Listen, we're going to be sunbathing by the pool again in a few minutes, and if we so much as *think* you're spying on us by the fence with your phone this time, we're gonna call the cops."

Mason opened his eyes as wide as he could without discomfort, feigning shock and innocence. "Ladies! Why would you ever suggest such a thing? Why, just because I *happen* to be in *my* backyard sunbathing at the same time as you *happen* to be sunbathing in *yours*... I ask you, is that a crime?"

They both glanced over his shoulder at his pool, which had been in disrepair for the better part of a year — tiles covered with a slick smattering of moss and muck while the water surface itself was almost completely obscured by lily pads and a thick, unspecified black film. Sure, he had loved the idea of an exotic, saltwater pool when he first moved in, but didn't take into account the sheer amount of money or effort it would require to keep up with it.

In the end, he'd decided he really only wanted to relax in his floating lawn chair in the pool instead of actually swimming in it, so he'd decided to let it go. Much to the dismay of Sandy, Mandy, and a handful of other surrounding neighbors.

Mason didn't care. He was happy enough, and until their court cases worked their way through the clogged and corrupt judicial system, he and his pool of yuck were staying put. Lawsuit or not.

"Just leave us alone! Pervert!"

"Hey!" he yelled back, pointing a meaty finger up at

them. "It was *you* gals who were spyin' on *me* here! Attemptin' to take a sneaky peek at my pecker!"

"Ew! Stop talking!"

Mason pointed a meaty finger up at them. "So don't *you* be threatenin' *me* about playing peek-a-boo!" He placed his hands on his hips and sneered. "Although, Imma be honest wit you, I'd be glad to show you *mine* if... you know..." He gyrated his hips in a circular motion, attempting to accentuate his extreme flexibility.

Both women simultaneously brought their hands to their mouths, gagging and retching as if they were about to throw up. They turned and bolted back inside just as a small dog darted out between their legs, stopping at the balcony's edge. Looking like a filthy mop with peg legs, it looked down at him and barked happily.

Stupid dog, Mason thought, glaring up at it.

He'd found it in his yard more than once, scattering its organic Tootsie Roll deposits about like an Easter Bunny on crack. Despite his scolding it and shoving it back under the fence, it retained an inexplicable affinity for him. It was as if the stupid thing was infatuated with him, no matter how much he hated it.

What was its name again? Stamps? Stitches...?

"Staples!" one of the girls yelled, arriving in the doorway. "Come back here!"

She stooped to pick the dog up, giving Mason an eyeful of cleavage in the process. When she realized what was happening, she straightened upright and glared at him, eyes blazing with fury. "Come on, Staples, sweetie. You're going on a playdate with Muffles tonight! Let's get you away from that... that *disgusting* excuse for a man."

After she'd disappeared inside, Mason closed his eyes, unsuccessfully trying to reconstruct the frozen image of her in his imagination. He frowned, realizing the negative commentary that followed had effectively spoiled his fantasy. Walking back to the side of his pool, he elaborately prepared the lounge chair for his leisure time.

Bottle of water? *Check.*

Sunglasses and favorite baseball cap? *Check.*

Sony Walkman, headphones and the dial tuned in to his favorite radio station? *Check.*

Oh yes. Mason was ready to rock and roll.

For a second he considered going back inside to retrieve his camcorder, on the off chance an opportunity presented itself next door. He decided against it this time, however, since Mandy... or Sandy... *whoever it was...* had directly threatened him if he ever did it again.

One of the other neighbors must have seen him the other month. Bunch of nosey rubberneckers. As if they weren't getting an eyeful as they were watching him watching the girls. He frowned and glanced around the yard, checking to see if anyone was being nosey again today.

And there was.

Three houses down from Mason, a guy stood on the outside balcony, staring directly at him. He wore black slacks, a black, buttoned-up, long-sleeved dress shirt and a black baseball cap. He was looking right at him, not even looking away when he was spotted, which made Mason feel even creepier.

"Hey, pervert!" Mason yelled. "Take off, you Hoosier! 'Fore I call the cops!"

The man's face broke into a grin. Then he laughed at

him, shrugged his shoulders and disappeared back inside the apartment.

Mason swore under his breath, glancing down at himself in his super-tight Speedo. What was that sicko hoping to catch a glimpse of, anyway? The bombshell twins?

Or *him?*

He swore again as he eased himself down into the lounge chair, careful to balance it perfectly so he wouldn't end up in the sludge again. It was one thing to neglect a pool until it became nasty. But swimming in it? Out of the question.

Mason settled back into his chair, adjusted his glasses and hat and pushed off from the side with his pool paddle / back scratcher. As the chair slowly trudged its way through the water, he turned on the Walkman and closed his eyes. AC/DC's "Highway to Hell" played on the radio, and Mason smiled, quickly falling asleep.

Mason jolted awake. He bolted upright, then grabbed hold of the armrests and steadied himself back down before he could fall in. He opened one eye just enough to get a socket full of sun, instantly regretting it. He closed his eyes and frowned.

Pulling one headphone off his ear, he heard the frantic squeals of one of the girls next door. She was crying hysterically and yelling for Staples.

Stupid dog, Mason thought. *Heaven forbid something happen to that mutt.* His sunburned lips spread into a solar-baked smile. Maybe it made a poopy in one of their princess slippers, instead of popping out pooplets all over his stinking yard.

Dang dog.

Mason placed the earpiece back and dialed up the volume as Dire Straits sang in his ears. He sucked on the straw in his water bottle, placed it back in the holder and swiftly fell back asleep.

Mason jolted awake. Again. His arm jerked out wildly, knocking his water bottle into the murky water surrounding him. He opened his eyes just in time to watch it sink below the surface. Mason closed them again, leaning back and groaning dramatically.

He felt horrible. Sunburned and dehydrated, downright crispy, like a piece of turkey jerky that'd been nuked in the oven too long. He tried to swallow, but his mouth was too dry. It hurt to even try.

How long had he been asleep?

The sun was behind the fence, beginning to set, so he determined he was out for, what... two, maybe three hours? He must've been more exhausted than he thought he was.

That was when he noticed the static.

Instead of the best variety of classic rock and yesterday's hits that just kept coming, Mason's head was filled with the harsh sound of raspy static. Pulling the headphones off his ears, he was suddenly all too aware of another sound close by.

Staples.

Barking non-stop, and somewhere close.

Dang it! The poopin' pooch was in his yard again!

He opened his eyes and angrily searched around for the

mutt. It didn't take long to find it, standing at the edge of the pool, three feet away from him, barking frantically.

Mason was furious. He started cursing at it for a few seconds before stopping abruptly. His eyes fell away from Staples and he frowned as he saw what was happening in the rest of his backyard.

It was completely overrun by ants.

Something was wrong, though. Something he was seeing didn't make sense. These ants weren't the typical red ones Mason had dealt with in his yard a few hours earlier. Similar in color, sure, but these ants... these ants were the size of rats.

And there were *hundreds* of them, all swarming through some kind of mist under the fence, crazed and crawling over themselves in their pursuit of Staples.

The dog looked around and started whimpering in terror and confusion. A pair of ants drew closer and lunged, mandibles clicking audibly like a broken metronome. Staples yelped and turned back toward Mason. Then it leapt into the pool.

"Aw, crap..." Mason muttered.

Mason used his paddle to pull himself over to the dog as it struggled against the thick sludge and lily pads. Its head began to slip beneath the surface just as Mason reached out and wrapped a hand around the dog's throat.

Without a hint of gentleness or compassion, Mason lifted Staples out of the water by its neck, plopping it into his lap. The dog's long nails felt like hot razorblades, scratching mercilessly against his sunburned thighs and chest as Staples scrambled to smother him with happy kisses of appreciation.

"Stop that! Stop!!" he protested.

He pushed it back repeatedly, finally getting it to settle

down and stop lacerating him. Mason extended the paddle to push further away from the pool's edge until they were dead center, buffered by three feet of muck on every side.

The colossal wave of ants continued their feverish rampage, surging out of the mist over the entire backyard and beyond. In every direction Mason looked, a shifting, liquid shroud of rust-brown engulfed absolutely everything.

Apartments. Trees. *Everything*.

The majority of the insects scurried past the pool without giving them a second glance, eagerly heeding some distant directive. A select hundred lingered, remaining rooted on the sidewalk, encircling the pool on all sides, their cold, unwavering gazes focused squarely on the savory snacks in the center.

And as the sun slowly sank behind the horizon, plunging the two of them into a fog-filled darkness far more terrifying than anything either had experienced before, Mason's mind echoed with a lone, pulsating pang of confusion and regret.

Perhaps he never should have peed on that anthill.

Author's Note

Now, you may be wondering if I'm obsessed with ants, considering one of the key stories in *Squint* a few years ago. (No spoilers...)

On the one hand, I have to say no, I most certainly am not. I never studied them at length and didn't really pay much attention to them growing up. However, since living overseas in Indonesia for a large chunk of my life, I'm now much more familiar with ants than ever before.

This story wasn't inspired by true events, however. No, this one was inspired by Jeff Strand's *Mandibles*, which is a horror / comedy novel about a town being overrun by... what else? *Giant ants.* (His are considerably larger than these were, I should note. And slightly nastier.)

So you could consider this a kind of an unofficial side story to his, taking place in tandem with the events of his story. It's also a nice way for the keywords Jack Kardiac and Jeff Strand to show up in the same sentence, so that's kind of an added bonus.

If you're a fan of ants and giant 70's epic disaster movies, be sure to check out *Mandibles*. This short story is an ant appetizer. (Antppetizer? Sure, why not.) *Mandibles* is the full course meal.

Blackballed

JACK KARDIAC

blackballed

I'D JUST LOST my eighth game in a row when I spot
Walker and Rod outside the dimly lit bar. Even through the
smoky haze it wasn't too difficult to ID them, given their
sheer size and girth. That, plus the telltale bulges beneath
their jackets.

Great. Looks like my luck just ran out.

They make eye contact with me through the grimy
window and I frown, letting out a deep sigh. A part of me
considers bolting for the exit, but decide it would probably be
better to stay put. Despite my afternoon losing streak, I'm
feeling surprisingly lucky today.

Inside, the room is filled with the scent of stale beer and
cigarette smoke, the low hum of conversations blending into
the soft murmur of music playing from the jukebox. Pool
balls collide with a *crack*, punctuating the air's occasional
burst of laughter, mingling with the clinking glasses at
the bar.

Sinking my hands deep into my jean pockets, I calmly

await their approach. As usual with these guys, it's not without fanfare.

Pushing through the narrow doorway, Walker bumps into some guy in a slick, black suit trying to exit. They stop and exchange glances, and then the big bull proceeds to poke him in the chest with a fat finger, cursing like a true Philly native before grabbing the guy by the shoulders and shoving him outside.

The stranger regains his balance, turns around and grins. Seriously! He *grins* back at them and then turns and walks away.

Smart man.

The two thugs squeeze past the ongoing pool games like greasy tankers plowing through a swampy shipyard, coming to a full stop at my table. I notice they've positioned themselves at the corners opposite me. Walker's clean-shaven, professional mug is in direct contrast to Rod's unruly neck beard fighting for freedom from his flannel shirt. Apparently the mob doesn't have a consistent appearance policy when hiring these days.

I nod. "Walker. Rod."

"Mitch," Walker says. He juts his chin toward me. "Shaved your head, I see."

"That I did."

"Think it'd help you blend in or somethin'?" Rod grunts.

"Something like that."

"You look like a freakin' cue ball, you're so white."

I smile. "Thank you. I'll take that as a compliment."

"You shouldn't."

I ignore him. "So tell me, what brings you boys all the

way out to Indiana? Here to catch the Indy 500? 'Cause if you are, you're kinda lost..."

"Ain't catching the Indy," Walker says, glaring at me. He looks like he's still bitter about his brother's black eye back in Florida. I should probably apologize for that. I won't.

"Naw, we're catching *you*, Mitch," Rod says, grinning. He swings his denim jacket open just enough so I can see how serious he is. I stare at the piece and start to chew on my lip, wondering if maybe I made a mistake by sticking around so long.

The bathroom door behind me opens and a short, stocky kid walks out, wiping his hands off on his shirt. He stares at me for a second, like he's surprised to see me standing there, hands in my pockets. Then he looks over at Walker and Rod before returning back to me, saying nothing.

After an awkward pause he shrugs, grabs the triangle and starts racking up the balls.

I stare at the table. The smooth indigo blue surface is uncommon these days, but I have to admit I'm partial to it. It's unique. I like stuff like that. I start to lift my hands out of my pockets to help the kid when Tweedle Dee and Doofus both flinch, hands darting inside their jackets.

"Whoa, boys..." I say calmly, freezing. "All's I'm doing is helping him rack the balls."

"Nuh-uh," Walker says, shaking his head. "It's really in your best interest you leave your hands right where they are."

"Walker," I chide. "Come on! What, are you afraid I'm gonna—"

"Man said No," Rod growls from the other corner.

I study the two of them for a few seconds before finally rolling my eyes. Exhaling an exasperated, exaggerated sigh, I make a show of shoving my hands back into my pockets, as deep as they'll go.

They both relax, letting their jackets fall back into place, resuming identical stances: hands clasped in front of them like they think they're trying out for the Secret Service or something.

To my right, the kid reaches across the table, retrieving various balls from the pockets and plunking them loudly into the rack. He appears pretty oblivious to the gravity of the situation, and I wonder how long this is going to go on before it either becomes super awkward or critically serious.

It gets serious before it becomes awkward.

"Hey kid," Walker says, his annoyance resounding clearly in his voice.

The boy drops a ball into the rack and grabs another from the pocket beside him. He turns his head and looks at Walker, confused. "What?"

"Do you mind?" Walker asks.

The kid leans back from the table and stands erect, cue ball in one hand, eight ball in the other. "*What?*" he repeats, slightly annoyed.

"Go find another table, punk. The adults are tryin' to have a conversation here."

I feel the kid bristle next to me and decide it's time for me to intervene. "Okay, everyone just... calm down, here... maybe I should make a few introductions, huh?" I start to lift my hands out of my pockets but they both twitch again, reaching to their sides. I shove my hands back down.

"We don't give a flying fig who junior here is, so how 'bout we—"

"Yeah," I interrupt. "I get that. But you *should.*"

"What?" Rod says.

"You should," I repeat.

"We should *what?*" Walker says, growing increasingly annoyed.

I lean forward over the table. "You *should* care who he is."

Rod laughs. "Yeah? And why's that?"

"Well, I'll give you three reasons."

They both exchange glances and then stare back at me. Walker shrugs. "Whatever."

"Fine," I say, smiling. "Well, for one, this kid's name is Mickey."

"As in 'Mickey Mouse'?" Rod sneers.

"As in 'Mickey Mantle.'"

"Great. Hiya, Mickey," Walker says, cocking his head to the side. "Now beat it."

"Second," I continue, ignoring Walker's rudeness. "His name really *is* Junior."

"Thought you said it was Mickey," Rod says, frowning. "Which is it?"

"Both, actually."

"Who the hell cares?!?" Walker exclaims. "Get on with it!" He glares at Junior, who's calmly taken a few steps back from the edge of the table, hands behind his back. I pretend not to notice that he's planted his feet, and I back up two steps to give him a cleaner line of sight.

"And number three," I say with a grin. "He's ambidextrous."

Blank stares look back at me.

"*Ambidextrous*," I repeat.

They continue to gape. Walker shrugs.

I look over at Junior and sigh, shaking my head sadly.

Then I glance back at the two thugs. "What I'm saying," I say, my smile growing wider as I'm no longer able to contain my glee, "Is my kid can pitch with both hands."

Walker seems to grasp what I've said a second before Rod does, but it's too late. Before either one can go for his gun, Junior has hurled both balls, one right after the other, at approximately seventy miles per hour each.

There's a muted *thunk-thunk* as they slam into their foreheads, followed by somewhat-synchronized pirouettes as Walker and Rod gracelessly spin around and crumple face-first into the floor. Peanut shells flutter away in their wake as people around the bar start yelling and scrambling for the exits. In the commotion, Junior and I calmly step out the back exit into the alley.

Once we're in the truck and pulling onto the highway, I look over at him and smile, shaking my head.

"Well, I suppose that went about as well as could be expected." I reach over and punch him in the shoulder. "Thanks for the assist."

My son nods and grins. "You bet, Pops."

Author's Note

This story is a continuation of Mitch's plight from *Orange, Black and Blue*, which originally popped up in my first short story collection, *Snapdragon*.

At a little over 1,300 words, it doesn't qualify as flash-fiction like the original did, but it's still short and sweet, a nice 5-minute read that plunges the reader into the world of bad bets, bumbling Button men and baseball.

And yes, I had ChatGPT provide me with "a B-word that describes a gang member or mafia enforcer" so I could tweak the consonance up above. The result? The word that starts with "B" and describes a gang member or mafia enforcer is "Button man." A "Button man" is a term used to refer to a low-level member of a criminal organization who is often involved in carrying out acts of violence or enforcement on behalf of the higher-ranking members. It is sometimes used as a synonym for "hitman" or "enforcer."

So there you go. Now you can look smart when you start using the name "Button Man" as you talk about mafia goons with your friends.

JACK KARDIAC

Super Secret

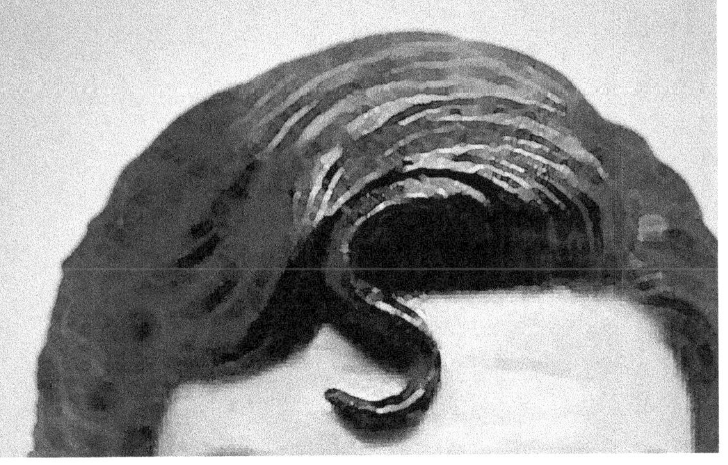

super secret

I'M GRINNING like a schoolboy as I walk through the mini mart's parking lot, an overstuffed bag of groceries nestled in each arm. I honestly can't recall a time in recent history when I've been as content with my life as I am right now, in this very moment.

Ms. Moore waddles a few feet ahead of me, fishing around in her oversized handbag for the keys to her station wagon. She's still ecstatic I was willing to accompany her all the way to her car in the parking lot.

"You understand how it is," she says, "What with the crime rate rising on account of them city-folk moving out here to the suburbs." She turns back and looks at me, shaking her head in disapproval. "It didn't used to be this way, you know. No, used to be a gal could get her groceries and never have to worry about things like that around here."

"Yes, ma'am," I said, nodding my head. I understand her perspective, but a large part of me feels somewhat guilty at her words, because that's exactly what my wife and I did a few months ago — moved out of the chaotic metropolis of the city to enjoy some quiet, country living.

Well, that, and just to get away from the constant crime. Ms. Moore is right, however; it seems to be getting worse everywhere these days, city *or* country.

"Ah, here they are!" she exclaims, retrieving a large keyring from her purse, dangling a minimum of twenty keys on it. She miraculously finds the correct one on the first try, inserts it into the lock and swings open the station wagon's wide side door.

"There you go, Ms. Moore," I say after I place the bags inside, ensuring they're going to stay upright on the trip home. I shut the door and smile at her. "See you at church tomorrow, ma'am?"

"Oh, posh!" she says, waving me away with a hand. "Don't you go 'ma'amin' me, Joe. I'm only sixty-five, you know!"

"I... did not know that..."

"Thank you again for carrying my groceries to the car, though." She eases herself into the driver's seat. "You tell your Momma that she raised you right, you hear?"

I blush, but manage a genuine smile. "Yes, ma'am. I'll do that," I say with a cordial nod.

"Again with the *ma'am*...!"

"Right! Sorry ma'am... er... just... Sorry."

"That's better. See you tomorrow, then." She backs out and drives away, not waiting for a response.

I wave as she pulls into the street, then take a few extra seconds to appreciate the brilliant red sunset exploding on the horizon in the distance. I close my eyes and breath in deeply, holding it for a few seconds before exhaling, soaking up the sun's rays. Sunsets always have a calming, almost alien effect on me. As if they have a way of somehow making me feel smaller in the world, almost weaker, to a degree.

I relish the feeling. It's as if the universe itself takes a fleeting moment to remind me that the pace of the planet doesn't actually move at the speed of sound. At the end of the day I'm just one man, and can only do so much to make a positive impact on the world and those around me.

Some days it seems all of humanity suffers from hurting hearts, and no matter how much I've tried to plug up the leaking gaps in the dam, there's always going to be a new one springing elsewhere. Always. It never ends, and it can get overwhelming. Draining. Sunsets give me perspective, a new frame of mind. They bless me with the daily mental and emotional reset button I so desperately need. Despite my tender heart and God-given talents, in the end, I'm only one man.

My wife keeps me grounded. She ensures I stay "down to earth" so I won't spend too much time with my "head in the clouds." It was initially her suggestion that I take some time off from work, an unofficial sabbatical so we could stop the insane, insistent pace we were finding ourselves trapped in every day. We needed to be still and *rest* — together — even if only for a month or two.

At first I balked at the idea, protesting that I was too critical to the team, to our success, but we both knew she had hit a nerve. She's good like that. When I stopped resisting, I had to take a step back and really examine myself, my mindset. As gently as she could, she challenged me to take a closer look at my self-identity, separating who I truly am from the man the world *wants* me to be.

In the end, I had to conclude that she was right in her assessment. As much as I want to believe it, I'm not indispensable or invulnerable to exhaustion. I had needs, just like everyone else, and if I pretended I didn't it wasn't going to end well. Thankfully my coworkers gladly reassured me they'd all in during my absence, continuing to fight the good fight while I indulged in some long overdue off time.

As I walk back to the front doors of Dee-N-Cee's Mini Mart, I laugh, mulling over the words.

Off time.

Vacation.

I'd heard the terms used by others constantly over the years, but I never thought to apply them to my own life. For as long as I could remember, my life moved like a locomotive, barreling along like a speeding bullet, barely staying on the tracks. I had to admit to myself that a large part of me *liked* living that way. I did. Seeing the needs of others and lending a helping hand in an emergency was a kind of adrenaline rush to me. It made me feel good, inside and out.

It was only when it was suggested that I might be addicted to these feelings that I considered slowing down. Not so much for myself or my own health, but for the sake of our marriage. It was a sobering day when I recognized, as a direct result of my brisk pace and commitment to my work, the two of us had never really celebrated a proper honeymoon.

She hadn't corrected me or protested when I mentioned this one night, but simply stared out the window blankly, as if a silent, secret pain was slowly resurfacing.

That was all I needed to see.

The following week we lined up an extended stay in a

remote cabin in the country, and I applied for a job at Dee-N-Cee's, working as a clerk. Granted, we didn't need the money and the languid, sluggish pace was the complete opposite of the speed I'd become accustomed to moving, but that was exactly why I loved this job so much.

I'd always wanted to do something more with my time on this earth than *work*. And now, with fewer hours and less fires to put out, I feel like I'm an actual, honest-to-God *human being*. Making real connections. Spending time in the country and seeing the same friendly faces, day in and day out, helped jog my earliest memories about what truly mattered in life. It reminded me of who I was, who I wanted to be, and why I first felt called to my vocation in the first place.

Today, I'm at peace.

Today, I finally feel like I'm *home*.

This is my new life now, and I'm genuinely, inexplicably satisfied with it.

The door chimes softly overhead as I walk in, and I'm instantly accosted by the stark aroma of hot dogs spinning on their rollers by the check-out counter. Even after working at Dee-N-Cee's for nearly a month, I'm still amazed how pieces of meat can slow cook for hours and *not* become tough as jerky. I stare at the tubes, mentally counting off the different strains of bacteria undoubtedly swimming in the juices.

"Welcome back, boy scout," a voice says from around the end of the counter.

I walk over and see my manager, Dee, working on a

crossword puzzle. She reaches out, retrieves a hot dog from atop the rollers and shoves an end into her mouth, crooked teeth severing the leathery skin.

I frown. "Uh... boy scout?" I ask, pushing my glasses back up the bridge of my nose.

"That's right," she says, grinning at me. "Escorting ol' Ms. Moore out to the parking lot. Just like an oversized boy scout, you are!"

"Um... well, she looked like she could use the help, so I—"

"You know she's got the hots for you, don't you?"

I blush. "I... did not..."

"Ah, I'm just teasing you, Kenton," she says through her second mouthful. "Thing is, you're the best employee I ever hired. Reliable, on time and super-friendly to the customers. You stick around a little longer and this place is gonna end up being the most popular attraction in town!"

She lowers what's left of the hot dog and frowns. "You *are* planning on stickin' around, right?" It's not a question. "I mean, I know you said you wanted to just do it month-to-month and all, but... well, like I said... you're super. Manager's thrilled to have you around."

"I thought... you... were the manager."

"I am." She takes another bite and grins at me.

I clear my throat. "Well, I'm not planning on leaving anytime soon," I say, smiling back at her.

"Well, thank the stars! That's some good news, what that is."

"I'm just glad you took me on. Not everyone's willing to hire a stranger like you did."

"Eh, you seemed like a pretty good guy, and I was

desperate for help as it was, so... yeah... don't go gettin' a swollen head there, big guy."

"Gee, I... thank you?" My smile clouds over with confusion.

"Whatever," Dee says, shoving the rest of her hot dog into her mouth and returning to her crossword puzzle. "Plus, you look super-cute in that tight yellow T-shirt."

I feel my face flush, shaking my head. "Um..."

"Ah, I'm just messing with you again, Kenton! I know you're married to that hot wife of yours. An' you know I've been happily hitched to Cecil for the past forty-four years. Doesn't mean I can't mess with your head once in a while."

"Dee," I say. "I just have to say I think you're probably the strangest boss I've ever had." I shake my head again.

"And let's keep it that way, shall we?" she says, giving me a thumbs up. "Looks like it's gonna be a quiet night around here, what with the high school football game going on across town. Stocked the bathrooms yet?"

"Done."

"Beer shelves?"

"Yes, ma'am."

"Swept the floor?"

"While you were taking your nap, yes."

She gives me a menacing scowl. "Don't you get smart with me, tough guy."

"My apologies," I say. "I didn't know messing with heads only went one way."

"Yeah? Well, now you do." She wags a greasy finger to scold me. "Parking lot trash?"

"The lot's been swept clean, cans emptied and new liners

inside," I report. "I also filled the bins with fresh washer fluid and restocked the paper towels."

"Wow. You did all that while I was out?"

"I did."

"Crud, you're fast."

"I aim to please." I stand erect and salute her, fighting the grin spreading across my face. I really am having fun at this job.

"Uh-huh," she says, eyeing me skeptically. "Well, tell ya what. I've been meaning to repaint those cement guard posts by the pumps for the past few months. Since it's so quiet tonight an' you're stuck in efficiency overdrive, seems like now might be a good time to tackle it. Whaddaya say?"

"I'd love to. Where do I start?"

"Got two cans of that Krylon royal blue paint back on the second shelf of the utility closet. Should be a large brush beside 'em." She looks up from her crossword. "I can grab you some newspapers to boot if you'd like. So's you don't splatter all over the pavement."

"I think I can manage," I say over my shoulder as I walk into the back storage area.

"I'm sure you will," she mumbles absently, returning her attention to her crossword puzzle while reaching over to pluck another dog from the display.

I hear the faint front door chime as I navigate my way to the utility closet in the back. I've been slowly attempting to clean up and organize the storage area, but I didn't want to do too much too soon. As Dee's already keyed into, I'm nothing if not super-efficient. I can't help it. Sometimes I think perfection was hard-wired into my DNA. Honestly, I can't *not* be efficient, even if I tried.

Spotting the cans of paint on the shelf, I hang one on each hand and stick the paintbrush into my back pocket. I'm pushing through the swinging doors in back when I begin to sense something's wrong.

I walk around the candy display on the end cap and stop directly in front of the dairy case. Dee stands at the counter, arms raised into the air, face filled with fear. Her eyes involuntarily dart to me, and that's when I realize a moment too late what's happening.

A skinny teenager whips around the end of the aisle, gun leveled at my chest. I can see the punk is clearly strung out on something, probably hoping he can score some cash to get his next fix. And what better place to hit than a sleepy mini-mart while the rest of town — law enforcement included — is preoccupied with the game?

The kid is jumpy, though, and I know what's about to transpire the moment we make eye contact. It all happens as if in slow motion, and my mind processes every single second as it unfolds.

The muzzle explodes, blasts of lightning and smoke shooting into the air. I look at Dee, staring at her in mock shock and terror, and I can't help but feel a strong sense of sadness for what's about to happen. This past month has been one of the best months of my life, and one I've vowed never to forget. To have it all end like this, so suddenly... well, it just doesn't seem fair.

As the bullets speeds toward me, I think about my wife back home. Tonight we'd been planning to have a late dinner together at the local diner. Genuine, artery-clogging, Southern-fried food with all the fixings, followed by a heaping helping of apple pie. *A la mode.*

My heart sinks as it becomes increasingly clear in the unfolding moment that date night is about to be canceled. She was right, of course. About everything.

This job? This quiet, secret life I've painstakingly created? It isn't real. She warned me, told me flat-out that the day would come when reality would impress itself on me once again, reminding me of who I was, and why I've always done what I do.

I close my eyes as bullets rain down on me like bees of lead.

The milk display behind me shatters instantly.

The cans of paint in my hands each explode in tandem, creating random splatters of blue across my chest, almost completely obscuring the yellow of my T-shirt. I hear the imperceptible snap of a cable splitting apart just overhead. The bright red poster advertising the latest soft drink falls free, floating gracefully down toward me, two edges draping themselves across my suddenly sticky shoulders like a crude cape.

I feel my shoes dampen and glance down to see I'm standing in a river of milk flowing freely from the shattered case behind me. As I stare, my broken glasses and blonde wig fall away and land at my feet. My stubborn, jet-black lock of hair suddenly pops out over my forehead once again, hanging down to create my famous curl.

I look up and stare at my reflection in the faded mirror behind Dee, sighing at the bizarre yet unmistakable pattern the paint has created on me. The distinct outline of an iconic shield and a splattered "S" are now emblazoned across my chest, and my mind can't help but calculate the astronomical odds of everything unfolding in this exact sequence of events.

I sigh, looking at the faces of Dee and the kid. Both stare back at me, wide-eyed and frozen, mirroring identical reactions of shock and recognition. My shoulders sink as I come to the realization that my vacation has come to a swift and abrupt end.

Then my frown slowly transforms into an unstoppable grin.

Lois was right.

It's time I went back to work.

Author's Note

It may surprise you to know that when I was a child, I didn't really enjoy reading. All the stories I was required to read for school honestly weren't that enjoyable. Plus, I was being *forced* to read them, so a lot of the joy of reading was inherently sucked out of the experience.

Then one day when I was around ten, my family visited some college friends of my parents up in North Dakota. The other kids wanted to take my brothers and I out snowmobiling, but I didn't really want to, so while Eric and Kolby both went, I opted to stay inside...

...a single decision that changed the entire course of my life.

You see, the mother of the house felt bad and didn't want me to be bored, so she ushered me into one of the boy's bedrooms and pointed to where his comic books were, insisting I should read some.

So I did. And quickly fell head-over-heels, madly in love.

The characters! The dialogue! The action!

It was all so... marvelous! Amazing and *Fantastic* and **Incredible!**

When the kid came back inside he was justifiably horrified that his mother had given a strange kid access to his secret stash. When I showed him how I had the utmost respect for the pages, however, turning them gingerly from just below the upper corner, then carefully returning each issue to its protective sleeve, he had a change of heart. At the end of the night he gave me a stack of comic books to take home, as my very own!

That day changed my life, and I've been a fan of comic books ever since. If you can't already tell from my writing style, superheroes and powers play a big part in my stories. I can't explain it, but it just feels "right" when I breathe life into these everyday heroes.

So when I had the idea of writing a short story based on one of the most famous comic book icons ever created, it just felt... right.

As usual, there are plenty of clues along the way (the title, the cover, keywords, etc.), but hopefully I had some of you guessing until the very end!

Blind Date

JACK KARDIAC

blind date

4:35PM

Sandy,

I thought you should know that I'm going to be keeping a record of my entire night. 😃 I also want you to know if this blind date you set up doesn't work out? I am going to just die. 💀 Do you hear me? D.I.E. And you should know I'm going to totally blame you for it, girl.

"Mandy, you're too cooped up all the time. Sure, you're a mechanical engineer and math prodigy, but you look like a supermodel hottie, girl! 💃 You need to get out more! Go on a date! Breathe some new life into that stuffy heart of yours!"

That's what you said, remember? Sure, you noted I've got the brains to match the body, which I appreciated, but you said I'm slowly suffocating myself, "cramped" up in my high-rise corner office all the time, day after day. That I should "get out" and "live a little," right? (Those were your words, Sandy, not mine.) 😜

So I just wanted to make it official, right now and in writing. Well, in text, which is kinda like writing…

I, Mandy Miner, being of sound mind, super fashion sense and über hot body, hereby swear that if this blind date ends in an absolute disaster (and it probably will), I will officially hold my sister, Sandy Stein, responsible. ✌ (That's supposed to be a Scout's Honor thing, with two fingers, but I can't find it, so… just pretend)

There. Now Imma get ready for this thing and get it over with already.

6:04PM

You didn't write back. 😠 Is something wrong with your phone, or are you ignoring me? Don't do that. Write back already. 💋

Anyhow, he's late.

He is late, Sandy. 😠😠

Lateness is not something I admire in a man. Lateness is akin to carelessness. Or at least that's what Mom always said. And Dad? He reminded me just last week that if I'm not at least ten minutes early to an appointment, I'm late.

And that's what this guy is, Sandy.

Late.

By over four minutes, too.

You know me, Sandy. You know I have high standards. Dates get graded. It helps me keep things in perspective, to kind of remove my heart from the mixed-up emotions these kinds of situations can create and evaluate them from a distance.

I make it easy. Every date gets an easy 10 points possible — if they don't screw up.

And out of 10 points possible?

This guy's getting a -2 so far.

The guy I went out with last week? Brad — Brian? — whatever. He got a total of 3 points. He was on time, which gave him an easy point, right there. (No, I'm not saying I'm easy, you Nasty Girl! But when it comes to making points with me on a date, I'm not hard to please, either.)

I gave him another point just for having a clean, detailed car. I'm talking spotless. It was clear he'd put a lot of time and effort into making it look nice. So sick and tired of dates opening a door only to have me sit down in their personal dumpster. I don't care how nice your Corvette looks. If I spy even one crunchy, stale french fry on the floor — you're not getting a second date. Ever. 🚫

But that guy? Über clean car. Immaculate.

Too bad it smelled like butt. 💩🕳️

Seriously, Sandy, I'm not even kidding.

The car was impressive as hell, but the smell. 💨 Pee and You. Ew? You? How do you spell that? Pee-yoo? Sure.

As soon as I sat down I told him to roll the top down. I was literally gasping for relief. Pretended I loved the feeling of fresh air blowing through my hair.

I hate fresh air blowing through my hair, Sandy. 😾

My hair was perfect until then.

I could have just died. ☠️

Bzzt! Minus two points. ⚡ So he was back at zero. 

He took me to Fargali's, that fancy new Italian restaurant on Seale Drive? Four points, right there. ✔ The toasted ravioli was decent, but the chicken marsala was to die for! The aroma itself was divine, and I'm pretty sure I turned him on just by leaning over and inhaling it, you know, with my eyes closed and all.

Or maybe he just liked staring at my cleavage.

Whatever.

So he's at four points, right? Then he surprised me. Instead of going out to see The Last Whisper (the play we had talked about), he said he's taking me to a smaller show that he thinks I'd like better. I was pretty skeptical, 'cause, you know me, I'm a picky girl to begin with. I just know what I like, what's the point of settling for anything but the best?

That, and I really don't like surprises.

So I smiled and pretended I was excited, and we headed back into his Butt Mobile and drove (windows down) to Huffington Point. You know, where they have those small, intimate shows for indie bands and singer-songwriters and whatnot? Yeah, that's the one.

So my interest was piqued even more and I gave him an extra point for that. He was at five at that point, which was pretty dang good for a blind date, Sandy!

We walked inside, sat down and do you know who's playing that evening?

Duncan Sheik.

Duncan. Sheik.

DUNCAN SHEIK, Sandy!!

You know, that guy who sang "Barely Breathing" back in the early 90's? Sure, some people might refer to him as a "one-hit wonder," but not me. I've been following his musical career for years, and I'm not the least bit ashamed to say that I simply adore that troubadour! The man took my breath away!

Scored four more points for Brad. Or Brian.

Whatever his name was, he was at a total of eight, okay? A Blind Date record (and this was despite the funky car crap).

Sure, it was a short concert, but I was loving every minute of it. Even let the guy put his arm around me, as if we were a genuine couple out for our anniversary or something.

I didn't mind. It was cold inside the place anyway, so I was glad to let him provide the extra warmth I needed. Plus, he smelled pretty fantastic.

Now, lemme ask you something: how can someone who smells so good not have a stinking clue that his clean car smells like butt?

Maybe it's me. 

Maybe I'm just super sensitive to smell?
You know I can't help it. I just know what I
like, and I like things that smell nice.

So anyway, the concert ended and he took
me back home, we had great conversation
and I was really kinda enjoying myself. Then
he pulled up and parked in front of the
wrong house. I was about to tell him that he
missed my driveway by like, three houses,
when the guy leans in and kisses me.

KISSES ME, Sandy.

On the lips.

So I punched him.

Right in the sternum. And then when he
pulled back, gasping for air? I popped him
one in the eye, just like Daddy taught us.
Ka-Pow!! 

He started whining and wheezing and I took
the liberty of letting myself out of the car,
slamming the door hard. And as I was
walking back to my house, he gets out of
the car and starts to call after me,
apologizing.

Then he made his biggest mistake of the
evening.

"Candy," he whines, "I'm sorry! Please! Can
we talk about this?!?"

Can you believe that?

Candy?!? 😾😾

So I turned around, drew a deep breath into my lungs and I yelled back, "My name is Mandy!! And no, we can't talk about it. We're done! Goodnight and goodbye."

And I walked up the steps and inside.

Looking back, I think the whole scenario was kind of sad. I mean, the guy had so many positive points to start with, but he almost lost all of them by being a kissy-face freak in the end. So why did I leave him with 3 points?

Because he took me to Fargali's, Sandy. ✔️

And as we both know, the cheesecake at Fargali's is heavenly. Smothered in raspberry sauce? Just to die for. 💕💀💋

Okay. Now it's 6:23pm and still no...

Hold. Doorbell just rang.

Be right back.

...after I finish ripping someone's heart out. 🚫🖤

Plus, my thumbs are starting to hurt so Imma take a break. Byeeeee....

- Mandy

(Why did I sign my name? As if you don't know it's from me…? Pfft) 😆

7:02PM

Sandy, I know you're going to be surprised by what I'm about to say, but I think I may have overreacted a bit. I know, I know… Daddy says I'm a passionate gal and I feel everything intensely, which is true. And yes, the guy was super late. But when I was fuming earlier I didn't anticipate he'd actually have a good reason for being late.

And he did. 😁

So here's the thing, when he knocked on the door I was all prepared to give him a piece of my mind and tear his heart out. But when I threw the door open and saw the blood on his hands, I knew I should probably shut my mouth and let him be the first to speak.

He started by apologizing for not only being late, but for his appearance as well. He was dressed in slacks and a silky white, tight button-up shirt. I usually don't pay attention to a guy's body, but this guy was looking pretty good from the neck down. 😎

From the neck up… eh, I guess kinda so-so. 😕 Sandy hair that could've used a comb, and flat, brown eyes. Yeah, he isn't much of a looker, to be honest.

Anyhow, his hands were both lined with scratch marks across the palms, and I quickly rushed him over to the sink to rinse them off. With the water running over his hands, he proceeded to tell me how he'd been all ready for our date (and actually left at 5:30pm to make sure he'd be early). But on the way over he saw an old lady by the side of the street, sitting by a tree outside her house and sobbing.

He admitted that he drove on by at first, but the more he thought about her, the more he couldn't get that image out of his mind. Said he asked himself what he would want someone to do if they saw his mother crying by the side of the road? (He actually became teary at this point, and I'll admit it — it kinda choked me up.)

So he turned around and pulled up to the curb and asked her what was wrong. She waved him off at first, out of embarrassment, but when he got out of the car and approached her, she ran into his arms and started bawling. Can you believe that?

After a bit he was able to peel her away and determine what the problem was. And Sandy, you're not going to believe what she said! She actually told him that her cat was stuck in the tree! Can you believe that? An old lady crying over a cat stuck in a tree? That's just classic. Straight out of that scene from The Incredibles, right?

So anyway, he asks her if she has a ladder in her garage, and when he retrieves it he climbs up to coax the cat out of the tree. He said it was super cute and super friendly and scampered right over to him, but when he grabbed it and started to go back down the ladder, the thing freaked out and started clawing the crap out of him.

He said he barely made it down without breaking his neck, but soon he was on the ground, cat safely in the lady's arms again. She offered to bandage him up and reward him for his efforts, but he declined, knowing he was already super late for our date.

Sandy, isn't that just insane?!

I can hardly believe it myself, but to be honest he does look pretty messed up, with his hands full of scratches and all. After I bandaged them up he asked again for my forgiveness, and I held my breath and pretended I had to think about it.

I told him that I was touched by what he did, and I thought we should still give our date a shot. Grandma was right; if you find a man who knows how to treat a woman and who loves animals? You've got yourself a keeper.

I think I just might have found a keeper, Sandy.

Will write more later.

Right now, we're going on a date!

8:36PM

Sandy, this is the worst date of my entire life. 😠

The worst. 😈

Where do I even begin?!

Okay, so the guy saved the cat and made Granny do the happy dance. I loved that, but then he lost some serious points when we went to dinner.

"And where did you go to eat, dinner, Mandy?"

Arby's.

He took me to Arby's.

Arby's, Sandy! ARBY'S!

I couldn't believe it.

I thought he was just joking with me when we pulled into the parking lot, like maybe we were going to park there and actually walk across the street to siZZles, that steakhouse I've been dying to go to. 👟

But no, he was dead serious. Said he wanted to start a "grounded relationship" with me, where we weren't putting on airs or pretending to be something we're not. He said he didn't want to date a girl if she was only interested in his money, so this was his way to sift through the stifled "fancypants fakers" and uncover the "meaty girls."

Sandy. Those were his exact words.

Uncover the meaty girls.

I Am Not A Meaty Girl.

Why did I ever let you talk me into this date?

Anyhow, at that point I realized I was completely trapped with the guy ('cause he was my ride home and all). So I took a deep breath, put on my best I'm A Blonde Idiot smile and ordered the most expensive item I could find on the menu. Do you know what that is, Sandy? Neither did I, so I asked the kid behind the counter.

"What's the most expensive thing on the menu?" I asked.

"Meat Mountain." He started grinning at me, and it was creepy and cute at the same time.

"Excuse me?" I said as I looked up at the menu display behind him.

There was no "Meat Mountain" up there.

"Mean Mountain," he repeated, eyes bouncing down to my chest the entire time. 🍑🍑•• I ignored him. Turns out it wasn't on the menu because it's a "secret" item. Comes with every kind of meat they sell, all sandwiched between two buns. Super expensive.

I knew I wouldn't even come close to finishing it, but I didn't care. This guy said he wanted a "meaty girl"? He was gonna pay for it. 💰💰💸💸

I ordered two. (The second one "to go.") 😛

I told him that I completely agreed with him, and how I found it refreshing to meet someone with the same values as mine.

Ugh. I wanted to barf inside. 🤢

Plus, there was this creepy-but-hot guy in the back corner, wearing a sweet black suit and tie, sipping on his Frosty and just staring at us. It was super creepy, Sandy. 🕵

So, that's it. instead of eating siZZle's award-winning prime rib with a side of sautéed mushrooms and their elegant, grilled herb potatoes, I ate a quarter of a Meat Mountain.

At Arby's. ‼️

Heck, I would've had a better time at The Perky Peach. Or even Nacho Wong's, for that matter!

I feel like I'm dying a slow, torturous death, here, Sandy.

Grrrr....

And what's up with the dark clouds outside of town? It looks like some weird London fog rolling in or something. Super creepy.

I say that a lot, don't I? Super creepy.

It's fun to say.

Super. Creepy.

Oh, and I figured out why you're not texting back. You're working at the hospital, so your phone's probably locked up down in the lockers. Whatever. I'm still gonna write, probs so I can stare at my screen instead of acknowledging this disaster. Ugh.

9:17PM

Okay. Now, I know you're going to think I'm completely schizophrenic or have multiple personalities or whatever, but here's the thing: I think I misjudged Morris. And here's why:

He may have just saved my life.

(And Muffle's as well.)

Let me explain.

We finish eating at Arby's and he asks if I want to go see a movie. I kindly decline and force out the best fake yawn I can, then tell him I needed to get to bed early because you and I have an early morning coffee breakfast thing planned, and I don't want to be too tired.

Yes, Sandy, I lied.

And totally threw you under the bus. Thankfully, he doesn't know you like I do, so he had no idea you're gonna be partying all night long after your shift and probably won't see your next breakfast until Sunday at noon (if you'll even be sober by then, you naughty girl!).

So just as we arrive back at the house and he's pulling up to the curb, something scuttles in front of his car and we hit it. WE HIT IT, Sandy! We both screamed (I'm pretty sure his was higher-pitched than mine), and he pulls over to the side of the street and stops the car. We open our doors and walk around to the front of the car to inspect the damage, and I scream again.

Sandy, you're not going to believe what it was.

Wedged between his tire and the wheel well on my side of the car is an ant. AN ANT, Sandy! Only this thing was the size of a dog!

And I mean a LARGE dog! Not like Muffles or Staples, but BIG, like… well, not Clifford, but you get the idea.

Morris jumped back when he sees it, wheezing and wriggling around, trying to get free. And I'm all freaking out, because, well, THERE'S A GIANT ANT stuck in his car! It was wiggling and screeching and I swear, it was staring at me with those cold, black eyes. Ew. 👽

Did you know ants don't have eyelids?

They don't, so it just stared at me the whole time. Super creepy. ⚫⚫

I was looking over Morris' shoulder, and I saw another ant run around the corner of the park, which was all foggy and stuff, like a thick steam bath at the sauna. Then a whole bunch of them run out of the mist and I screamed and he started screaming, and we both dove back inside his car while the whole street just erupted with giant freaking ants, like a volcanic wave of bug lava. 🌋🐜🐜

ANTS EVERYWHERE SANDY! It was insane! 🐜🐜🐜🐜🐜

So we're sitting in his car, panting hard and struggling to catch our breath, when Morris slams his foot on the gas. There was some resistance at first, and then we hear a loud thump and the tires crawl over the ant as we drive away. I look back out the rearview window, hoping to see a smushed ant on the pavement behind us.

It wasn't dead, but it wasn't moving fast, either. Just like, limping along or something. Then it was surrounded by all its ant friends and they started taking it apart. 🤢

Sandy. It was so disgusting. I can't even. 🤮🤮

So Morris drives like a maniac and he gets the bright idea to turn on the radio. The broadcast guy is super frantic, and we can barely understand a word he's saying 'cause he's so hysterical.

He's crying, and says there's some kind of a monstrous, foggy cloud thing blowing into town and gigantic ants of all sizes are coming out of it.

He's screaming for everyone to get out of town, to find shelter or something, and that's when he starts sobbing uncontrollably. 😭 A second later we hear him scream, and not a manly yelling or whatnot. This guy is shrieking like a girl, Sandy! 😱😱

Then there's this… sound… Like clicking and ripping or something, the microphone gets bumped a bunch of times, and a terrible, suffocating silence sets in. Dead air. 💀💀💀

I turn to look at Morris and I'm about to say something when I see it. Up the street a bright yellow school bus appears at the top of the hill, only it isn't just yellow. It's yellow and red and brown, 'cause it's covered with giant ants! 🚌🐜🚌🐜

The driver's honking the horn, swerving from side to side in the street, and they're getting closer. Heading right for us.

Morris sees it too and gasps, then starts screaming until I slap my hand over his mouth. We watch as the bus, covered in ants, speeds right past us in the street and disappears from view down the hill.

I take my hand off his mouth and start to hyperventilate, telling him how I'm too young to die, how I'm not ready, how I want to get married, have kids, watch little league soccer games and get into fights at the PTA — everything that pops into my head. And suddenly he nods his head and smiles this weird, distant smile. He looks over at me and tells me he can save me.

I didn't get it. I stared at him and shook my head. What was he even talking about? I explained to him that no one could be safe at this point. The world was swarming with giant ants! We were all dead, it was just a matter of time.

But he shook his head and smiled, and that's when he told me he had — you're never gonna believe this, Sandy — a bunker under his house.

A bunker!

Of all the guys I go on a date with, I end up with a survival nut on the very day of the "misty ant apocalypse." What are the odds of that?!? I figure I must've done something right to deserve him.

So he's about to pull back into the street when I scream, tell him to stop the car. I tell him I can't just leave Muffles behind. He looks at me like I'm crazy, so I explain how when I first got her as a puppy, I didn't know whether to call her Oodles or Muffin, so I went with Muffles. 🤭

He still doesn't get it, though, and tells me I'm crazy and he isn't about to die because I want to save some stupid mutt.

That's right. He called her stupid. 😠

So what do I do? I reach over, pull the keys out of the ignition shove them into my purse. I hear him screaming after me as I bolt out the door, running up to the house, fumbling with the door code until I hear the click and I fling it open.

I didn't even have to call for Muffles, she was right there by the door, waiting for me! So I snatched her right up, ran back to the car, jumped in and handed back his keys.

Well, you can imagine how mad he is at that point, yelling at me for "risking our lives" over a stupid dog. I don't want to waste any more time, so I apologize, lean over and kiss him quick. 💋 Then I tell him to "shut up and save us already."

He stared at me for a few moments, then looks down at Muffles and frowns. When I point out the windshield at the oncoming ants and scream at him to do something, he finally wakes up enough to start the car and drive. We pull out of the driveway and tear off down the street.

Wow, this is a long text. 😳 Sorry, Sandy. I should probably put this in some kind of note app, but I guess I want to make sure someone reads this, you know? Plus, I can always copy it into something else later, right? 😎

Anyhow, I begin asking questions about the bunker, why he thinks it can save us and for how long. He basically tells me to shut my mouth so he can focus on driving and get us there without getting overrun by an army of ants. 🐜🐜🐜

Well, you know me. I've never been one to respond well to verbal abuse (apocalypse or not!), so Muffles and I ignore him the rest of the way there, giving him the complete silent treatment. I don't know if he noticed or even cared, but it was necessary. I wasn't going to put up with crap like that from anyone, whether the guy was saving my life or not. 🚫

Morris wasn't lying, though. Within less than five minutes we arrive. He doesn't slow his car down, but jumps the curb and tears up the grass beside the house, smashing through the thin fence until he's in the backyard.

Takes the keys out of the ignition, grabs a duffle bag from the back seat and dumps all his exercise clothes and shoes out of it. Then he grabs Muffles and stuffs her inside, zipping the bag tight. I'm about to yell at him when he holds his hand up to silence me.

So rude. 

Then he says if I want my dog to live then we have to protect it.

He jumps out of the car and I run after him, until he stops in front of a beat-up, broken-down tool shed in the corner of the yard.

My heart sank. 

That was it? That was his big plan? 

Hiding out in his backyard shed?!? 

I mean, the date was a disaster up to this point, but being locked inside a shed with this loser? Well, let's just say that I decided then and there that if it was up to us to repopulate the world one day? The world was going to come to a swift and sudden end. Because I would have rather died than get frisky with this jerk.

He hands me the Muffles duffle, opens the rusty shed doors, and we sprint inside, shutting them behind us. I turn around and see Morris throw aside a dusty tarp to reveal a trap door in the floor. It was surprisingly clean compared to the rest of the shed, and had a massive turn handle thing on top. He punches a code into a keypad and the wheel unspools itself automatically, ending with the door popping up from the floor a few inches. He grabs the lip and flings it open to reveal a narrow set of steps leading into darkness.

It was terrifying, Sandy. Absolutely terrifying. 😱

I mean, come on. Every horror movie involving abducted girls and basements suddenly bubbles up in my mind, and I freeze, staring down at the blackness below. A second later I feel his hand on my shoulder and he shoves me. Hard. 😠

I barely have time to catch myself on the edges before my feet find the steps below, and I stumble through the hole and fall to the floor, Muffles bouncing in the bag with a yelp.

When I look back up, the latch is closing and then the world goes black again. I scream, furiously cussing him out for what he's done and start to jump up toward the steps when I bump into him. He tells me to calm down, that he's looking for a light.

Well, I was already amped up, though, so I kind of, accidentally slugged him in the stomach.

He didn't like that.

He grunted, and then lifted his arm to punch me back.

He was going to punch me, Sandy!

He stops himself, but as I dodge I fall back to the ground, knocking the wind out of me. I try to catch my breath, and that's when the reality of my situation sunk into me, like a sneaky stinger just under my skin.

I was now trapped inside an underground bunker with an unhinged, borderline-abusive maniac.

Yes, this is officially the worst date of my life.

12:13AM

Okay, where was I? Oh, yeah. The jerk almost punched me. I lost my breath. It wasn't pretty.

Anyhow, after he managed to get the lights on and we were able to kind of calm down a bit, get our heads together. The room was small and cramped, maybe fifteen feet by twenty feet. There was a cot in a corner, a small toilet beside it and rows of canned goods on the shelves.

Sandy. I just about puked. 

This was his bunker? This… dump? This was where I was going to spend the next few days or weeks or months until we were rescued?

I started to cry. 

He sat up and glared at me, his hands cradling his soft stomach. He told me to calm down. I told him exactly what he could do with his crappy "bunker."

Then he smiled.

Not like a creepy, "I've got you in my clutches now" kind of smile, but a "I've got a secret and it's awesome" kind, if that makes sense. And now that I look back, it was kind of awesome.

Sandy, I don't even know how I'm ever going to send this to you or if you're still alive or being eaten by crazy, gigantic ants, but I need to keep writing. Because you are not going to believe what happened next.

After I finish ranting, Morris smiles at me. That's when I knew he was psychotic. I start digging around in my purse for my pepper spray as he walks past, toward the cot. Just when I find it and flick off the safety, he places his hands on the wall behind me and pushes. It swings aside to reveal a separate, much larger room behind it.

A five-star, Hilton-worthy suite.

Sandy, this place is to die for.

Morris explains that he didn't want to take the chance that someone else might somehow stumble on his real bunker, so he took the extra precaution by making it ultra-secure with the false front. I didn't know what to say, so I just picked up Muffles in the duffle bag and walk past him, avoiding eye contact.

As soon as I cross the threshold I notice the difference. Instead of the cold, cement floor behind us, this room has plush, white carpet. Granted, it's shag and I'm not a fan of shag carpets (what is this, the 70's?), but compared to the concrete? I can put up with a little shag.

The soft, warm glow of the lamps spread throughout the chamber, giving off just enough light to make it comfortable without being glaring. But what amazes me the most is how huge the place was! I estimate it's at least two thousand square feet, with a central living room and two side rooms, a bathroom and a bedroom. (But I'm telling you right now, Sandy, if this guy thinks I'm sharing a bedroom with him, he's nutso.)

Still, the place is classy beyond belief. I was about to ask him how he managed to do all of this when he explains that he's been preparing for the zombie apocalypse for the past fifteen years, making this his full-time project outside of work. He shrugs and tells me that it works just as well with giant, man-eating ants as it would for the walking dead. 🐜🐜🐜💁💁💁

I unzip Muffles from her bag and set her on the floor, where she starts to wander around and sniff the air, then stops and inhales with extreme interest the back leg of a nearby barstool. Morris gasps and lunges, snatching Muffles up in his hands. He rushes her toward one of the side rooms, and I run after them, screaming. But then he opens the door to reveal an incredible, luxurious bathroom. He kind of carelessly dumps Muffles onto the tile, but I was so enraptured I didn't really care. 🖤🖤

He sees my awe and grins. Then he starts to share the details of the room, and I instantly begin to fall in love. A Kohler DTV shower complete with a wall-mounted LCD touchscreen to control water pressure, temperature and chromatherapy. (You know, the ambient lighting above it? Yeah, it's cool.) That would have been enough to melt this girl's heart, but then he goes on about the 7.1 surround sound system, heated floor tiles and towel racks, and the ionic mister and Tornado body dryer.

Sandy. It has everything I've been dreaming of when I pour over those Crutchfield catalogs during my lunch breaks. Everything. 😌😌😌

I suddenly have a newfound respect for Morris and his toys, and I immediately ask for the full tour, shutting Muffles alone in the bathroom without a second thought. She'll live.

He leads me to the living room and points out the three overstuffed sofa options: plush microfiber, buttery suede or Ettinger leather. This is in addition to the DreamWave massage chair in the corner. Then he picks up the remote, presses a button and the wall comes to life. The wall, Sandy! 😄😄

The entire wall is an LCD screen, so it was virtually invisible until he turned it on. It is absolutely massive, and I'm in love. He motions to the bookshelves beside it and explains how it's stocked with an up-to-date collection of both DVDs and digital movies through his server, with ceiling-mounted speakers from the Bose and Harmon Kardon collaboration line. When he noticed me noticing my chair's vibration, he brags that he installed subwoofers into the furniture structures as well, to add an immersive "4D" experience.

When I ask about the noise levels, he says he anticipated having to keep the sound down to avoid outside detection, so he installed a solid six feet of sound-absorbing foam surrounding the bunker, to prevent any indoor noise from ever escaping. Pretty impressive! 🏆🏆

Next we wander over to the kitchen, where he introduces me to the touch screens on the stovetop as well as the refrigerator, all equipped with mini Bluetooth speakers as well. The pantry is easily the size of my bedroom at home, and stocked with enough food to last a family of four for two years. I couldn't help but choke up a little at that, not only from thinking about our parents back home but also about the idea of being stuck here for that long.

Nope. Surely this will blow over in a few days. Right? 

Sandy, please write back ASAP. I'm not kidding. I need to know you're okay.

The bedroom is equally impressive, with its own widescreen display, private bathroom, a sauna and a built-in jacuzzi. I think he may have said something about the bed even having vibrating capabilities, and that's when the unwanted images crept into my head. I told him I insisted I have the room to Muffles and I. He balked at first, but relented when I explained to him I wasn't about to share a bed with a perfect stranger. (Now or ever.)

We wander back into the living room where I grab the remote and start flipping through channels to find the news and figure out what in the world is going on. Every channel is static. Every one of them. I sat down and shook my head.

That's when he sheepishly explains that he had intended to get the cable working this past week, but he'd been so busy at work he hadn't gotten around to it. So whatever we had on the bookshelf is all we have in terms of entertainment.

I try to dial out on my cell, obviously but I have no bars. I ask him what the wifi password is so I can get online and find out what I need to know. (Plus send you this update, of course…)

Well, that's when he explains that the Internet was going to be part of the cable package.

The package he hadn't hooked up.

Arghhh…

At this point I closed my eyes and took a deep breath.

No TV. No radio.

No phone. No wifi.

No news.

No way to communicate with the outside world whatsoever, in or out.

This is just great.

But not a problem, I say. We'll be out of here in a matter of days, so no big deal, right?

He frowns, and tells me this isn't entirely true.

Turns out that when he designed this place? He wanted to be sure it was safe and secure and not subject to a person's "emotional whims" from the inside. Then he explains that in every zombie movie he's ever seen, the people who get killed first are the ones who don't stay put. "The idiots who venture out from their safety and security before the threat has sufficiently passed."

So he designed his bunker to seal the occupants in for a minimum of a month.

A month, Sandy.

A month!!

I'm stuck down here with this idiot for another four weeks.

This is the worst day of my life. Worst month of my life.

I was about to ask what else could go wrong when I looked around the room and saw them. Or rather, didn't see them. I rose and started to inspect the corners and ceilings. They weren't there, Sandy. Either this guy had installed them in a super-secretive, high-tech way like the rest of the place... or he was a complete and utter moron. 😌😌

So I turned around and asked him point blank.

"Where are the air ducts?" ⁉️

He just kind of stared at me, so I broke it down for him.

"The air ducts?" I asked again, raising my eyebrows. "How did you manage to solve the internal air filtration problem when you designed it?" ⁉️

"What?" he asked, confused.

"This is a sealed, underground bunker, right?" ‼️

That's when the color completely drained from his face.

🙂

Turns out this guy is a moron. But not just an average moron. No, Morris is a Grade A, First Class Moron of the Highest Caliber. 💀💀 💀💀

He tried to wave off my question, insisting we probably had plenty of air to survive for the next two months, but I was already doing the math in my head.

"How big is the bunker?" I asked.

"Why?"

"How big?"

He paused. "3,000 square feet."

"How tall are the ceilings?"

"Eight feet."

A few seconds later I had my answer...

...we're all going to die down there.

He blew me off and insisted I was crazy. Said I was overreacting to the situation and that I should look around myself. That the place was huge, and we'd have plenty of air to go around. Idiot.

I laid it out for him as clear as I could, in plain English and speaking slowly so he'd hear every word.

Two people in an enclosed space. (With furnishings, remember.)

Each breath we take has a volume of 1/64th of a cubic foot.

The current air supply is 3,000 square feet, and with an 8 foot ceiling this lends to approximately 1,536,000 breaths. At best. ✅

A person typically takes 20 breaths a minute. ✅

Every 24 hours we're taking 28,800 breaths. ✅

28,800 breaths per person. Per day. ✅

That leaves us with just over 26 days to live. ✅ 😫 😫

Maximum.

😨 😰 😩 😫 🥴

Sandy.

This is the worst date of my life.

And my last.

Author's Note

IT'S BEEN a long time since I wrote this, but I think I was inspired by The Walking Dead. Not a huge zombie fan (or a fan of gore, for that matter), but you watch enough scenes set in that apocalyptic world and eventually you're gonna ask "What if…?"

By the way, the whole "cat retrieval" scene was real, only it wasn't in a tree. We had some rats throwing a nightly party in our attic while we lived in Indonesia, so I borrowed a neighbor's cat and shoved it up there in the early morning (before it got too hot) for a few hours to see if it wanted a snack or three.

A few hours later I coaxed it back to the attic opening and managed to grab it, but it wasn't thrilled at being so high off the ground and kinda freaked out. I was *thisclose* to having a Nick Fury eyeball-slashing disaster.

Lesson learned: wear protective eyewear around crazed attic cats, kids.

BORKEN

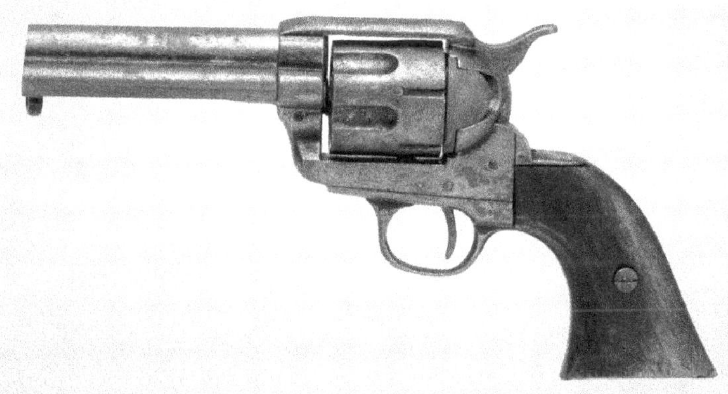

JACK KARDIAC

borken

FOR TWO DECADES NOW, Jerry Crone had been the proud proprietor of King's Pawn Shop, but time hadn't managed to shrink the length of those arduous days. Enduring behind the counter for a grueling ten hours — minus a fleeting forty-five minutes for lunch — had Jerry ready to call it a day and head home. The clock's ticking hands felt like they were in a race with his aching foot, and he eagerly anticipated the soothing touch of his wife Helen's skilled massage. Maybe even catch a football game if one was on TV.

Jerry glanced up at the clock, inhaled deeply and sighed.

5:51pm

Sometimes it felt like the last ten minutes of every day were the last ten minutes of his life. Although he had to admit the job itself wasn't especially grueling or physically demanding. He loved what he did, and having the opportunity to work alongside his son was icing on the proverbial cake. Sure, Tyler wasn't always the brightest tool in the box, but he was his son, and Jerry loved him no matter how many lunkheaded mistakes he might make. God might have shortchanged him in the smarts department, but he'd been extra generous when it came to the heart.

He looked across the checkout counter and noticed a man browsing the hand tools aisle. Young, about mid-to-late 20's if he ventured to guess. What piqued Jerry's interest was how the guy was dressed in all black. Black sneakers, black pants and a button-up black shirt. Even his perfect hair was jet black.

Jerry frowned.

The guy was too old to be in high school, but if he looked a few years younger he could've passed as one of those gothic punks or something. What were they called again? Bono? Elmo? Emo?

Yeah, that was it. Emo.

This guy looked really emo. Downright morbid, when he thought about it. Jerry considered putting on a smile as he approached him, but in the end decided he was just too spent and settled for simply being polite and direct.

"What're you looking for?" he asked.

The man didn't respond, but picked up a small shovel off the rack and examined it, turning it over in his hands.

"Hey," Jerry said, a little louder.

The man looked up at him, startled. "I'm sorry?" he said, eyebrows raised.

"Anything I can help you find?" Jerry stared at him, patience running thinner by the second.

The man smiled. "No, thank you. I'm just browsing." He cocked his head to the side. "You know, killing time while I'm waiting for an appointment."

Jerry nodded, unmoving. "Uh-huh. Well, we're about to

close up shop, so I'm afraid you're gonna have to kill it somewhere else."

The man's smile disappeared. He sighed, then reached out and hung the shovel back on the rack, staring at Jerry the entire time. "Fine," he said, clearly annoyed. "I'll do that." He started walking toward the front door.

"Open tomorrow at eight," Jerry called after him.

The man came to a halt, casting a brief glance back at Jerry. "Well, it's a small town and the night's still young. Maybe I'll see you around before then."

Jerry's brows furrowed as he frowned. "I seriously doubt that."

With a nonchalant shrug, the man said, "Eh, we'll see..." He pivoted and strolled through the front door out into the night.

Jerry's gaze remained fixed on him through the plate glass windows. The man reached the curb, paused, and propped himself against the streetlight, his eyes scanning up the street. He had no reason to feel like he did, but the guy just gave him the creeps. Maybe he'd open up late tomorrow, just to steer clear of encountering that guy first thing in the morning.

Jerry turned and started walking back to the office when the door chime rang. He glanced over his shoulder to see two more men enter. Frowning, Jerry looked up at the clock.

5:57pm

He let out an exasperated sigh. The door should have been locked by now, specifically so he could avoid the awkwardness of ushering customers out after closing. Where was Tyler, anyhow?

"Tyler!" he bellowed toward the back storage area.

A brief silence ensued, and then a face appeared,

partially hidden by the plastic dividers that hung from the doorframe.

"Yeah?"

"What the..." Jerry began, shaking his head. "What are you *doing* back there? Front door's not locked, Tyler. It's time to close up, son."

"I know," Tyler said, walking toward him. "But I had to make a crap."

"Use the bathroom," Jerry corrected.

"Huh?"

Jerry sighed. "We're in the shop, Tyler. With paying customers."

Tyler stopped walking and looked around him. "So?"

Jerry lowered his voice to a hushed whisper. "So you didn't have to 'make a crap,' Tyler. You had to *use the bathroom.*"

Tyler looked back at him and shrugged. "Okay," he said. "So... anyhow... I had to use the bathroom to make a crap..."

Jerry closed his eyes and shook his head.

Oh, lordy...

"...an' I'll tell you one thing," Tyler continued, shaking his head. "That's the *last* time I eat a large order of Komodo Fajita's at Nacho Wong's. Those things practically burned a new butthole back there."

Jerry opened his mouth to speak, then thought better of it and closed it.

"And we were outta toilet paper, so I had to use the paper towels by the sink."

Jerry's eyes widened. "You didn't flush them, did you?" he asked, alarmed.

"What?"

"Tell me you didn't try to flush the paper towels down the toilet, Tyler."

Tyler's face flushed and he looked away, staring intently out the window. "Uhhh..." he said quietly, his voice trailing off.

Jerry let out a deep, heavy sigh that seemed to come from the depths of his being. He closed his eyes, his hand instinctively rising to cover them as if shielding himself from the world. "Oh, lordy, Tyler..."

"No! It's okay!" Tyler said, holding up his hands. "But I forgot to... wash my hands... so I'm just gonna... go do that now." He looked at his father and nodded vigorously. "Imma go wash my hands now." With that he spun around and walked briskly back into the storage room.

Jerry strolled over to the front door, his hand extending to secure the lock. The mysterious man in black remained silhouetted on the sidewalk, back turned to Jerry as he nonchalantly leaned against the post. Outside the formerly serene twilight skies were starting to cloud up overhead, as if they were preparing to unleash a thunderous fury in the next few minutes. He'd have to hurry things up if he intended to make it home without getting drenched.

Locking the door, Jerry walked around the counter and retrieved the plunger from beneath it. Lord knew he'd probably be needing it in the next few minutes, not to mention a couple of bottles of Drano, assuming Tyler did what he suspected he'd done.

Jerry's steps faltered as he made his way toward the back room, his attention snagged by the sight of the two men who had entered earlier. The shorter one, sporting sandy blonde hair, emitted an aura of dishevelment, as if he hadn't showered in a week. A greasy yellow t-shirt clung to his frame, and shorts sagged in desperate need of a belt. He looked nervous, almost anxious, with his fidgety demeanor and darting glances.

The other figure stood tall, with a wiry build and eyes sunk deep into their sockets, giving him an appearance of pale parchment. Draped in an overcoat and sporting combat boots, Jerry thought he bore an uncanny resemblance to the infamous Columbine shooters from the late nineties.

Neither of them resembled typical shoppers, that much was certain.

"We're about to close, folks," he called out. Watching both men closely, he positioned himself at the aisle's end. "Is there something you need help with?"

The shorter man's gaze snapped towards him, eyes widening as if he'd just realized they weren't alone in the store. Meanwhile, the taller flashed Jerry a smile, a grotesque display of teeth stained in a motley array of grays and blacks.

That's when Jerry recognized him.

This guy was the one the cops arrested for dealing drugs near the high school a few months ago. What did they call him? Chemical Herk? Jerk? No... Hank! That was it!

Chemical Hank.

That's what they'd called him.

Jerry tried to hide his alarm.

"Bullets," Hank said, nodding.

"I'm sorry?"

"Ah... I mean, BB's. Do ya'll sell BB's here?"

"BB's? As in, for pellet guns?"

The man nodded. "Yeah. That's right. Can we buy BB's here?"

Jerry paused, eyes bouncing from Hank to his friend and back again. "Sure," he said. "Over in aisle 6. Follow me."

He walked down the aisle and hoped Tyler would have the smarts to see there was a potential situation brewing in the shop. The kid might have dyslexia and ADHD and Lord only knew what else was floating around in his DNA cocktail, but if there was one thing Tyler excelled at, it was marksmanship. He'd won Top Shot in the state fair contests three years straight. Even though Tyler could shoot an antenna off an ant, Jerry personally hoped it wouldn't come to that.

When he walked around the aisle corner he stopped. In front of the gun counter sat an old man, slumped over in his chair. The guy looked like he'd been ripped right out of the pages of an old west adventure magazine.

Wide-brimmed white cowboy hat, buttoned-up shirt and leather vest, faded jeans pulled over a pair of worn and weathered boots, his brass belt buckle glinting in the harsh fluorescent lighting. Despite his rugged appearance, he's slouched over in a deep sleep.

It was Chester Chambers.

"Oh, Lordy," Jerry muttered, shaking his head.

"That guy dead?" the short guy asked from behind him.

"I sure as hell hope not," Jerry muttered. He pointed up ahead of them. "BB's are up on aisle 6, to your right. You guys got five minutes."

They walked past without saying a word, and Jerry

watched them closely, eyes narrowing. *First emo weirdo, then these two tweakers show up and now I gotta deal with Chester. This day just keeps getting better and better...*

He walked over to Chester and held a finger under his nose. A second later the old man's hot air washed over it, and Jerry stopped holding his own breath. The old duffer was still alive, thank God, but now came the fun part.

"Hey," he said. "Wake up, Chester."

No response.

Jerry had forgotten how deaf the old guy was. He leaned in closer to him. "Wake up, Chester!" he yelled.

Chester snorted, then shook his head. His mouth opened slightly to reveal a set of perfectly straight, tobacco-stained yellow teeth.

Jerry reached out and shook his shoulder gently. "Chester!"

The old man's eyes flew open, widening as they locked onto Jerry's. His initial fearful confusion morphed into a fiery anger. Chester leapt to his feet, his right arm disappearing beneath his vest in a flash.

Jerry lunged forward, clamped a hand on Chester's arm and gripped it tightly as he shook his head. "Whoa, there, sheriff! No need for that, now!"

Chester struggled with him for a few seconds, then looked from Jerry to the rest of the shop and back at Jerry. His body relaxed, tension dissipating. "Jerry?" he asked.

"Yeah, Chester. It's me."

"Wha... wha's happening?" he slurred, lowering himself back in the seat.

Jerry continued to hold onto his forearm, gingerly pulling it away from the man's vest. He reached out with his other arm and took Chester's hand in his. He reasoned it would not only be a calming gesture, but it's more difficult to grab a gun if you're already holding something in your hand.

"You're in my shop," Jerry said. "It's closing time."

Chester frowned, his annoyance evident. He took a deep breath and scowled. "Shouldn't wake a man up like that, you know. Liable to get yerself shot that way!"

"Well now, I wouldn't have to wake you if you weren't *asleep*, Chester!" Jerry said, exasperation showing in his voice. "What are you doing here?"

Chester cupped a hand around his ear, leaning forward.

"I said," Jerry yelled, "WHY ARE YOU HERE? I'M CLOSING THE STORE. TIME TO GO HOME!"

Chester shook his head. "Waiting," he mumbled.

"WAITING FOR WHAT?"

"For Junior to give me my damn money."

Jerry shook his head in confusion. "Junior?"

"That's right."

"Tyler?"

"What's that?" Chester said, turning his head slightly.

"YOU'RE WAITING FOR TYLER?" Jerry yelled.

"I don't know what his name is! But he owes me money and I'm not leavin' 'til I get it!" He stomped a boot as if to enforce his point.

Jerry stood up and shook his head.

Unbelievable.

"TYLER!" he yelled.

There was the sound of shuffling in the back storage area and Tyler suddenly appeared. Both forearms of his flannel shirt were soaking wet.

Jerry stood in stunned silence, a surge of emotions

swirling within him — a bubbling blend of confusion and frustration. He shook his head, his thoughts a tangled mess he no longer wished to unravel. Raising his hand, he beckoned for Tyler to join them.

Tyler's gaze dropped to his hands, his cheeks flushing a bright shade of pink. Wiping them on his jeans, he walked over to the counter where they stood. "What's goin' on?" he inquired.

Jerry pointed to Chester. "Chester's here," he said.

Tyler looked down at Chester and nodded. "Oh. Hey, Chester."

"Says you owe him some money."

Tyler's face looked like someone had just accused him of sniffing glue. He shook his head from side to side, frowning, until his eyes lowered to the counter between them.

"Ohhhh..." he said, smiling as if suddenly remembering something.

Jerry's eyebrows raised. "And?"

"And what?"

"Why's he here?"

"Yeah, so, he sold me that gun." Tyler jutted his chin at the gun on the counter. It rested on a rumpled piece of paper with the word BORKEN scribbled in large block letters across it. Covered in dust and clearly not well maintained, the gun wasn't much to look at. But the one thing that stood out to Jerry was the fact that he didn't immediately recognize the make.

Which meant it was most likely old. Or rare. Or both.

And old and rare meant it was possibly valuable.

"How much you want, Chester?" Jerry asked.

"What?"

"HOW MUCH?"

Chester frowned and moved his mouth around like someone had snuck a spoonful of curdled milk into it. He stood up and turned around to face the counter, staring down at the gun.

"Well, I don't know. Thing belonged to my grandpa, an' I just found it again in the attic yesterday. Been cleaning up since Matty died last summer, you know. See, I was meaning to do it a few months ago, but—"

"Two hundred dollars," Jerry said.

"What?"

Jerry held up two fingers. "TWO HUNDRED."

Chester looked at Jerry's hand, then over at the gun. After a few seconds he nodded his head, shrugging. "Sounds fair to me..." he muttered.

Jerry moved around to the opposite side of the counter, passing Tyler before deftly popping open the cash register. Reaching inside, he withdrew a neat stack of bills, placing them meticulously on the counter before shutting the register again. "Write him a receipt, please," he instructed Tyler.

Tyler grabbed a pen and a stack of receipts and started to scribble. As he glanced up momentarily, he caught sight of Hank and his companion watching them from around the bend of the aisle. Ignoring them, he finished writing. "Sorry," he said as he handed the paper to his father.

"Later."

"I was just—"

"Tyler. We'll talk about it *later*," Jerry insisted, taking the paper from him and handing it along with an envelope to Chester. Hank and the other guy emerged from the aisle and now stood in line behind him, a small box of vibrant plastic pellets in hand.

"Thank you for your business," Jerry said loudly and shook Chester's hand firmly. He turned to Tyler. "Can you please see him out while I ring these guys up?"

Tyler nodded and walked around the counter, motioning for Chester to follow him. He involuntarily gazed back at the two strangers and frowned. He'd never seen them in the store before, and although he couldn't pinpoint why, they gave him a bad vibe. He just didn't trust them.

As Tyler escorted Chester to the front of the store, Hank placed the box of pellets down on the counter in front of Jerry.

"You know these won't work in BB guns, right?" Jerry asked.

Hank looked at him blankly. "Why not?"

"Because these are the rubber pellets, made exclusively for the toy guns." He pointed to the label on the box. "See? Says right there."

"I think they'll do the job," Hank said, looking away and sniffing.

"They're gonna gum up your gun."

Hank shrugged. "Don't care."

Jerry's gaze lingered on the man momentarily before shifting to his companion. The friend's impassive stare was disconcerting. Finally Jerry shook his head and sighed.

"Alright, then," he said, scanning the barcode. "That'll be $6.36."

He reached under the counter and grabbed a bag. Tyler

returned from the storefront and joined his father behind the counter, frowning at the two men.

"What about that?" Hank said suddenly.

Jerry stuffed the box into the bag and looked up. "What about what?"

"That," Hank said, jutting his chin toward Chester's gun on the counter.

Jerry looked over at it and back at Hank, confused. "What about it?"

"How much?"

Hank abruptly reached over and snatched it off the counter before Jerry could respond. He began to examine it, turning it over in his hand as though he were scrutinizing its quality.

Jerry glanced over at Tyler and back at Hank. "That's not for sale."

"Why not?" Hank held it up and pointed it at Jerry, then squinted and stared down the barrel of the gun.

Jerry swallowed. He knew it wasn't loaded, but having a gun pointed at him — loaded or not — infused him with a reasonable sense of unease.

"Because..." Jerry said slowly, "It needs to be cleaned, for one thing, and secondly—"

"I'll take it." Hank lowered the gun and opened the barrel. His face suddenly lit up and he grinned widely.

Jerry glanced down and saw the reflective glint of casings in the barrel before Hank slapped it back into place.

Crud, Chester...

His shoulders sank with the heavy realization that there was now a coked-up meth-head standing in his store with a loaded gun.

"An' I think I'll take what's left in the register, too," Hank said, aiming the gun at Jerry again.

Jerry turned to Tyler and sighed. "You didn't clear the gun first thing?" he asked sadly.

Tyler's face flushed and he stared at the gun in Hank's hand, then back at his father. "I... I forgot!" he stammered. "I had to..." He paused, glanced across the counter and back at his father. Tyler lowered his voice. "I had to *use the bathroom* to make a crap, remember?!?"

Jerry closed his eyes and shook his head.

"Open the damn register, man!" Hank yelled, taking a step closer to the counter, reaching up with his left hand and nervously picking at a scab on his cheek.

"I am, I am..." Jerry said, punching in the buttons on the keypad.

"And don't try to be smart, or I'll blow a hole in you!"

Jerry glanced at the gun. "I really don't think you want to do that," he said, shaking his head. He fought the urge to smile as the register drawer popped open.

"Don't tell me what I do or don't want!" Hank screamed. "Just gimme the money!"

Jerry grabbed all the bills and held them up in his hands. "You want a bag for this?"

"What? No, I don't want a bag! I ain't getting blitzed by no stupid dye pack!"

Jerry laughed. "This is a pawn shop. Not a bank. I don't even have dye packs. But now that you mention it, I should probably go buy a few..."

"Give him a bag," Hank's friend interjected.

Hank looked over at him and frowned.

"What?" the man said, shrugging. "I don't wanna try to carry all that stuff by hand."

Hank nodded and looked back at Jerry. "Do it," he commanded.

Jerry retrieved a bag from under the counter and started to shove the bills into it.

"Stop!" Hank yelled, waving the gun.

Jerry stopped.

"You do it," he said to his friend. "An' you and the kid just... back up!"

Jerry raised his hands and Tyler followed suit. They both took a step away from the counter until their backs bumped into the cabinets behind them.

As his friend checked the bills and shoved them into the bag, Hank smiled at Jerry and Tyler and flashed his rotting grin again. "Guess Borken's a pretty good gun, huh?"

Jerry stared at him and frowned. His mind replayed the words in his head, but they still didn't make any sense. "I'm afraid I don't understand," he said, shaking his head.

Hank jutted his chin toward the counter at the piece of paper with the word BORKEN scrawled across it.

"Borken," Hank continued. "This gun. I mean, it ain't a Colt or Wesson, but I like it." He held it up and admired it, nodding his head. "It kind of has a Wild West thing going on."

Tyler was about to speak, but Jerry's gentle nudge on his shoe silenced him. He glanced up at his father, his brow furrowing in confusion. Jerry shot him a meaningful look, then redirected his attention back to Hank.

"Yes sir, Borken is definitely a classic, alright. We don't get a lot of those in here, that's for sure."

"I bet not."

"Stupid name, though," his friend said.

Jerry smiled. "You're right about that."

"Sounds like that Swedish Chef on that TV show," Hank's friend said. "The puppets."

"Muppets," Hank corrected, looking at him.

"What?"

"They weren't called the *puppets*. They're '*The Muppets*.'"

"Whatever. I'm just saying Borken sounds like something that Swedish Chef guy would say." He opened his eyes wide and flailed his arms around stiffly. "Borken! Borken! Shmorky Borken!"

"Stop it," Hank snapped.

"What? It's true!"

"Knock it off."

The other man scowled, dropping his arms back down. He glared at Hank. "The hell, man…"

Hank locked eyes with him, then looked down at the ground and shook his head. His expression grew darker, more serious. "Frog freaked me out," he muttered.

"What?"

"The frog," Hank repeated. "Always freaked me out as a kid."

"Who? Kermit?"

"No, not *Kermit*!" Hank snapped. "The *other* one!"

His friend frowned. "*What* other one?!?"

"The little one. Ribbit…"

"Ribbit?"

"Yeah, Ribbit," Hank said, shaking his head. "Or Rabbit… Robbit…"

"You mean Robin?" Jerry volunteered.

"Yeah!"

"Like Batman and—"

"Yeah! Yeah, it was Robin!" Hank growled, his face hardening again. "*Hated* that frog."

His friend looked over at Jerry and Tyler, then back to Hank. He shook his head and shrugged, picking the bag off the counter. "What about them?"

Hank snapped out of his reverie and looked up at them. "Guess we should kill 'em, huh?"

"Please, don't," Jerry protested, shaking his head.

"Even if you do, you won't get away with it," Tyler added, sneering at them.

"Oh yeah?" Hank asked. "And why's that?"

"Because," Tyler said, beaming. "We got you on *video*."

Jerry's eyes widened for a second before they closed tightly. He felt his heart sink inside him as Tyler's inept words hung in the air like a fragrant fart.

Hank frowned. "You serious?"

"Uh-huh," Tyler continued. "An' when the police come they'll see that video and they'll figure out real quick it was you guys who killed us."

Hank looked over at his friend and back at Tyler. "What if we say we don't believe you?"

Tyler laughed. "Then you'd be stupider than I am!"

"You say you got video of us?" the smaller man said. "Prove it."

"I will!" Tyler said indignantly. He walked briskly toward the back of the store. The other man grinned, dropping the bag of cash by Hank's feet and following him.

Jerry opened his eyes and watched them walk away, shaking his head in disbelief.

"That kid," Hank said, nodding in their direction. "He yours?"

"Yes sir, he is."

"Not all that bright, is he?"

Jerry opened his mouth to speak, but then closed it.

Hank snickered. "Uh-huh."

They waited in silence for a few more seconds before Tyler and the other man reemerged from the back room. His son was still grinning as the other man walked over to Hank holding a VHS tape in his hand.

"See?" Tyler said, looking at Hank and pointing to the tape. "Told ya!"

Hank took the tape and dropped it into the bag by his feet. "Yeah, you guys sure did show us. Guess you were right."

"That's right! We were!" Tyler said, nodding in satisfaction. He looked over at his father, staring back at him blankly. "What?" he said, a look of confusion crossing his face. "Why're you staring at me like that?"

Jerry shook his head and looked back over at Hank. "Alright. You got the gun, the money *and* the tape. You're home free now. I won't even report it. Too much of a hassle, to be honest."

Hank laughed. "Well, thanks for the offer, but I think I'll go ahead and be extra careful."

"You gotta kill 'em, Hank," the shorter one said, standing a few feet behind him.

"I *know* that!" Hank snapped. "What do you think I'm doing?!"

"I'm just sayin'..."

"Let me handle this!" Hank barked.

"Please," Jerry said, crossing his arms and leaning against the wall. "You boys really don't want to be doing this."

"I agree," Tyler said. "You really oughta not shoot us with—"

"Shut up! You don't think I never killed someone before? Huh? This isn't like my first time or nothin'.'"

Jerry shrugged and smiled. "Alright, then. But may I request that you shoot me first?"

Hank's eyes bounced around in his head as he pondered the idea, then he nodded and smiled. "Sure. Why not?"

"Thank you."

Hank thrust his arm forward, aiming the gun at Jerry's chest. There was a soft *click* followed by a blinding flash as the gun discharged in his hand. Hank screamed and dropped the weapon, the sound of it clattering to the floor piercing the following silence.

The man standing behind him yelped. He brought a hand up to the side of his head where his ear used to be. "Ow!" he yelled, his voice a mixture of pain and disbelief. "What the—!" Blood started seeping through his fingers as he pressed them against the wound.

Hank's gaze shifted down to the gun at his feet. Scattered around it were the mangled remnants of his three lower fingers, looking like blood-soaked sausage links that had been absently discarded.

He screamed again.

Using his remaining hand, the other man shoved Hank forward and together they fled down the aisle and through the front door. Jerry and Tyler watched in amusement, then looked over at each other and burst into laughter.

"Buncha dummies," Tyler said, wiping a tear from his eye.

Jerry smiled, and nodded his head. "Well, I have to tell you, son. I never once thought there'd come a time when dyslexia would save the day."

Tyler's smile slowly faded, replaced by a look of confusion. "I don't get it."

Jerry reached across the counter and retrieved the piece of paper, holding it up for Tyler to see. "Why'd you write this?"

Tyler shrugged, looking worried. "Cause when Chester brought it in and I looked it over I saw right off how it was all crusty and busted up on the inside. So I did like you always taught me to do, and wrote 'Broken' so you'd know later on."

"Okay," Jerry nodded. "And I appreciate that. But you didn't write 'BROKEN'."

"What? Sure I did! Says right there!"

"Tyler," Jerry said, shaking his head and grinning at him. "You wrote 'BORKEN'."

Tyler stared at the word, his lips moving silently as he spelled out the letters in his head. Suddenly his face broke into a grin. "*BORKEN?* Well, *that's* funny! Is that why he kept saying 'Borken' all the time?"

"Yeah, well, we just got lucky is all," Jerry chuckled, handing the paper to Tyler. "How about we don't talk about our video surveillance system when we get held up, huh?" He extended his hand to his son.

Tyler smiled and gripped it, shaking firmly. "Deal."

Jerry's smile faded as he glanced down at their clasped

hands. He noticed the dampness of Tyler's shirt and the moistness of their handshake. He quickly let go, a slight grimace on his face.

"Alright," he said. "That's enough excitement for today. I'm going home."

"Me too."

"Uh-uh. Not 'til you fix that toilet, you're not."

Tyler frowned. He turned and started walking to the back when he felt a hand on his shoulder.

"On second thought," his father said, coming alongside him. "If it's not overflowing, maybe it can wait until after dinner. What do you say?"

Tyler smiled. "I like that idea."

"Thought you would." They started walking toward the front of the store when Jerry suddenly stopped, looking back at his son. "Tyler?"

"Yeah?"

"It's *not* overflowing... is it?"

Tyler shook his head. "Not yet."

Jerry grimaced and nodded. "Good enough for me."

Author's Note

This story, much like my short story *Snapdragon*, was inspired by a single word: BORKEN.

I'll be honest, I'm not a big singer. In the shower or perhaps in the solitude of my office? Sure, I'll sing along to something. But unless I'm over-the-top in love with a song and melody, I'm just not much of a crooner.

Which sometimes makes it slightly (read: *incredibly*) awkward when I'm at church, where everyone else seems to passionately love every song we sing.

Every. Single. One.

Me? I have a hard time singing the same words over and over and over again, no matter how much I identify with the lyrics. So suffice it to say that I typically find Sunday morning worship services to border on... (gasp) boring.

That is, until one Sunday when the lyrics up on the screen contained a mistake.

I believe the line was supposed to read "broken for us" or something, talking about Christ's sacrifice on the cross. Only it read "borken for us."

Hands down, it was the most hilarious thing I'd seen in weeks. Maybe months.

Ever since that pivotal moment, the word BORKEN started crashing around in my head, the nagging questions soon followed. In what kind of scenario would the word BORKEN be funny, or at least really mess things up? Or both? What's typically broken? Vending machines... ATM's... roads...

All true, but what would make for a good *story?*

The answer? A gun.

A *BORKEN* gun.

Couple that with an inept robbery and you have the makings of a pretty hilarious, ironic short story.

A DATE WITH DEATH
JACK KARDIAC

a date with death

DONNA DAVIS HEFTED the second overstuffed bag of groceries from the minivan and smiled. Today was going to be a great day. She knew this without question, because of the simple fact she'd been meticulously planning today for over a week. Everything was set to go, minute by minute and hour by hour.

The kids had been dropped off promptly at school at 7:21 am, after which she'd successfully secured their groceries for the week in a record twenty-seven minutes. She reasoned it would've been at least five to six minutes less if the checkout scanner hadn't died in the middle of it all. Instead, Donna ended up having to rescan her entire cart in the next lane over, but even with that setback she'd still been able to finish relatively unperturbed and sooner than expected.

Tucking a strong-willed bag of dog food under her elbow, Donna reached out and gripped the van door, tugging it just enough to engage the automatic mechanism to shut it, all while carefully clutching the bag beneath her arm. Her grin grew wider.

Oh, yes, this was going to be a great day.

As she approached her house, Donna mentally ticked off the delightful highlights that awaited her once she put the groceries away and cleaned up the kitchen.

One hot, uninterrupted shower. *Check.*

A thirty-minute exercise and stretching session. *Check.*

Leisurely browsing the used bookstore up the street (for a *minimum* of an hour). *Big Check.*

Brunch with Owen at the Mexican restaurant she'd been dying to try. (Complete with a nicely chilled sangria, of course. Possibly two.) *Check.*

An hour and a half Thai massage. *Check.*

And last — but most certainly not least — a nap. A glorious, hour-long nap.

Checkity Check-Check.

Oh yes, today was going to be a day Donna would blog about later. Guaranteed.

"Mind the water."

Donna glanced over and saw her next door neighbor, Edna, tending the garden in her front yard. A sprinkler tractor was leisurely trudging up her lawn, winding its way between the houses, cheerfully spritzing both sides of their property. The sidewalk leading to Donna's front porch was generously soaked.

"Don't want you to slip, now," Edna continued, pointing to the damp steps.

"Thank you, Edna," Donna said, smiling. "You're always looking out for me, aren't you?"

"Just doing my job," Edna said, nodding. "As a good neighbor. And I do apologize for the mess, dear. I was expecting you to still be out and about this morning, so I figured this was a good time to get the watering done." She shrugged sheepishly. "Suppose I was wrong."

Donna hefted the dog food higher and waved her hand dismissively. "Oh, it's no problem! Really! I actually love it that you water our yard too. Lord knows how often it slips my mind! You know, with the kids and all."

"Of course."

Edna groaned as she began to push herself to her feet. "Do you need some help with those, honey?" she asked.

"Oh, no," Donna protested, walking up the porch and opening the door. "I've got it. Thank you, though! You're always so kind-hearted!"

"Well, okay then..." Edna groaned again as she lowered herself back to the ground, refocusing her attention on her gardening. "Have yourself a great day, now."

"Thank you, Edna. You too!"

Donna slipped inside the door and lightly kicked it shut behind her. She smiled.

That woman is so nice.

She and Owen had moved to Indiana a little over a year ago, and Edna was the first to welcome them to the neighborhood. Donna had never really been a fan of banana bread growing up, but Edna's recipe had won her over at first bite. Who would have imagined adding dark chocolate chips could make such a huge difference? It was heavenly!

Over the next five minutes Donna flew about the house, putting the groceries away and stuffing the empty bags into the pantry to recycle later. Opening the drawer containing her scented wax tarts, Donna perused her selection.

Berry, minty, grassy, homey... so many scents to choose from. She took her time, careful to select the absolute best aroma that matched today's mood.

There it was.

Autumn Sunset.

Donna flipped the tart over and read the description: an earthy mix of pumpkin and cloves, with just a hint of blood orange to warm your heart and brighten your day.

Perfect.

She grinned and grabbed two tarts, carefully arranging them in her warmer. Donna knew there wasn't much point in arranging pieces of wax which were destined to melt into a unified, mottled glob, but she just couldn't resist. She liked life to be tidy and tranquil, even if she knew chaos could only be chained for so long.

She glanced over her shoulder at the leftover breakfast mess in the kitchen.

Speaking of chaos...

Dirty plates, cups that needed washing and a frying pan — freshly coated with residual bacon fat now congealing into thick, salty sludge.

Donna sighed.

The mop bucket sat in the corner, full of cold, dirty water from when she'd cleaned the kitchen last night. Some days the eternal list of things left undone could become overwhelming, as if she were trapped in a twisted time loop designed just for homemakers.

Cook. Clean. Laundry. Sleep.

Cook. Clean. Laundry. Sleep.

COOK! CLEAN! LAUNDRY! SLEEP!

Rinse and repeat.

Day after <u>day</u> after *day* after *DAY*.

And chauffeur, she reminded herself. *Can't forget that part...*

Donna stared at the kitchen for a few more seconds before deciding to ignore it all. Completely. Honestly, who would really care if her kitchen remained a disaster for a few more hours? She wasn't expecting company anytime soon, and would it really kill her to live her life for once? For just a few hours?

No.

No, it would not.

Taking out her phone, she connected to the home stereo and started her favorite playlist — an eclectic collection of upbeat pop songs expertly mixed with choice instrumental soundtracks. Owen had installed the system himself, touting the enjoyment of having unseen speakers spread throughout the house so they could hear the same song in every room, everywhere they went. True, Donna hadn't appreciated it at the time, but as she darted upstairs and started running the water for her shower, she had to admit Owen was right. The uninterrupted flow of music was somewhat majestic.

The shower ended up being everything she had hoped for, rejuvenating her even more than she'd anticipated. Maybe it was just her excitement for the day, infusing her with a renewed sense of energy and purpose, but Donna was living in the moment, and this day — along with everything it held in store — belonged to *her*.

After toweling off, she changed into her favorite yoga ensemble of a dark maroon tank top and form-fitting black sweatpants. Perfect for exercising *or* lounging around the house. Thirty minutes of excruciating exercise, some serious stretches and she'd be ready to take on the town.

As soon as she descended the stairs, Donna knew something was very wrong. She winced, wrinkling her nose up as the odor invaded her senses.

What is that SMELL?!

She stepped into the kitchen and walked to the wax warmer. Perhaps something had soured with the wax during production? A bad batch? She didn't think so, remembering how fantastic it had smelled thirty minutes ago when she'd unwrapped it, but maybe the heat had somehow altered it?

Donna leaned over and inhaled deeply. There was the faint aroma of oranges and spice, but the other odor in the air vastly overpowered it. She frowned. It wasn't the wax.

Her eyes wandered across the room to fall on the second suspected culprit: the trash compactor.

Lifting the lid, she glared at the crushed cartons and refuse inside it, leaning over and sniffing somewhat hesitantly. It wasn't pleasant, but not nearly as ripe as whatever rank funk was floating about. Still, the bag was nearly full and Donna reasoned it might be time to take it out. She expertly manhandled it into the air, tying it off in seconds with all the flair and finesse of a rodeo cowboy harnessing a heifer. Leaning it against the kitchen island, she resumed her search.

The food disposal in the sink was clear, as was the fish tank tucked into the kitchen's back corner. Okay, they weren't *clean* clean, per se, but none of them had the sharp tang of the stench. No, whatever it was, it was descending into the distinct scent of decay — something akin to the aroma of Death itself.

She leaned over the pan of bacon grease. If anything, the fragrance actually *improved* when she inhaled. Donna frowned.

So it wasn't the dishes.

Or the fishies...

Or the disposal...

Or the trash.

But... what *was* it, then? Had some poor creature crawled under the house and died?

Donna groaned, envisioning Owen belly crawling beneath the subfloor, searching for the carcass of a crusty critter. She hated the idea of asking him to do that, but she was beginning to get desperate. Granted, she had planned to leave the house anyway, but she had no intention of walking back into... *this*.

Heck, no. She'd rather stay in a hotel.

A hotel!

At this Donna perked up and smiled. What better way to end the day than to stay in a hotel! With Owen! Surely she could find a sitter for the kids, right? *Edna always said she'd love to watch over them.*

Donna opened the fridge and started inspecting plastic containers, seeing if one had been left open by chance. Even if it had, she knew it wouldn't account for the smell *outside* of the refrigerator, but she was quickly running out of alternative explanations. She decided to move a few of the more questionable items onto the counter, just to be safe.

Spaghetti.

Some kind of soup. She thought...

An unfinished take-out box of nachos from that weird Mexican-Chinese restaurant around the corner. What were they called? Komodo Nachos?

Strange name. Addictive snack.

After a minute Donna decided she needed to stop herself before she quickly ended up sacrificing her morning on the altar of cleanliness. Before shutting the door, however, she stooped down and stared at an unidentified white cylinder on the back shelf.

Donna frowned, then squinted and moved closer into the fridge.

Is that what I think it is?

She reached in and pulled out a roll of toilet paper.

Laughing out loud, Donna shut the door and stared at the inexplicable roll in her hand. *Who in the world puts a roll of toilet paper in the fridge?* A better question was *why* they would ever do that? She shook her head and smiled, anticipating the conversation she was going to have with her family over dinner tonight.

The most obvious suspect was her thirteen-year-old daughter, but her husband was also known for absent-mindedly putting things in wrong places. Like the tub of ice cream they found melted in the laundry room last summer. *That* had been a mess!

Donna placed the roll on the counter beside her and froze. Something was wrong. Something had—

"Milk's expired," a voice said from behind her.

Donna gasped and spun around.

A man sat at the dining table, casually holding an open carton of milk up to his nose. His skin was pale, and the beginning of a five o'clock shadow crept across his face as he stared at her through faint, blue eyes. His immaculate, jet-black hair looked as if it required weekly trips to a stylist just to maintain it. Dressed in black tennis shoes, black socks, black slacks and a buttoned-up black dress shirt, the man's supermodel good looks and professional attire would have normally impressed Donna with how attractive he was. Instead she was borderline panicked, paralyzed in her kitchen, staring at him.

The man lifted the carton and sniffed it again, inhaling deeply before exhaling and grinning. "Now that..." he said, "is good stuff." He held up the carton and wiggled it in his hands, eyebrows raised. "Care for a hit?"

Donna didn't move.

She felt her heart beat triple time inside her and glanced over her shoulder at the phone on the counter.

The guy was at least twenty feet away from her, on the opposite side of the dining table with multiple chairs positioned around the room between them. Donna would easily be able to reach it and dial 911 before he could attack. Even if he *did*, she knew she was more than capable of defending herself.

"Don't waste your time," he said, shaking his head. "It's already dead."

Donna lunged forward, running across the gap and grabbing the receiver. She dialed 911 faster than she ever thought possible.

Silence.

She slammed the phone down, picked it up and tried again. Still nothing.

"As I mentioned…"

She ignored him and grabbed her cell phone off the counter where she had left it. Donna watched him out of the corner of her eye as she brought up the number keypad. He didn't move, but simply studied her, as if he were mildly amused.

"That's not going to work, either, Donna," he said, shaking his head and smiling. "You don't seem to understand the situation: you're in a dead zone."

She looked up at the corner of her cell phone. No bars. Which was impossible! They were less than a quarter of a mile from the nearest cell site! Ever since they moved here they never — not once — had less than full five bars of connection.

Wait. Did he just say my name?

"Did you just say my name?" Donna asked angrily.

"I did."

"How do you know my name?"

He laughed. "How do I *not*? I mean, you *are* Donna Lee Davis, are you not?"

She stared at him, unmoving.

"Lives on 7734 Moneta Lane, married to Owen Davis for the past fifteen years — majority of them happily, I'd say. Three spunky kids, a minivan and a dog and a languishing blog that hasn't been updated in months." He leaned in closer over the table. "Am I getting closer?"

Donna's eyes searched the room, trying to take in everything that was happening. His presence, everything he was telling her, it didn't—

"You don't realize it, Donna, but you and I? We have an appointment today."

She frowned. "*What?!*"

"You and I," he repeated, pushing his chair back and standing up behind the table. "We have an appointment."

"What are you... I don't—"

"It's true! I'm not lying to you."

"WHAT ARE YOU TALKING ABOUT?! WHO ARE YOU?!" Donna screamed.

He stared at her and dropped the carton onto the table. It bounced once and tipped over, the white contents spilling into a sudden puddle on the table, dripping through an unseen center seam onto the carpet below.

The man looked down at the mess and back up at her. He smiled. "Well, don't go and cry over it, Donna. It was bad anyway."

"You're insane."

"No," he said, shaking his head. "I'm actually not." He walked around the end of the table and pretended to admire the house plants decorating one of the shelves. As he strode past he reached out, brushing them lightly with an extended finger. As if performing a synchronized swim routine, with a single touch each one immediately browned, shriveled up and died.

Donna stared at him, growingly increasingly alarmed. Reaching behind her, she quietly opened the nearby utensil drawer and lowered a hand into it. Searching for her favorite Cutco knife, her hand wrapped around a handle and she pulled it out in front of her.

A spiked meat mallet.

Good enough.

The man watched her the entire time, seemingly oddly disinterested. Instead he continued his preoccupation with the rest of her plants, retouching a few fighters until they were all terribly and truly dead.

He retrieved a family portrait off a shelf and held it up. "Good looking family you got here. You have the complete set, don't you? A girl and two boys. Typical American family. I love it."

"Please put that down."

He cocked his head at her and thought for a second, then nodded. "Alright. But only because you said *please*." He reached out to put it back on the shelf when he suddenly stopped, peering closer at his reflection in the glass.

"Wow," he said, turning his face to the side. "Huh. I've never looked like *this* before. This is... really different." He looked back at Donna.

"I mean, to be perfectly honest... I never really know *what* I'm going to look like when I show up. Sometimes I'm a crusty old fart, next day I come complete with these creepy black wings sprouting out of the center of my back. They look super cool, I'll be honest. Pretty heavy and not fully functional, but *man*, do they certainly scare the living crap out of folks when I spread 'em!"

He looked back at his reflection and brought his lips back, examining his teeth. "Oh yeah. I *like* this a lot! Beats the heck out of the old skeleton, scythe and robe thing I was stuck with for a few centuries. Although, let's be honest — the Black Plague was an absolute *blast*."

"What is *wrong* with you?"

He frowned. Sighing, he placed the frame back on the shelf. "Look. Donna. I may be just the messenger — or the chauffeur, if you will — but that doesn't mean I don't enjoy my work. I *do*! And I'm very, very good at what I do."

"And what is it you do, exactly?"

He snorted loudly.

"Really? You still don't get it? Even now?" He reached out and touched a nearby electronic photo frame. Donna watched as the picture of her eldest daughter riding a horse flickered twice on the screen and died.

She looked at him, shaking her head. "So... hold on... you're telling me..."

"That's right," he said, shrugging. "I'm Death, Donna. And I'm here for our appointment."

Donna laughed out loud, then brought her hand up to her mouth and back down. "Well," she said. "I suppose that explains why the house reeks so much..."

He spread his arms and grinned. "Smells like Death, am I right?"

"Yes, that's probably the most accurate way to describe it." She paused for a moment. "To describe *you*."

"Oh, please. Better than your fancy wax over there," he said, nodding to the warmer. "That stuff smelled like Heaven. Took me forever to overpower that crap when I first arrived."

Donna looked down at the mallet in her hand and back at the man. "I'd like you to please leave now," she said firmly.

"Oh? You'd like me to—" he started, feigning surprise. "So I should... just... you know, skedaddle on out of here? Show myself out, perhaps?"

He jerked a thumb at the front door, then turned and

walked away, exaggerating his steps and stopping just before he reached for the knob.

"Nah, on second thought..." He turned to face her, frowning. "I think I'll stay."

"You're not welcome here."

"Lady, *you're* the one who invited me!" he retorted.

"I... what? What are you talking about? I never—"

"Oh yes, you did!"

"When? How?!"

"Oh, I don't know... how about every other day last year?"

"What? I never—"

"Donna. Please. Let's not kid ourselves, here. Admit it. Some days you just want to curl up and die."

"Not today I don't!" she yelled, voice saturated with irritation and a fresh wave of indignation.

"Fine," he said. "Maybe not *today*, but do you have any idea how many times you wished I would pay you a visit last year alone? Any at all?"

She stared at him and frowned, crossing her arms. Donna didn't like the direction the conversation was headed, but she wasn't about to let him know it. She remained silent, glaring at him.

"One hundred and ninety-six times." He raised his eyebrows and shrugged, giving her space to let the sum total settle in. "*One hundred. Ninety-six.* Donna, that's almost every other day."

"What? Are you saying I wanted to die one hundred and ninety-six times last year? Is that it?"

"Lady, that's *exactly* what I'm saying."

"Well, I'm sorry, but I don't believe you."

He chuffed. "Imagine that."

"Prove it."

"Excuse me?"

"I said 'prove it.'"

"You want me to prove it?"

"That's right."

He grinned and strode over to the other side of the kitchen island, standing by the mounted TV. Donna positioned herself opposite him, keeping her distance while reaffirming her grip on the mallet.

"Man, I absolutely love technology in this age! Makes my job *so* much more entertaining, you know?" He smirked. "Not to mention how many people die each year from electronic distractions alone. Walking into traffic, texting while driving... simply phenomenal." He reached out and pressed the power button, the screen blinking to life.

A list of icons appeared and hovered on the screen. He reached out and tapped a black one, glowing with a sickly green hue. It expanded and a text document soon appeared. He waved his hand up and the text scrolled in response, words blurring as they sped past the screen.

"Ah. Here we are..."

He cleared his throat. "*January 27th. I'm such a horrible mother. I lost it again, biting their heads off like a witch. This is why it'd be better if I were dead. They could all start over again, with a new one. A wife and mother who isn't so freaking damaged or neurotic.*"

He moved his hand lower. "*February 6th. I continue to die a slow death, day by day. Perpetually dying, but never dead. I want a different life. Or a swift death. I don't care which one anymore, I just want things to change.*"

"Please stop," Donna said, eyes lowering to the floor.

He ignored her.

"*April 10th. What's the point? I quit, I quit, I QUIT!
September 20th. I'm tired of breathing. I'm ready, Lord. Come
now!*"

"Stop," Donna repeated.

"Or *this* one... this is one of my absolute favorites," he
grinned. "*August 18th. It's not that I want to die, but if I
happened to be hit by a bus I wouldn't complain.*"

"Stop it!!"

"Hold on," he said, shaking his head as he glanced at the
screen. He held up a finger. "Just one more..."

Donna couldn't contain her fury any more. She flung the
mallet toward him as hard as she could. It slammed into his
shoulder and bounced off, clattering loudly across the wood
floor in the hallway.

"Ow!" he shouted, shooting her an angry glare. He
reached up and rubbed his shoulder, looking down at where
it had struck. There was a fresh rip on the upper seam of his
shirt. "Dang it, Donna! You just ruined a good shirt!"

Donna didn't respond, but started searching the kitchen
for other objects to use against him. The knife drawer was on
his side of the island now, so that option was out. She reached
behind her, never breaking eye contact with him. Grabbing
the first thing she felt, she brought it around in front of her.

The roll of toilet paper.

He looked down at it and snickered. "Well, now you're
starting to treat me like crap."

"Lord knows you smell like it."

He laughed. "Well, he would know, now, wouldn't he?"

"Whatever." He pursed his lips for a few seconds, staring
at her.

When his frown disappeared completely, Donna wondered if he was going to attack. Then one side of his mouth raised and he sneered at her, nodding to himself.

"You know what? I don't usually do this, but I'm gonna make an exception for you." His eyes narrowed angrily. "All because of your... ah... *hammer* time, back there." He jerked his thumb toward the mallet on the floor.

Donna didn't move, keeping her eyes fixed on him. She was preparing to bolt away once he made a move. Glancing out the window over his shoulder, she saw Edna standing and stretching her back, facing the street. If only she could get her attention, maybe she could call for help! May she could break the window somehow and—

He saw her staring out the window and stepped in front of it to block her view. Donna locked eyes with him, doing her best to hide her secret hope.

"As I was saying," he continued. "I don't usually like to play with my food, but I'm pretty sure you could use a little more seasoning, if you will." He reached up and touched the screen once again, bringing up the icons. Tapping one with a sick, yellow hue, he licked his lips in anticipation of what was about to happen.

"Funny thing about being Death, Donna. Every once in a while I get a glimpse into people's lives. Not only what they are today, but what they likely *will* be. Yours is especially heartbreaking, I'm pleased to report."

He scrolled to a video segment and hovered over the play button. "Today I'm the ghost of Christmas future, and this, Donna Davis, is your life!" He winked. "*Without* you, that is."

He pressed Play.

Donna watched the screen and saw her friend Mary appear on it, crying uncontrollably. Her heart broke, seeing her in so much pain. "What is this?"

"This," he said, "is Mary after her husband leaves her for another woman, in just a few months. Without you around, she has no one to talk her through the heartache, no one to console her, no one..." he grinned, "to stop her."

Donna watched as Mary stopped sobbing and walked to a nearby closet. Retrieving a shoebox from an upper back corner, she removed a revolver, checked to see that it was loaded, and quietly shuffled up the hall to the bedroom.

"No..."

Mary opened the door silently, slipped into the room and stood over the bed, staring down at her sleeping husband. A second later she abruptly raised her arm and fired three times before turning the gun on herself.

Donna looked away, flinching as she heard the final shot, followed by the sound of Mary's body falling to the floor.

"Gotta love the two-for-one specials," he said. "Thankfully they're becoming much more common these days." He tapped the screen and another video popped up. This one showed a toddler crying in a busy amusement park.

Donna didn't want to watch, but she couldn't look away. The child continued to cry, searching the faces of strangers walking by, looking frantically. A man suddenly came into view and picked him up in his arms, telling him everything was going to be okay.

Donna saw the child was confused and afraid as he stared up at the stranger's face, then continued quietly crying for his mother before the video faded to darkness.

He clucked his tongue. "Mmm... if only you would've

been there next week to reunite that boy with his lost Mommy, Donna. Things might've turned out much... *different*... for him." He shook his head in mock sadness before his grin reappeared. "Alas, I'm afraid you're just not going to make it to the park on Tuesday."

"The hell I'm not." Donna stared at him, the anger and emotions swirling up inside of her, growing.

"Next." He swiped his hand to the left and tapped the screen. A scrawny, pimply-faced teenager appeared on the screen, and Donna immediately recognized him as one of the volunteers at the local library. Donald? No, David.

He had just finished shelving some books and was returning to the front desk when a customer approached him. Donna couldn't hear what they were saying, but it was clear from the body language that the customer was upset, waving his arms and pointing at David repeatedly.

David stared at the man calmly, shaking his head as the gentleman continued to rant, becoming more and more aggressive with each passing second. Then David walked away off screen... returning a moment later with a gun.

The man's demeanor changed immediately. Terrified, he held his hands up in front of him in protest as David shot him twice in the chest. Then he jumped up on the counter and started firing randomly at the other library patrons, even stopping to reload when he ran out of ammo. The picture paused.

"You know this young man, don't you?"

Donna didn't answer, glaring at him.

"Sure you do. And here's how it plays out: because there's not going to be a Donna Davis there to diffuse the situation, *this* guy..." He pointed at David's angry face on the screen. "...

is going to go on a sweet rampage. And lemme tell ya, the library's only the beginning. David's gonna take out an amazing *thirty-four* People! Completely random strangers who don't deserve it! Why? Because he is just *sick* and *tired* of the constant crapfest that is Life."

He stopped and raised his eyebrows, pointing an accusing figure across the kitchen. "Just like you, Donna."

"That's enough," Donna said. "You've made your point."

"I have a point?" he asked, confused. "Well, that's surprising. Here I thought I was just ripping your heart out."

"You are such a—"

"Speaking of hearts, though, you should know Owen's going to get a little bit lonely when you're gone... but only for a short while."

He giggled and touched the screen. Owen came into focus. He was dressed in a tuxedo, and stood in the center aisle of a church, surrounded by groomsmen and bridesmaids. A moment later a woman came into view and took his hand, beaming.

"Tiffani?" Donna asked, mouth gaping wide.

"Is that who that is?"

"She's the bimbo who works with Owen at the office. But she's a complete ditz! He said so himself! Owen would never fall for her!"

"Oh, but he *will*," he said, shrugging his shoulders. "Men do such silly things when hearts become lonely. But don't be too jealous, dear Donna... the honeymoon is short-lived."

He sped the video forward and stopped it. Donna heard her children crying, huddled together in a dark room while Tiffani yelled at them from outside their locked door.

The next scene showed Tiffani talking to Owen,

manipulating him into buying her a new car. He squirms in his chair, trying to explain their limited budget and her excessive spending. The woman is relentless, however, mercilessly pressing on until he finally gives into her demands with a sad, defeated sigh.

At first Donna's heart had started breaking as she watched her children being mistreated, but the more she watched Tiffani on the screen, the more she heard her children's cries, the more enraged Donna became. The roll of toilet paper never had a chance, crushed to the core within Donna's furious fist.

"That's enough." She glared at him through calculating, cold eyes.

"Think so? What, you don't want to see how your mother ends up? Or how about your sister, perhaps? She's quite the—"

"I said enough!"

Spying her phone on the counter, Donna snatched it up and hurled it toward him. She missed completely, connecting with the dead center of the screen instead. It shattered loudly, the phone falling to the floor with a *thunk,* followed by the *tic-tic-tic* of black glass shards.

He looked over at the TV and back at Donna, glaring angrily. "I have to say, I am *really* getting sick of you throwing things, lady! Show some class, why don't you?"

"Get out of my house," she growled. "*Now.*"

He shook his head. "Uh-uh. Sorry, but you're stuck with me until the end. Which..." he glanced at the watch on his arm. "Is right about now. So how about we wrap this up, shall we? Why don't we go upstairs, draw you a nice, hot bath and—"

"*Excuse* me?"

"Ah, ah..." he scolded, holding up a finger. "Allow me to finish, please."

Donna didn't move.

"We'll draw up a nice, hot bath. Some relaxing music, a bunch of bubbles, the whole bit. Then I'll drop a stereo in your lap, and — *snap, crackle, pop* — we'll stick a fork in you and call you done." He grinned at her. "What do you say?"

"I say," she whispered. "You can go to hell."

He stared at her across the kitchen island, shaking his head sadly. Sighing, he spread his arms out wide in surrender. "Look, I think I've been a pretty nice guy so far. Have you even *read* some of the Darwin Awards out there? Granted, you technically wouldn't count since you've already created three clones, but seriously! I offer to let you go out with some dignity in a common household accident, but you're kind of being a jerk about it all!"

"You think dying naked in a bathtub is dignified?"

"Sure! Why not? Okay, to be perfectly fair I can't really say I get the whole dignity concept, but—"

"I don't want to die!" Donna snapped.

"Oh. Sure, not *today*," he countered. "As in, 'I don't want to die *today*, this very *instant*.' But guess what, *Donna*? I give you another twenty-four or thirty-six hours and you'll be sobbing in your soup, putting in another request and dedication. I guarantee it."

"No, I won't. Not anymore."

"Oh really? Do you have any idea how many times I've

heard *that*? How many millions — no, *billions* — of times people have tried to bargain with me? The *oh-so-sincere* promises of permanent change?" He shook his head in disgust. "It's ludicrous. You people are ridiculously stubborn! So freaking passionate about what you want, when you want it. But then when the stress starts to squeeze you and life sucker punches you in the gut, you're itching to pull the plug. Every one of you." He snapped. "Just like that."

"I'm not going to die today."

"Yes. You are."

"No, I'm not. I refuse to."

"You refuse…" he chuckled. "That's so cute. It truly is. But your future awaits, Donna…"

"The future's not written yet."

"Oh, please! Don't get all 'timey-wimey', space-time continuum on me! What, you been watching *Back to the Future* movie marathons again? Drinking some of Doc Brown's Kool-Aid? *It's a movie*! It's not—"

"I don't care. I'm not dying today."

"Donna. Stop. Just… stop. *Look at you.* You can't fight *me*. And don't you dare try to cheat me. Yeah, I'm a pretty laid-back guy, but I *really* hate cheaters."

"Then I suggest you buck-up, buttercup, because I'm not going down without a fight."

He shook his head. "You can't fight fate, Donna."

She looked at his ripped shirt, remembering how he yelped when she'd struck him with the mallet, how he'd flinched away from the shattered TV screen.

Donna put the pieces together in her mind and couldn't stop the smile from forming across her face. "Thank you for your opinion," she said, staring at him coldly. "But I think I'm going to choose to actually fight for my life." She shrugged. "You know, because I'm just kind of ridiculously stubborn like that."

He nodded, mulling over the weight of her words. "So be it," he said, frowning.

A second later he darted around the kitchen counter, lunging after her.

Donna grabbed the carton of leftover spaghetti beside her and flung it into his face where it burst open immediately, splattering him with frigid pasta and marinara sauce.

He stopped cold, cursed and lifted his hands to wipe his eyes clear. A chunk of garlic was trying to lodge itself under his left eyelid, and he swore as it began to burn.

He abruptly reached out for her, oblivious that Donna had launched an aggressive attack. She ran toward him and delivered a swift sidekick to his stomach, sending him careening across the kitchen.

As his lower back slammed into the counter and he slipped to the floor, Donna's suspicions proved to be true, even better than she had hoped for: he had winced in obvious pain. As powerful as he was, he wasn't without limitations.

He could be *hurt*.

And Donna Davis had every intention and ability to hurt him.

Scrambling to his feet, the man stood upright, reassuming a fighting stance. He squinted through his left garlic eye, blinking uncontrollably, as if it were having an independent epileptic seizure.

"So," he said between breaths, "Looks like we have ourselves some kind of martial arts training, have we?" He reached up and removed a strand of spaghetti from his hair, flinging it against the window above the sink.

"Karate? Tae Qwon Do? Brazilian Jiu Jitsu? Maybe a little old school, Matrix-style Kung Fu?"

"Don't you want to know," Donna snarled, arching an eyebrow. The corner of her mouth raised into a sly smile. She knew her fight was as much mental as it was physical, so if she could inject any kind of uncertainty or self-doubt in this guy's façade, she would.

Out the window, Donna caught sight of Edna in her garden again. She glanced to the front door and back at him. He was still too close. She'd never make it past him in time.

Taking a step toward him, she reached out and retrieved the heavy pan off the stove, a greasy spatula falling onto the floor at her feet. She raised the pan over her shoulder and brandished it like a bat.

He laughed. "Are you being serious right now? A *frying pan*? Don't you think that's a little too Disney? Even for you?"

"Mother knows best," she growled, holding it higher over her shoulder. The bacon grease started dripping down her arm and seeping between her fingers, but she didn't care. After losing access to the knives on his side of the kitchen, this was unquestionably the most formidable weapon she had at her disposal.

"'*Mother knows best,*'" he repeated, nodding. "I like that! I have to tell you, Donna. I am *really* going to enjoy killing you."

"Feeling's mutual. Now are you going to get the hell out

of my house, or do I have to bash your brains in? Assuming you have any..."

"So very witty," he said, then took a step closer. "You're forgetting something, however."

"Such as?"

"I've done this many, *many* times before. And I know how it's going to play out."

"Think so?"

"I tell you true," he said, in the best gypsy accent he could muster. "Vatch this..." He walked toward her briskly, malice in his eyes.

Donna swore under her breath. She pulled the pan back and swung her arms forward as fast and as hard as she could, aiming for his face.

Something shattered behind her.

She instinctively turned to see the frying pan spinning around on the counter, having shattered the fish tank and clattering into the sink. Broken glass and water flooded onto the floor along with Nemo, Pumpkin and all the other fish her children had collected over the past year.

Donna turned back around just as he swung his hand forward, slapping her hard across the cheek.

She yelped and stumbled backwards, catching herself against the refrigerator. Trying to shake off the blow, she turned quickly and resumed a fighting stance, but he didn't advance. Instead he stood there, casually leaning against the sink, arms crossed.

Grinning at her.

Donna fought back the tears attempting to flood forth from the surprising strike. She shook her head, struggling to focus on him. Her cheek started to tingle and grow numb, as if it were swelling to gigantic proportions on the side of her face, like an aggressive tumor. The distinct sensation reminded her of the last time she visited the dentist.

"I feel like I have to be honest with you, Donna," he said, taking a moment to appreciate his manicured fingernails. He looked up and leaned toward her.

"I'm holding back," he whispered.

Donna glowered at him.

"I don't usually play around like this, but as I said before... I *really* like you!" He shrugged. "There. I said it. *I like you*. Will you go with me?"

"Go to hell."

"No, I meant 'go' as in, what kids used to say in middle school back in the 80s, dating and all. Oh, never mind. You're clearly not in the mood for jokes, so I should probably stop wasting mine on you."

"Please do," Donna said, reaching down and grabbing the bag of trash leaning against the island. She hoisted it over her shoulder as if it were a gunny sack, silently praying there was something — anything — inside it that could inflict some serious damage.

"Donna. You look downright ridiculous. Like some kind of demented Mrs. Claus, itching to dole out punishment to all the naughty children."

"I am," she declared, stepping around the island and swinging the bag at him. He tried to evade it, but it was too late.

The bag smacked hard into the side of his head, knocking it sideways. He reached out to grab it, but Donna had already pulled it back, just out of reach. She spun in a tight circle, adding momentum as she made her second rotation. As the bag slammed into his stomach, something inside it shattered. Donna brought up her foot and kicked the bag into him, hoping for the good fortune of slicing into his stomach with whatever it was.

He grimaced, reached down and gripped the bag with both hands, ripping it open with a feral yell. Trash exploded across the kitchen — snotty tissues, uneaten sandwiches, empty snack bags, junk mail...

...and the gloriously shattered remains of an empty pickle jar.

Taking advantage of the chaos, Donna stepped in closer and kneed him in the groin. As he bent over she bounced her foot off the floor, slamming her knee into the bottom of his jaw. He yelped as his head snapped up, a bloody tooth launching out of his mouth, bouncing twice on the countertop before disappearing somewhere under the microwave.

Donna turned to run, but his hand shot out and locked around her wrist. For such a skinny, pretty boy appearance, his strength was shocking, and she winced as his grip tightened.

"Let me go!" she screamed, trying to hit him with her other hand. She felt her wrist start to go numb under his touch, just like her face did when he'd slapped her earlier.

He twisted her arm hard, forcing her stomach against the sink counter. "Stop it!" he screamed. "Stop resisting! What is *wrong* with you, lady? I'm giving you exactly what you've been begging for all these years! Why do you have to make it so damn difficult?!?"

Donna ignored him and stretched her free arm ahead of her, grabbing the nearest thing she could find to fight back.

The hot wax warmer scalded her skin as she wrapped her hand around the base of it and picked it up.

Throwing it over her shoulder, it smashed against his head, his nose breaking with a sickening, satisfying *POP!*

The numbing grip on her arm loosened instantly. He screamed as the hot wax splattered across his face, adding a scant, scalding layer to his wide-open eyes. He started scratching madly with his hands, trying to peel off the residue as it burned and bubbled on his skin.

A primal scream of raw fury flew out of Donna's mouth. Grabbing a forearm in both hands, she shoved his hand down into the sink disposal before he realized what was happening. Reaching across the counter, Donna flipped the switch, the sharp blades inside roaring to life.

He shrieked as his arm spasmed wildly in the narrow opening, fingers, bones and muscles suddenly shredded into a bloody, pulpy mess.

Donna let go and ran.

He tried to kick her, but instead his foot connected with the bucket beside them, dumping dingy mop water across the linoleum floor.

Donna slipped in the soapy water, her legs flying out from under her as if they'd been yanked upward by an invisible cord. Her back slammed hard against the unforgiving kitchen floor, knocking the wind out of her.

She moaned and rolled over to her side. Out of breath and in a world of pain, Donna lay there on the wet floor, trying to catch her breath as pieces of pickle glass dug into her back. She blinked her eyes rapidly, fighting to stay awake. A few inches in front of her, tucked under the cabinet corner, lay Nemo, his desperate gasps for breath perfectly synchronized with hers.

Above her the sink disposal stopped its angry squealing, and Donna lifted her eyes.

He stared down at his arm and screamed again. What had once been an immaculate, manicured hand had been reduced to a mangled, blood-soaked, shredded stump. Donna thought she saw one finger still attached, dangling by a tendon or two, but she wasn't positive. He looked down from his hand to where she lay on the floor and his face changed from one of horror to pure, unadulterated fury.

"*You!*" he hissed.

His foot flew forward and he kicked Donna across the face, her skull snapping back. Having foreseen the fierce attack, she'd managed to roll with it, but still suffered a broken nose and a pounding headache as fresh blood gushed to the floor.

Donna cradled her head in her arms, curling up into a tight ball to protect herself. Eyes watering and head pounding from the kick, she heard him step over her and walk to the pantry, its opening announced by the telltale squeak of the door.

"Tried to let you die with dignity, Donna," he said, grabbing a plastic shopping bag she'd stuffed inside it earlier. "You could've fallen down the stairs... had a simple heart attack... Heck, I would've even been okay with letting you punch out peacefully in your sleep during an afternoon nap. But *nooooo*... you just *had* to have your way, didn't you?!"

He walked back to where she lay and grabbed her by the hair, pulling her upright. She reached out with her hands, weakly lashing out at him. He let go and punched her twice in the face, sending a new series of sparks behind her eyes. Donna moaned and stopped struggling, arms falling limply beside her.

He grabbed her hair and pulled once again, her legs instinctively lifting her into the air to minimize the pain. She willed her arms to reach out and try to stop him, but they refused, flailing in the air, grasping nothing.

He pushed her back against the counter and she heard the snapping sound of the bag as he opened it, filling it with air. She opened her eyes just as he pulled it over her head and twisted the bag behind her, creating a tight seal against her skin.

Donna panicked, kicking her legs behind her, missing completely. She reached around with her hands, searching wildly, but it was useless. He was perfectly positioned behind her, out of reach, and his grip was too strong.

"Stop resisting!" he yelled. "Why won't you just die, already!" He tightened his grip on the bag. Donna felt it dig into her neck even more.

She reached up with her hands, hoping to tear an opening in it, but his bloody stump continually blocked her, knocking her tired arms away each time. Donna's heart sank as she realized she wasn't going to get out of this. Her death was all but inevitable at this point. Aside from some kind of divine intervention, Donna Davis was going to die.

He lifted a knee and pressed it into the center of her back, pulling the bag tighter behind her, blocking her every attempt to reach it. This was supposed to have been an easy run, a quick "get-in-and-get-out" assignment. Not a "get-maimed-and-dismembered" situation. This day couldn't end soon enough.

As he felt her body slacken, an explosion of bright light burst into the room from outside the kitchen window. Luminescence flooded the room a brilliant white, and he raised his bloody stump to shield his eyes, his grip on the bag loosening slightly. He removed his knee from Donna's back and lowered his leg to the floor, trying to regain his balance.

The light began to fade, and he squinted through the small window. As his eyes adjusted to the room, he discerned a figure standing outside, next door. It had the appearance of an old lady dressed in gardening clothes and a gaudy sun hat, but he saw through it all in an instant, and his eyes widened at the sight, recognizing her for what she was.

"Impossible!" he whispered. "What is she doing *here*?"

Outside, Edna frowned at him, then raised a dirt-coated glove in front of her, holding a single finger up. She wagged it slowly from side to side, shaking her head in solemn disapproval.

He stared at her through the window, his mind searching for answers even as a swelling lump of terror began to grow inside him. He was so distracted that he failed to see Donna's hand searching the sink, fumbling about until finally coming to rest on a familiar handle.

Donna twisted and swung, the back of the cast iron pan slamming into the side of his skull with a resounding *clunk*.

He went sprawling across the kitchen, glancing his head against the marble corner of the island before spinning and falling face-first into the trash collection on the floor.

He stopped moving.

Donna reached up with her other hand and ripped the bag off her head, gasping for air. She threw it to the ground and wrapped both hands around the pan's handle, hefting it over her shoulder as she took a step forward, staring down at his limp body. She breathed deeply, her vision quickly clearing even as her head continued to pound with painful throbs.

A black pool of blood seeped out from beneath his head, forming a large puddle on the wood floor around him. Donna instinctively winced at the thought of having to clean the stain later, then realized how ridiculous the idea was. She wasn't in clean up mode, she was in survival mode. Who cares about a little blood in a situation like this?

She continued to stare down at his body for a full two minutes, pan raised and ready. He never twitched, never moved, never even breathed.

It was over.

A rush of emotions overwhelmed her, and Donna sank down against the cabinets, the pan clattering to the kitchen floor beside her. She stared at the dead, breathless body of Nemo, then leaned back and wept as the pool of bloody, soapy water soaked into her sweatpants.

Somehow, against all the odds that she knew weren't in her favor, she had won. She'd won the right to live, and no matter how bad or complicated her life might become in the future, Donna vowed to never take it for granted again.

Somewhere in the room her phone chirped and buzzed. Donna spied it a few feet away from her on the floor, face down. Glancing back at the still body of her attacker, Donna dug through the trash and found her phone.

He didn't move.

She held her phone up, frowning at the fresh crack across the center of the screen. It flickered and chirped again as another text message arrived. It was her daughter.

HOPE YOU HAVE A GREAT "DONNA DAY" TODAY, MOM! PRAYING FOR YOU!

It was followed by a random collection of emojis, ranging from pink hearts to cats to Chinese symbols. Donna smiled. She loved her family's bizarre sense of humor, which always seemed to show up in her life at just the right times.

Her phone chirped again, the new message reading:

P.S. CAN I GO TO A MOVIE WITH BRIAN TONIGHT? AND MAYBE BORROW $20?

Donna smiled.

Borrow? Typical.

TALK LATER she texted back. LOVE U 2. THX 4 PRAYERS.

Donna lay the phone in her lap and sighed deeply, staring at the body across from her. He still hadn't moved, but something had changed.

Something wasn't right.

Reaching down beside her, Donna grabbed the frying pan. She studied his body for a few more seconds before she realized what was seeing. She sucked in a breath, her heart clenching inside her.

It was his hand.

His left hand.

It was completely healed.

She sat up straighter to get a better look. The fingers on his mangled hand were now all reattached and repaired, perfectly manicured nails visible even from a few feet away.

Donna leaned back, breathing deeply, silently, trying to

refocus her thoughts. She reached up and grabbed the counter with her free hand, pulling herself to her feet and leaning against it. She dropped the pan onto it with a loud clang, then continued to stare at him.

"So... you're not actually dead, are you?" she asked.

He didn't move.

"Answer me, please." She banged the pan against the sink.

His body jerked, and she watched his back rise as he inhaled deeply. "No," he mumbled from the floor. "I'm not."

Donna frowned. "So what now? Do we have to do this all over again, or—"

"I'd really rather not, if you don't mind," he said, his words slurred as they slid out of his squished cheek. "May I please get up, or are you going to beat the crap out of me if I do?"

"That depends," Donna said, shrugging. "Are you going to get the hell out of my house?"

"I am."

"Is that a promise?"

"It is."

Donna squinted at him. "Can you even make a promise like that?"

"I can. I'm a man of my word. I promise."

"That's nice," Donna said, smirking. "So, you're promising me that your promise is good, is that it?"

"Something like that." He raised his right hand off the floor a few inches. "Now may I please get up? It's really quite unpleasant down here."

"Whatever. Get up and get out."

"Thank you."

He slowly pulled his arms up beside him, then pushed himself up to a kneeling position, pausing to stretch his neck from side to side. From what Donna could tell, he was completely healed from head to toe, without a mark or scratch on him aside from his clothes. His clothes were ripped, covered with trash and caked with blood.

Donna smiled at that.

He glanced over his shoulder at her and glared.

She raised an eyebrow, lifting the pan up off the counter and slapping it against her other palm as if it were a baseball bat.

He sighed, looked away from her and nodded. Standing slowly, he limped a few steps away from her into the dining room. Stretching from side to side, his body popped and cracked a few times as pieces seemed to slide back into place. Turning to face her again, he tucked his shirt back into his pants and frowned.

"Well," he began, shrugging. "I would say this has been fun, but I have to be honest. You pretty much ruined my day, Donna."

"Glad to hear it. Feeling's mutual. Now get out."

He nodded and started walking toward the front door before stopping, staring out at the front yard and frowning. He turned around and pointed across the room, walking in the opposite direction. "I think I'll use the back door, if you don't mind..."

"Whatever. Just leave already."

"Right. I'm going."

When he reached the patio door he turned the knob and started to walk through but suddenly stopped. Popping his head around the door, he grinned at her. "See you in thirty years or so."

"Not if I see you first," Donna said, glaring back at him.

Just after she heard the door latch shut, Donna reached down for her phone and began to dial. Dropping the pan into the sink, she pressed the phone up to her ear, her eyes starting to fill with tears.

"Hello?" she said, her voice quivering with emotion. "Owen?"

"Hey there," Owen said. "I've been trying to call you for the last half hour..."

"Yeah," Donna murmured. "I've... been kind of busy."

Owen paused. "Honey? What's wrong? You sound like you're crying."

She sniffled for a moment and laughed, "Yeah, I am."

"Are you okay?"

"Oh... it's nothing. I'll be fine," Donna said, shaking her head. "It's just... it's kind of been a really rough morning, is all."

"Was it the kids? Did something happen on the way to school?"

"No, no, the kids are fine," she said, smiling. "They're fine. We're all fine, actually. I'll be okay... I promise."

"Are you sure? Because I could come home if you want, instead of just meeting for lunch."

"No, I'll be alright. I promise."

Donna paused for a moment as she stared around her

kitchen, the endless amount of trash and glass and water and blood starting to overwhelm her again.

Then she smiled.

"Hey, honey?"

"Yes?"

"Remember last year when you wanted to give me a month's worth of that cleaning service for Christmas?"

"Sure."

"And I said no, that it was just too expensive?"

"Yes, I remember," he said.

"Well, I think I've changed my mind. Today's Christmas." She reached over the sink and pulled the strand of spaghetti off the window. "Make the call."

There was a short moment of silence on the other end of the line, and then she heard him laugh. "Alright. Sure thing. I'll call them right now."

"Thanks, babe."

"Anything else? I could—"

"Nope," she said. "That's really all I need for today." She paused, staring up at the broken TV screen across the room. "Well... hold on, there's just one more thing, I guess."

"Name it."

Donna's face became taut, her eyes narrowing into a single, focused scowl.

"Tell Tiffani I'd like to have lunch with her tomorrow."

Author's Note

Life can be beautiful, but some days it can also be utterly and completely overwhelming. Things don't go according to plan, people fuss and fight, and an otherwise perfect day can be ruined in mere minutes. It's easy to let our emotions overpower us and cloud our perspective, causing us to despair and entertain thoughts we would normally never consider.

What if one day we actually received what we foolishly asked for? What if all those hot-headed, misguided pleas for an appointment with the Grim Reaper were actually adding up, to one day be cashed in?

What if...?

Those two words are the golden seeds of great stories.

What. If.

I knew what I originally wanted to accomplish with the story, but as usual the specific details didn't become clear until I actually sat down and started writing. The kitchen fight scene wasn't fleshed out nearly enough, but the more I envisioned it unfolding in my head, the better I got to know Donna's character, what she was capable of and what she would do to survive.

I especially enjoyed the fact that Donna didn't have any super powers, unlike the majority of most of my other female leads. She's just a boss lady. A formidable woman not to be trifled with, hidden beneath the veneer of a typical housewife. (I suspect that's more than likely the case with the vast majority of homemakers out there.)

Long live the Donna Davises of the world!

THE HITCH

JACK KARDIAC

the hitch

IF YOU FIND yourself in the right place at the right time, you may find your life is changed for the better — forever. On the other hand, being in the wrong place at the wrong time can also get a guy killed. And the second I saw the man was missing three fingers, I knew there was a fairly good chance I was going to die that day.

It took me a few repeated attempts to get Tyler out of bed and ready to head to the auction this morning. He mumbled something about having watched the *Lord of the Rings* extended trilogy and playing Halo all night, but I kindly informed him it wasn't my problem. I'd told him the day before that we were going into town "first thing in the morning," so if he chose to squander his time turning his mind to mush, that was his prerogative and his predicament. Not mine.

Needless to say, we were late at the auction house. I'd already spoken to Bernie, the owner, the night before, so it wasn't a big deal. We have a long history, Bernie and I, going all the way back to grade school. It was just good fortune that we found ourselves working together so often, what with my owning a pawn shop and his running an auction block. Our wives like to cackle and crackle on about our long hours, but do we hear them complaining when they cash our checks?

No, sir, we do not.

Now, after all the crazy crap at my shop the other night, I was determined to take a few days off of work. I'd also decided I wanted nothing to do with the gun Chester had sold us. Granted, I was grateful the thing misfired rather than burying a bullet into my brain. Still, I wasn't inclined to take the time to tinker with it and make it work.

Tyler wanted to keep it around as a prop or something, considering it's from the Old West, but I told him straight up that wasn't an option. Antique or not, I didn't care for it. Something about it just felt... wrong. Like the thing was cursed or something. I can't explain it, all's I know is I didn't want anything more to do with it.

So I called Chester up this morning and offered to sell it back, but like a flaming idiot he'd already spent the money I gave him wrestling with the one-armed bandits at the nearest casino. Told him I was putting it up for auction in a few hours, but if nobody bid on it he could have the gun back for free. Well, he sobered up right quick, promising he'd be there. I suppose nothing perks up an old vet like the words "free" and "gun."

Tyler and I ducked through the back doors of the auction room and stood against the back wall, scanning the rows of chairs for a place to sit. The room was big enough to fit a little over a hundred people, and that morning it was stuffed wall-to-wall. I hadn't a clue what else Bernie was planning on selling that morning, but apparently it was drawing a lot of attention. I spotted a few other pawn shop buyers scattered in the crowd and watched as they took turns bidding on a compact chest of comic books displayed up front.

Tyler's interest was immediately piqued. I could feel his excitement just by standing next to him. To be honest, I'd never much been into comic books myself, but Tyler loved them from the day he learned to read. Well, seeing the opportunity and his interest, I calculated how long he'd been working for me in the shop, day in and day out, and decided to do something foolish and fatherly and just plain nice.

"Hey," I whispered, leaning over to him.

"Yeah?" he said, not moving his eyes off the chest on display.

"You want those comics?"

He broke his gaze away and looked at me, frowning. "What?" he said, confused.

I jutted my chin toward the front of the auction hall. "Those comic books. You interested?"

He still frowned at me. "Yeah..." he muttered.

I grinned. "Go ahead. You can bid up to $300 on 'em."

An expression of elation blossomed across his face. "You serious?"

"I am."

"You're not kidding with me?"

"I am not." I handed him my bidding paddle and smiled. "But don't bid $300 right off the bat, Tyler. Let 'em work up to it, alright?"

He grinned and nodded. "Got it."

"Good. Let's go take a seat. I think I see a spot in the middle, over on the left." We quietly made our way around the side aisle and then apologized to a group of cranky ladies as we wheedled past them to the open seats. Tyler didn't hesitate a second, raising his paddle high above his head.

"Fifty dollars!" he yelled.

The auctioneer turned his head and glowered at us. "We're already at a hundred and fifty, son."

Tyler blushed and looked around at the sea of frowning faces around him. He gulped, then raised the paddle higher. "Two ninety-nine!" he exclaimed.

Oh, Lordy, I thought, closing my eyes.

"Two ninety-nine!" the auctioneer repeated, and for the next thirty seconds there was an all-out bidding war in the room. Unfortunately, Tyler was quickly outbid, the set finalizing for $500, sold to one of the uptight ladies beside us, of all people. When I leaned over and asked her what she planned to do with them, she said she was going to give them to her grandchildren next time they came over to visit.

"Oh? They like to read comics?" I asked.

She frowned. "Oh, no. They can't read yet."

I blinked. "How old are they, may I ask?"

She beamed. "Jessica is four and Tessa Fay is two. She'll be three in six months."

I did my best to hide my horror as I envisioned two toddlers ripping the collectible comics to shreds. "That's nice," I lied with a smile, then turned back to Tyler, who was gaping at the woman like she'd just announced how much she enjoyed poking kittens with red hot knitting needles in her spare time.

"Dad!" he whispered to me loudly. "Did you hear that?"

"Don't stare," I whispered back.

"But did you hear what she said, Dad?"

I nodded.

"That's... that's just..."

"Shhhh... I know, Tyler," I whispered. "Eyes front, son. Ain't polite to stare at the crazy people, now."

He turned his head to the front, and I could tell he was about to burst into tears. I leaned over toward him, placed a hand on his shoulder. "Hey, for what it's worth, I'm sorry you lost, son."

"It's okay..." he mumbled.

"You want, we can hit a comic book shop on the way home. I'll still give you a hundred bucks to spend."

"Really?"

"Yeah, really."

He nodded. "Cool. I'd like that."

"Alright, then."

"Hey," he said, pointing ahead of us. "Isn't that Chester?"

I craned my neck to see where he was pointing, and sure enough, Chester was sitting by himself on the front row. He was slouched over just like he was in my shop last night, and I figured he was either drunk or asleep or both.

Tyler started to stand. "I'm gonna go say hi to him."

I reached over and grabbed hold of his arm. "Uh-uh," I said, pulling him back down. "That's not a good idea."

"What? Why not?"

"Well, for one," I said, "They're about to auction off our gun." I nodded toward the front of the room where an attendant was carefully carrying out the piece and placing it on the display podium.

"And second, you seem to forget that Chester's the jumpy sort. Didn't I tell you he's got PTSD?"

"Post-traumatic stress disorder?"

"Exactly."

"But he hasn't been in a war for, what? Thirty years?"

I shook my head. "Doesn't matter how long it's been," I said. "For some fellas, they might leave the war, but the war never really leaves them, you understand? Something happens to trigger 'em and it's like they're right back in it, no matter *how* long it's been." I raised my finger and pointed. "And Chester, there... well, he's a great guy, but he doesn't cotton much to sudden surprises."

"Cotton much?" Tyler repeated. "Are we in a Little House on the Prairie episode or something?" He snickered loudly.

"Hush up your butt," I said, punching him lightly. "Show's about to start."

Just before they started the auction, I glanced across the room and that's when I noticed something odd. In the aisle seat of the third row my eyes landed on someone I recognized. Someone from the other night.

I frowned. It was him, the creepy emo guy from my store the other night. He was still dressed in all black. Black dress shoes, black slacks and a button-up black dress shirt. I wondered what he was doing there, when suddenly he turned his head and looked right at me. I was about to look away when he grinned at me and nodded cordially.

I nodded back, then redirected my attention up front, trying to compose myself. It's a small town, a free country. Chances were good I'd see people from the shop around town, so it shouldn't have been that big of a deal, seeing him there. Still, based on my past experience, whenever that guy shows up somebody tends to get hurt.

The auction began, but before the caller even got started there was suddenly a loud commotion near the back of the room. I turned to see a security guy get shoved to the floor, followed by two men wearing ski masks, holding guns.

"EVERYBODY DOWN ON THE GROUND!" one yelled, waving his gun around the room. "NOW!"

The taller man stepped past him and pointed his gun at the floor in front of him. "CELL PHONES AND WALLETS TO THE CENTER AISLE! DO IT NOW!"

That was when my blood ran cold.

The man's bandaged hand was missing his three lower fingers.

Crud. These jokers were the same drug addicts who tried to rob me the night before. Chemical Hank and his buddy.

"Oh, you've got to be kidding me," I whispered as I sank to the floor, digging out my cell phone and wallet. I turned my face away from them so they wouldn't see me. The last thing I needed was for them to recognize me or want some kind of revenge for their screw up in my shop.

"Get down, Tyler," I whispered next to me. "Don't let them see you, alright?"

He frowned and turned his head to get a better look at them. I grabbed his neck and forced it down. "Head. Down. Pretend you're praying."

"I *am* praying!" he whispered through clenched teeth.

"PHONES AND WALLETS!" Hank yelled. "You have exactly... uh... sixteen seconds! So toss 'em to me now or you *will* be shot!"

The room erupted with whimpers and crying as a collection of phones and wallets started careening through the air and coming to rest in the center aisle. I looked over to see the lady beside me clutching her phone, trying to slip it beneath her thigh.

Idiot.

I reached over, pulled her phone out and tossed it into the middle of the room. She looked over at me, horrified, then glared and whispered a string of obscenities.

"You're welcome," I muttered back.

"Hey!" someone shouted.

It was Hank. I froze.

"Hey you!" he yelled, louder.

Oh crap, is this it? I thought.

Is this how and when I die?

I raised my hands and slowly started to rise off the floor when I saw Hank storm up the aisle to the front as his friend shoved wallets and phones into a duffle bag.

He hadn't been talking to me.

He was talking to Chester.

"I said get down on the ground!" he yelled, stopping a few rows back, aiming the gun at Chester's back. I saw a sliver of fluorescent orange near the muzzle, and for a second I wondered if he'd just shot him and I simply hadn't heard it.

I looked closer, then glanced over at the other guy's gun.

Just like Hanks, it was black and shiny, like it had been freshly painted. Apparently these two yahoos neglected to cover all the angles, forgetting the insides of the gun's orange muzzle.

The *toy gun's* orange muzzle.

I smiled.

These guys were even bigger idiots than I thought they were.

"I mean it!" Hank yelled, taking a step closer to Chester.

Chester didn't move.

He just sat there, head on his chest, breathing deeply. I

suddenly got a clear vision of how this scenario was likely to play out, and lowered myself back to the ground as fast as I could.

"Stay down," I whispered to Tyler. "And cover your ears,"

"What?"

"Ears," I said, pressing my hands into the side of my head. "Cover them." He follows my example, keeping his head down.

"That's it!" Hank bellowed, storming up the aisle with his friend right beside him. He lunged forward and jabbed the front of the gun hard into Chester's shoulder. "GET ON THE GROUND OLD MAN!"

Chester sprang to his feet in an instant. He turned around, eyes wide, face slathered in fury and fear. With shocking speed he reached into his vest and drew, shooting Hank three times in the chest.

Hank yelped and fell to the ground. His friend stared down at him, then stupidly raised his gun hand toward Chester. Three more shots fill the room and the second man collapsed onto the floor, falling on Hank's motionless body.

Chester stood at the front of the room, wide-eyed and shaking. He stared down at the two men in the aisle and then at the frightened faces around the room. Everyone was completely silent and still, terrified. They were all probably wondering the same thing I was: *were we just chucked outta the frying pan and into the blamed fire?*

Recognition slowly settled on poor Chester like a heavy overcoat. His shoulders sagged and he started to moan, lowering himself to the floor, gun falling out of his hand to carpet beside him. He shook his head vigorously. "I... I didn't know!" he protested loudly. "It was an accident! I swear!"

No one moved.

I stood up, hands raised over my head. "Chester? You alright?"

He looked over at me, eyes starting to water, hands shaking in his lap. "Jerry?"

"Yeah, it's me, old buddy," I said as I stepped over Tyler and edged my way out of the row, walking up the aisle toward him.

"Why'd they go an' do that?" Chester complained, frowning at the two bodies. "Why'd they haveta *jump* me like that?"

I walked over and picked up his gun, sticking it behind me into the back of my jeans. "I don't know, Chester. I guess some people are idiots is all."

"It was an accident!"

"I know it was. We all know it was." I motioned around the room at the people, slowly raising themselves off the floor, looking around in horror and confusion.

"Ain't nobody gonna blame you, Chester. You done good today."

He looked over at me, confused. "What? But I... I killed two men."

"No sir, you killed two *thieves*," I corrected him.

"I... did?"

"Yes, you did. These two men were trying to rob us blind, Chester. And you stopped them cold."

He looked over at them and back at me, shaking his head. "It... it was an accident."

"That's fine," I said, helping him to his feet. "Ain't no jury in the county gonna convict you for this, Chester. You're a hero." I started to clap, slowly, then turned and made eye contact with a few others around the room. They got the message and joined in, and within a minute the entire place was standing on their feet, filling the room with ample applause and cheers.

Chester's eyes welled up with tears, and he leaned into me. I caught him in my arms as he started to weep, letting out loud, sobbing cries, as if decades of bottled-up emotions had just been uncorked inside him. I held him as the man shook and shivered, giving him time and space to feel everything he needed to feel in the moment.

"You're a hero, Chester," I repeated quietly. "A hero."

Author's Note

I honestly don't know a lot of vets, so I'm not writing out of firsthand experience or insight into the PTSD that those who have served our country sometimes suffer from. It's also been a few years since I wrote this story, so I can't really say where the inspiration came from. Sometimes a story idea just "shows up," no catalyst or inciting event necessary.

As it is, I think it ended up being a nice add-on to *Borken*. Not a classic tale, but not bad, either. It was good enough, a short 10-minute tale to wrap things up a bit.

Note: I know it might be confusing, but not all the stories in this collection occur chronologically. The majority of them do, yes, but this one... doesn't. In fact, it takes place *after* the climactic events in *Extermination*.

Now, if you don't know what that means... don't worry, you will eventually. I promise.

Countdown

JACK KARDIAC

countdown

AS I SAVOR the last few sips of my second peach milkshake, Clara slumps into the booth across from me, emitting a deep sigh.

"Oh, it feels so good to rest my feet!" she moans. The deep creases around her eyes are always more evident when she's exhausted. Her lips are slightly pursed, as if she's nursing a hard candy. Once-black hair now shows strands of gray, as if she's skipped a few salon appointments.

"Long day?" I ask. The diner has almost cleared out, leaving only a handful of lingering customers. The glossy red booth upholstery glimmers in the sunlight streaming through the windows, saltshakers creating a dazzling array of disco dot constellations across the ceiling.

She shrugs. "Ah, no longer than any other. I'm just getting older is all, Honey. Standing around taking orders all day takes more out of me than it used to, you know?"

"I would imagine," I say, popping a fry into my mouth. "Is Bud going to get upset if he sees you out here, sitting with me?" I glance at the service counter behind her, but there's no sign of activity back there.

"Nah," Clara sneers, waving her hand. "He's busy watching some UFC match back in the kitchen. Guy hardly even knows I'm here today, 'cept when I give and take the orders." She smiles. "You know, just like when we're at home." She winks, and I can't help but smile at her.

"Clara, this place would fall apart without you."

She laughs. "Ain't that the truth?" She looks out the plate glass window beside us, lost in thought. Returning her tired, gray-blue eyes on me she stares as I finish my plate. "You alright, kiddo?" she asks. "Seem kind of quiet today."

I shrug. "I'm always quiet, Clara." Some of my brown, wavy hair wanders over my eyes and I blow it back with a quick puff, leaning back in the booth.

"I know that, but today you just seem a bit more... distant. Something got you down? You meet a man or something? Bum go and break your heart already?"

"No, Clara," I laugh. "I haven't 'met a man.' But you're never going to stop trying to set me up with one, are you?"

"Honey, if I was your age and had your looks, I wouldn't waste it sitting in a diner every other day."

"I *like* it here!" I protest. "And I like *you*. Even Bud. I like seeing you two, day after day, week after week. It's..." I pause, searching for the right word to accurately portray how I feel about them. "Comforting," I say, smiling. "I guess you guys are kind of like family to me. Plus, the food tastes good enough and hasn't made me sick. Yet." I pop another fat fry into my mouth.

"Good enough?!" Clara exclaims, reaching over to slap my hand. I dodge the attack and chuckle as she grins at me.

"Well, we love you too, sugar." She reaches over and steals a French fry from the edge of my plate, popping it into her mouth. Pushing off the table to her feet, she frowns, then looks down at me. "But don't hang around here on our accounts, okay? If the good Lord puts a man in your life who's worth your time, don't you be wasting it, hiding out in here."

I nod. "Thanks. I appreciate your thoughts, Clara. See you Saturday evening, then?"

She rolls her eyes and huffs. "In one ear and out the other," she says, shaking her head. She reaches over and gives my shoulder a light squeeze. "You take care of yourself, Sweetie."

"You too, Clara.

I watch her walk back toward the kitchen and smile. I've been coming here a little over a year now, and I love it more than the day I first stepped in. I'd walked past on the sidewalk on my way to the library, and every time I did I was so impressed by what I saw in Clara and Bud.

No matter how busy the diner was, the two of them were always smiling. Just one look at them and I could instantly tell they were not only happily married, but were the kind of couple who would actually grow old together.

They cared about their customers too. If it wasn't just right, they'd fix it. Bud's been known to go and recook a customer's entire order right when he gets a complaint. That's just the kind of guy he is. Great way to run a business, I think.

You could say I kind of gravitated here. Finding people like that — so in love with each other and life and who have a future together — well, I've found that's pretty rare. Some would call it a blessing from God, so I suppose I'm being a little selfish for wanting to experience a part of that blessing, week after week.

I finish my shake, pull out twice as much money as the bill calls for and tuck it under the edge of my plate. As usual, Clara will scold me later for "wasting my money" like this, and as usual I won't care. She puts in a lot of long hours for such little pay. Someone needs to let her know she's appreciated. Might as well be me.

As I'm leaving the diner I glance over and see that he's back. I hesitate, if only for a second. The man sits on a stool at the end of the counter, wearing all black again. Only this time he's sporting white tennis shoes. It's a stark contrast against his slacks and dress shirt, and I wonder if he's trying to attract attention or just having fun. Probably both.

He turns when he sees me leaving and nods politely. I lift a limp hand and wave back, then turn and step out onto the sidewalk, eager to get some distance.

The air outside carries the distinct scent of the street, mingling with the crisp scent of autumn in a way that's not wholly unpleasant. I smile, appreciating the setting sun as it explodes against the sky, an impressive array of orange, red and gold in the trees looming over the street. Inhaling deeply and exhaling, my grin grows wider.

This is it, I think. *The perfect time of year, at the perfect time of night, and I'm just thankful to be here, to be alive.*

I remove the white headphones from inside my backpack and slip them over my ears, moving my long, brown hair to the side to allow for a snug fit. Clara is constantly raving about my hair, calling me a small-town super model because of how thick and wavy it is. Of course, she loves it — *she's* not the one who has to contend with it every day. I suppose she has a point, though. And it beats being bald, I guess.

I grab my phone and open an app, turning on the audio-pass through feature. I adjust the microphone's sensitivity until I can clearly hear the world around me without being overwhelmed by it. As I walk down the street, I'm careful to keep my eyes low, avoiding eye contact. I kick myself for once again forgetting my sunglasses at home, so it looks like tonight I'm going to be doing this the old-fashioned way by being overtly non-social and as inaccessible as possible.

The sound of my steps on the sidewalk is a little too harsh, so I readjust the gain on the microphone. A small twist ensures the rhythmic pattern doesn't grate on my ears.

Children can be heard playing somewhere ahead of me, so I slow down my pace in response. I lift my head and glance. Two houses away. Three kids, kicking around a soccer ball. Two girls and a boy.

I glance over my shoulder, checking on traffic. It's rush hour, and there's already a steady stream of cars shooting past me. Which means I won't be able to just walk over to the other sidewalk and pass them over there. I take a deep breath and sigh, staring back up the street at the three of them.

I can do this. It's going to be fine. All I have to do is keep my head down, walk by quickly and it'll all be over.

Only I'm wrong.

Just as I'm passing by I hear one of the kids yell. I look up to see the ball rolling into the street. One of the girls runs to retrieve it, and one glance tells me she's the kind who'll chase it right into the street.

"Stop!" I yell at her. "I'll get it!"

I sprint up the sidewalk, stopping the ball with my foot a second before it jumps off the curb. Ignoring her, I roll it up onto my shoe like a professional, then kick it into the air where it drops into my open hand.

I hold it out, forcing a smile. "Here you go."

"Thanks, lady!" she says as she approaches me.

"You're welcome," I say, trying not to stare as I hand the ball back. My smile is a lie, my heart sinking inside me.

Oh, Lord, she's so young...

If the girl sees my sadness, she doesn't acknowledge it. Having happily retrieved the ball, she runs back to join her friends. I watch her go, eyes lingering on her long, blonde hair. *Too young...*

As I resume walking, my eyes start tearing up and I quietly curse myself once more for my lack of sunglasses. I need them for moments like these. Just because I'm drowning in sorrow doesn't mean the world has to see it.

When I arrive at the apartment complex a few minutes later, I'm immediately impressed with how upscale it looks. It's not surprising, being located in this part of town, but the intricate exterior design and the weather-worn cobblestone parking lot testifies to its classiness.

I remove my headphones, gingerly placing them into my backpack beside my camera and the manila envelope. Taking a deep breath, I zip the bag closed, approach the unit's front door and ring the buzzer. As I wait for a response, my mind starts to wander again.

Is this a bad idea?

So many times these moments have started out so sweetly, so innocently, only to turn sour in an instant. The hurt and confusion linger for days, sometimes weeks. Still, I tell myself that I at least have to try, to *keep* trying. If I could give just one person hope, *only one*, then maybe—

The door swings open and an older woman appears. She's wearing tan slacks and a slate blue sweater, gray hair cut into a cute, hassle-free pixie style. Most women her age are sporting high and tight buns, so I'm happy to see she's preferred to make her own way instead of conforming to the norm.

Maybe this time will be different...

"Hello," I say, smiling. "Are you Melody Yates?"

"I am."

"I'm Sephanie, your five o'clock appointment."

Her face brightens into a warm smile. "Of course! Please, come in!" She opens the door wide and steps aside, ushering me in.

An aroma of autumn spice immediately makes me feel welcome, at peace. I feel my body relax, the tension from the limited exchange a few minutes earlier slowly melting away as I bask in the comfort of a genuine, established *home*.

"Your home smells fantastic," I exclaim as she shuts the door behind me.

"Why, thank you," she says, motioning me toward a front room. "I always loved the smell of my grandmother's house when I would visit her in the country. She would constantly simmer something on the stove that smelled of citrus and spice and everything nice." She laughs, shaking her head. "I can never quite replicate the recipe just right, but it hasn't stopped me from trying."

"I would say you've succeeded," I say, walking from the hall into a small office.

"Well, that's very kind of you. Thank you!"

I nod and let my eyes wander around the room. It's painted a pale gray, with plush, blue carpet underneath. It's the kind of carpet that beckons you to indulge in it, to spread out on its softness and make floor angels like a kid. There's a wide desk in the back of the room, and a variety of books resting on the white, built-in bookshelves behind it. A long couch sits across another wall, flanked by two chairs and a small coffee table. A pen and notepad rest on it.

I smile. *Typical counselor's office.*

"The couch is yours to use as you see fit," she explains, taking a seat in one of the chairs. "You're free to lie down or sit up, or shift around if you're the fidgety type."

"I'm happy to just sit," I say, lowering my backpack to the floor before settling into a corner of the couch. Everything inside me wants to kick off my shoes and curl up into it, surrounded by the plush pillows, drinking in the ambiance. I resist the urge, opting instead to make the most positive, most professional first impression I possibly can.

From out of the corner of my eye I see a flash of movement in the corner of the room. I turn to look and am delighted when a trim, calico cat peeks its head out from behind her desk. It looks at me with curiosity, approaching me with slow, careful caution. After a few cursory sniffs, it hops up into my lap and snuggles against me as if we were long lost friends.

"Tandy!" Ms. Yates exclaims, concern coloring her face. "I'm so sorry! She doesn't usually come up to guests like that! You're not allergic, are you?"

"Not at all," I say, stroking Tandy's sleek coat. "And it's no bother at all. I love cats, actually. How old is she?"

"Just over five years. I rescued her from the shelter shortly after my husband died. We've kept each other company ever since."

"She seems like a very healthy cat," I say, looking down at her. "She'll live a long time."

"Ah, you know cats. I'll probably outlive her by a few years, but at least we'll be together in the meantime."

My face freezes, and I look away and nod, unsure how to respond. Tandy hops off my lap and wanders over to the door, disappearing into the hallway.

"So," Ms. Yates says, picking up her notebook and pen. "Please forgive me, but you said your name was Stephanie, correct?"

"Scphanie," I say, for what feels like the thousandth time.

"Sephanie?" Her face contorts into the same look of confusion I've encountered almost every day of my life.

"That's correct. Spelled just like 'Stephanie,' just without the T."

She scribbles it down in her notes, then smiles as she looks up. "I don't mean to pry, but is there a story behind it?"

"Behind my name?"

"Yes."

"Not an interesting one, I'm afraid," I say, shaking my head. "My parents actually *did* name me Stephanie after I was born, but when the birth certificate arrived they discovered it was missing the letter T. Instead of going through the hassle to correct it, they decided to just leave it be. So, Sephanie it was."

"That's very interesting. I've never met a Sephanie before."

"Neither have I," I admit. "I used to resent it when people couldn't get my name right, but now I've come to appreciate it. It kind of sets me apart, I guess."

"Of course," she says, writing on her notepad. There's an awkward half-minute of silence as she finishes writing before she stops, looking up at me. Her smile shrinks when she juts her chin up, studying me down the bridge of her nose.

"So, Sephanie. Would you please tell me a little bit about yourself? You know, so I can get a better picture of who you are, what you're like, that kind of thing?"

"Sure."

I settle back into the couch cushions and look directly at her, careful not to shy away from the instant intimacy. It feels awkward, but at the same time I'm reminded of conversations with my grandma, and I feel myself relaxing again, as if we're just two friends talking over a cup of tea.

"So, I'm twenty-two, happily single and living alone in a small, economical apartment. I'm an independent travel blogger and freelance photographer." I pause. "I especially enjoy strolling around parks, and just recently discovered Garfield Park here in town."

"Oh, I absolutely adore that park," Ms. Yates says, beaming. "I take my granddaughter there as often as I see her.

I nod my head. "And I love Italian food!" I blurt out.

"Me too," she says, smiling as she writes.

"Especially the fat-laden alfredo sauces," I confide.

She leans forward a few inches. "Me too," she whispers, then resumes her place in the chair.

I smile at her, recognizing that I genuinely do *like* her! Then my happiness fades when I remind myself I'm about to cross over the threshold, delving into my personal history where these relationships typically start to crumble. Maybe this time will be different, though. Maybe this time the response will be what I actually hope for, rather than what I always dread.

I inhale deeply and nod my head, mentally slipping over the edge for what feels like the hundredth time. It never seems to get any easier, no matter which direction I attempt to approach it.

Here goes nothing...

I begin. "So, when I was twelve years old my family and I were returning from Christmas dinner at my grandparent's house. Dad was driving, Mom was in the passenger seat and my little brother and I were in the backseat. It was just after ten o'clock and we were all pretty exhausted, but too excited to sleep because, well, Santa was coming in just a few hours.

"My brother announced that he was planning to stay up and try to catch him coming down the chimney. Mom, Dad and I all laughed at that, but we reassured him it was a great idea and wished him the best of luck. It was kind of a great moment in our family history, you know? I'll never forget it."

"That sounds nice."

"And I say that," I continue, "because a few seconds later

a drunk driver veered around the corner ahead of us, crossed over the center median and smashed head-on into our car."

"Oh, my..." Ms. Yates says, pausing her writing to look up at me. She's both saddened and shocked by the news, and I give her a few seconds to recover before I continue speaking.

"Even though I had my seatbelt on, I was somehow ejected from the vehicle. I was unconscious at the time, but they said I slid across the ice for thirty feet, breaking my leg and fracturing a few ribs in the process." I breathe in deeply and let it out slowly. "Unfortunately, I regained consciousness just before the gas tanks ignited. I watched helplessly as both cars caught fire and exploded. At that point I blacked out again, later waking up in the hospital." My voice catches. No matter how many times I tell this story, reliving it, it has to be told. All of it.

"Oh, honey," she says. "I'm so, so sorry you had to go through that." Her eyes are full of genuine compassion.

"Thank you," I say, nodding in appreciation.

"That must have been so tragic. And you were only twelve, you say?"

I nod.

She looks back at her notepad and frowns, shaking her head slightly as she continues to write.

"My grandparents raised me after that, helped me through high school and onto college. They both died about three years ago. She, from a sudden aneurysm, and then he died a few months later. They say it was pneumonia, but personally I think it was just a broken heart."

"Oh, Sephanie," she says, "That is a lot of tragedy for a young girl to have to endure." She scribbles something on her notepad. "I'm curious... is this why you wanted to see me today? Because you need help walking through the grieving process? It's different for each individual, you know. So, what might take one person a few months to recover could take someone else much, much longer."

I shake my head and smile. "No, actually. I've pretty well processed through their passing, to be honest. So, no, that's not exactly why I came to see you today."

"Alright."

"But... something happened to me just before my family died," I continue. "That's kind of what I'd prefer to focus on, if we could."

"Absolutely. We can talk about anything you'd like to. I'm here to help in any way I can."

"Thank you."

I take a deep breath and bite my lip, wishing I could figure out a way to make this part of the conversation even a little less awkward. "Just before my family died, Something... appeared... over them." I look across at her, trying to gauge her reaction. She continues to focus on the notepad, scribbling quietly.

"Go on," she says. "What did you see?"

I pause, knowing exactly how the next words I say will be received. There's no avoiding it. I have to tell her the truth, or else this won't work. I swallow, take a deep breath and continue. "Hovering over all three of their heads, a set of numbers suddenly appeared," I say, "like the displays of a digital clock or a stopwatch. And each of them displayed the exact same number."

Ms. Yates looks up from her notepad.

"00:00:52."

She writes the number down. I pause to take a breath.

"Ten seconds later we were hit by the car. Forty-two seconds after that," I say, measuring my words carefully, "my family died in the explosion."

I stop speaking and Ms. Yates stops writing.

She raises her head and we look at each other, both trying to determine what the other is thinking. Finally, she swallows, then breaks the silence.

"If I could, I'd like to repeat to you what I hear you saying. Just to clarify," she says.

I nod.

"Alright," she begins, taking a breath. "What I hear you saying is that you saw things..." she pauses to look over her notes, "floating... over the heads of your parents before they died?"

"Numbers," I correct her, nodding. "And over my brother's as well."

"And these numbers were... moving?"

"Yes," I say. "Well, no. They were stationary over their heads, but the digits themselves were counting down."

"Counting down?"

"That's correct. They were counting down to the exact moment of their deaths."

She inhales deeply, writing on her notepad again. "And you believe when these numbers reached zero was the moment your family died."

"That's right," I say, shifting my body on the couch, trying to find a more comfortable position. "Counting down from the moment I first saw them to the moment they died. Forty-two seconds precisely."

"You had a watch on?"

I pause, confused. In all the conversations I've had about this, no one has ever asked me this question before. It's both slightly offensive and simultaneously refreshing.

"I did..." I say slowly, "but I don't recall looking at it at the time of the accident. In fact, the face shattered against the pavement when I was thrown from the car."

"I see," she says, flipping a page and writing on the back side. I give her time to catch up and sit quietly, knowing she's juggling a lot at the moment. It has to be challenging to hear someone confide that they see fatalistic numbers, write down the account by hand *and* consider various professional responses.

"That's why I take photos," I volunteer, trying to speed up the process a bit.

She finishes writing her sentence and looks up at me. "I'm sorry, I missed that. Could you please repeat it?"

I nod. "I decided to go into photojournalism and media after the accident."

She looks confused. "And why is that?"

"Because when I take photos or videos, the numbers are gone."

"There are no numbers over people's heads?"

"No."

"They're not there at all?"

"Well, they're there when I see people with my eyes, but in the final photos I only see the individuals themselves. No numbers."

"I see."

"As I was growing up with this... ability... I found it difficult to spend much time around other people, especially those with low or fading digits."

"Fading?"

"Um... yes," I say, curling my hair behind my ear. "The majority of the numbers are kind of a light or baby blue shade. Those are the ones who have a lot of time left in their lifespan. When people are approaching the end of their time, the color kind of fades away until it becomes a pale white, and finally altogether transparent."

Her pencil moves furiously across the page, and when she reaches the bottom she quickly flips another over, resuming her entry at the top.

"I see the numbers just like you would on a digital clock. It took me a while to figure out what they represented, but after a while I quickly saw a clear pattern. The hour section represents years and the minute section is weeks. So, for example, if I see the numbers 3:16 over someone's head, I know they have approximately three years and sixteen weeks left to live."

I stop myself, wondering if I should share the last part. *I've told her this much,* I figure. *Why not get it all out?*

"So that's what the hour and minute sections mean. When I see that the readout has seconds appearing at the end, I know it's counting down the number of minutes that person has." I pause for a moment, looking down at my hands. "Those are kind of the hardest numbers to see, as you might imagine. Not because they're faint, but because... well..." I sigh again, staring at her. "Time is running out."

She starts to say something, but then stops herself, mouth shutting tight. She looks up from her notepad, her eyes blinking rapidly as she scours the room around us, as if she's searching for the right words to say next and doesn't want to mess them up.

"Okay… Sephanie… I'd like to hear more about the low numbers. Do you have any kind of a record or tracking system? What I mean to say is, do you believe everyone with these low numbers will die shortly after you see them? As in, have your predictions ever been wrong or inaccurate?"

"They're not predictions," I say quickly. "I'm not like a prophet or a fortune teller or anything. I'm not *predicting* when people will die. I just… see it. I just *know*."

"Fine," she says, searching her mind again. "We'll just call them 'numbers,' then, shall we? Have your numbers ever been wrong?"

"In the ten years I've been seeing them, there was only one time when the person didn't die on time." I wince as the words escape. "When they were *supposed* to, I mean. *Scheduled* to, that is."

I sink deeper into the couch, wincing at my poor word choice. I still forget how some people react to my story. I've told it so many times that from my perspective it's all simple, just matter-of-fact. But to them… well, to them it's all new and shocking and depressingly sad.

Her eyes, once warm and inviting, are now troubled as she looks at me, unmoving. She breathes deeply, then glances back at her notepad and writes something down.

"Could you tell me what happened that time?" she says, not looking up.

"Sure," I say. "It was a few years ago, a car accident while I was in Kentucky. I was walking through downtown Lexington after a movie, when a teenage driver ran a red light. It happened fast, and it was *loud.* The girl's economy car was almost completely crushed by the guy's SUV. Her head hit the steering wheel hard, and even from across the street I saw her numbers blink out and disappear."

"She died?"

I nodded. "Yes, she did. I dialed 911 on my phone when a second car pulled up to the accident and another girl got out. She saw it happen, and ran to the driver's side, opened the door and started to pull her out. I put down my phone and ran over to help. Together we carried her friend across the street and laid her down on the grass.

"The friend was crying and crying, and I was... kind of speechless. I knew it was too late for anyone to do anything at that point. The other girl's numbers were gone. Completely faded out. It was over. Of course, her friend couldn't see what I'd seen, so she didn't know it yet.

"She got down on her knees and started praying. And I mean, like, *really* praying! She wasn't panicked or freaked out or anything. It was... it was as if a switch had been flipped. Because one moment she was upset, borderline hysterical, and then she started praying this quiet, calm prayer, politely asking for God to bring her friend back."

At this point I stop my story and lean over, retrieving a tissue from the dispenser in front of me. I blow my nose and apologize. I never know when retelling it is going to bring back tears, but it looks like tonight is one of those nights. I'm glad, actually. I think it's important for Ms. Yates to see this side of me, the vulnerable, emotional side rather than thinking I'm some kind of death cheerleader or something.

Wading the tissue up in my hand, I take a deep breath and continue. "So after about two minutes of non-stop prayer, I saw a flicker reappear over the girl's head. The numbers were back, but they were different. I'd never seen anything like it before. Her new numbers were almost a neon blue, and they were glowing!"

"Glowing?"

"Yeah!" I nod, excited. "Glowing so bright I had to actually cover my eyes at first. A second later I heard a gasp, and when I looked back her eyes were open. She was alive! Breathing and crying and... *alive*! It was insane! She was *dead*, but because of her friend's prayer, she came back to life! It was all pretty surprising, to be honest."

I shrug again, nodding my head. "So, to answer your question, out of the countless number of people I've seen who *have* died on time, she was the *only* one whose countdown ever changed. *Ever*. But even then, I have to point out that the original time was still correct. She *did* die. She just... came back. But every other time the numbers are completely, one hundred percent accurate." I shake my head, staring down at the tissue in my hand. "I know... I know how this all sounds, and I wish I could say otherwise, but I can't. And I'm sorry, but I'm not going to lie to you."

"Thank you, Sephanie," Ms. Yates says, nodding. "I appreciate that." She writes in her notepad again and looks up. "Can you tell me how you feel about death in general?"

"Death?"

"Yes, please. Based on your story and the various

instances where you've encountered someone dying, I'd like to hear your thoughts and feelings about death."

I laugh, then cover my mouth. "I'm sorry."

Her eyebrows furrow and she starts to frown. "Did I say something funny?"

My smile widens, even though I try to suppress it. "You want me to tell you how I feel about Death?"

"If you would."

I smile again and shake my head. *Well, I'm in it this far. I might as well dive in headfirst into the deep end.*

"Well, to be perfectly honest," I say, shaking my head, "he's kind of a jerk."

She stops writing and looks over at me, confused. "I'm sorry?" she asks.

"Death," I repeat. "I said he's kind of a jerk."

She continues staring at me, her brain attempting to process what she just heard. When I realize the strain might be too much, I decide I should elaborate.

"He's pompous and conceited and smug. And he usually smells pretty horrible, like... well... like *Death*. He's not pure evil, *per se*, but he's not exactly a nice guy, either. He's just... Death. Oh, and he likes to complain about how he's not well-liked, how he's often misunderstood and how nobody ever wants him around — except for suicidal people. And even *they* usually have a change of heart when he shows up."

She looks at me, unblinking. "So, you believe death... is a person?"

I stop talking, look over at her and inhale deeply. I've seen that look before. It's the distinct look of sudden sadness, of pity. It's the face that whispers, *You poor, pretty girl with the broken mind. If only there were a way to fix you and rid you of all these illusions.*

I've seen that look before, and it kills me every time.

I look down at my feet and sigh. *Here we are again...*

"Look," I say, "I know what I sound like, okay? But Death is real, and I didn't even know it was a *he* until I started noticing him hanging around so much. He tries to change it up a lot, changes the way he looks each time, but I can always tell it's him. It's kind of hard to miss someone in a crowd when they're wearing all black, all the time, you know? You'd think he'd want a little more variety in his wardrobe..." I smile, even though I know she's not ready to laugh with me.

"To be honest, I think I freaked him out when he realized I could see him. I guess it's been a long time since someone could do that or something. So when he saw what I could do, he suddenly became super chatty, talking to me non-stop, as if he was the loneliest person in the world." I pause, tilting my head to the side as I consider what I've just said. "I guess it's possible he is, now that I think about it."

"And do you and... Death... talk often?"

I shake my head. "Not really. I still see him about twice a week, but we don't usually talk anymore. I don't really know what to say and I *really* don't want to hear anything he says. Sure, he'll insist that he's just the messenger, the chauffeur who's bringing people from this life to the next, but personally? I think he's lying. I think there's a part of him that secretly *enjoys* what he does. Thrilled with it, in fact. And I guess I still want to blame him for what happened to my family."

A soft chime from her timer breaks the silence, and both of us look over toward it in curiosity. Ms. Yates sighs and puts down her notepad for the first time since we first began, laying her pencil on top of it. Sitting back in her chair, she breathes in deeply and looks at me, eyes searching for something. When she realizes she's staring at me, she tries to force a comforting smile on her face, but it only lasts a few seconds before falling back into a frown.

"I am sorry," I offer, looking her in the eye. "I know this is a lot to take in at one time, and it can be overwhelming to some people. Even people who are professionally trained to handle things like this."

She looks like she's about to protest, but then stops herself, nodding slowly. I can't really get a read on her. *Is she about to cry? To offer advice? What's she thinking inside?*

"So," I say, crossing my legs and folding my hands across my knee. "Would you care to tell me what you think? About..." I wave my hand in the air and shrug. "all this?"

She takes in a breath and nods, but doesn't say anything.

"You can be frank, of course," I say. "I genuinely want to know what you think about everything I've just told you. I'm a big girl. I can take it."

She smiles at me, and it lights up my heart just seeing it. I really do like her. As awkward and painful as the last hour has been, I don't regret it. Not yet, at least.

"Well," she begins, picking up her notepad and opening it once more. "You've certainly endured some extreme trauma in your life. That's without question. And when a child at that age is subjected to that kind of trauma, it can affect her in a variety of different ways." She turns the page to read what she's written, then goes back to the first one.

"Because you asked for frankness, I'm going to be frank with you."

"I appreciate that."

She nods. "Sephanie, based on what you've shared with me, I believe you most likely suffered some significant brain trauma as a result of your accident with your family. Now, brain trauma is a very tricky thing to diagnose, mind you, but some of the things you described could be attributed to it."

"Such as?"

"Well," she swallows, clearly not wanting to say what I'm asking her to say. "Sometimes brain trauma can result in not only false memories immediately preceding an event, but also in seeing hallucinations for extended periods of time afterwards."

"Ten years seems like an awfully long time for me to hallucinate…"

"It is," she says, nodding. "And while it is uncommon, it doesn't mean it's without precedence."

I look at her and smile. "Ms. Yates, I like you. I really do. And I'm so, so glad I came to see you today. Thank you so much, not only for sharing your precious time with me, but also for your frank honesty. I've found that's rare these days."

"Well," she says, blushing, "I'm glad you feel that way. Many people don't really want to know what other people think, so to hear you say that means a lot to me. I appreciate that."

I reach into my backpack and pull out five twenty-dollar bills, holding it out to her. "A hundred dollars. Is that correct?"

She glances down at the bills and smiles. "Um… yes. But

don't you want to fill out the insurance forms? Most carriers will cover up to five sessions..."

"That's... actually not necessary," I say, handing her the money.

"Oh? So, you wouldn't like to schedule another appointment next week?"

"No, I'm afraid not. I just needed the one for today," I say, shrugging my shoulders and smiling at her.

Her eyes look at me sadly, and I can see the confusion percolating inside them. "I'm... was it something I said? Or did? I mean, I completely respect your opinion and I'm not trying to pressure you into anything, I'm just a bit... confused as to..."

I raise my hand and wave off her objections. "No, no, no! It's nothing like that! You've been *fantastic*. Absolutely amazing! You were everything I hoped you would be, actually."

"Then..."

"Then why am I not scheduling another appointment?" She nods.

"Because I didn't actually come here for counseling."

I let the words hang in the air for a few seconds, embracing the silence. Then I slowly reach into my backpack and retrieve the large manila envelope from inside. I look up and hold it out to her.

She's obviously fluctuating between curiosity and concern as she accepts it. Pulling it closer, she sits back in her chair and slowly unclasps the end. Reaching inside, she pulls out the large photograph I had developed earlier this morning.

The look of concern on her face melts away when she recognizes herself with her granddaughter, playing in the park last week. They're both running down a sidewalk, each holding onto a bright red balloon that perfectly balances the photo's azure sky and lush, green grass. It's actually one of the best photos I had ever taken in my life.

And also one of the most heart-breaking.

After a few seconds her look of joy begins to fade, slipping back into one of concern. Her eyebrows knit tighter as she stares down at the little girl in the photo, her eyes becoming anguished, almost tearful.

"Is it..." she whispers, voice cracking through the room's silence, "is it her...? Or me?"

I look over at her and I can't control it anymore. Tears start to well up in my eyes, and I can't hold them back anymore. I've been processing this image in my mind for the past week. Even though I've envisioned this very conversation repeatedly, prepared for it, the words are harder to say than I expected.

"It's you." I say, nodding my head slowly. "I'm so sorry."

Ms. Yates nods her head, taking in my words. She stares back at the photo, swallowing a few times before her eyes also begin to water.

"How long?" she asks, looking up from the photo.

I don't have to look over her head to read them. I've been aware of her numbers — *avoiding* her numbers — from the moment she opened the door. Even now they're fading from blue into a pale, misty white.

"Twenty weeks."

Her shoulders visibly sink at my words, and I watch as this woman's dreams for her future start to collide with a sudden, unexpected end of the road. She places the photo on the envelope and lays them both over her notepad. She doesn't move, but sits there in her chair, breathing deeply, trying to remain composed.

I shift from the couch to the chair beside her, extending my hand to grasp hers. Her touch is gentle and warm and everything I ever remembered about my mother's. We sit in silent communion for a few seconds, united by a shared sorrow as she processes the pain of what's to come. Finally, we reach for a few tissues to dab our eyes and noses.

"May I ask a final question?" I say. "Before I leave?"

She responds with a silent nod, tightening her grip on my hand.

"May I please pray for you?"

Tears well up in her eyes once more, and she nods fervently. We bow our heads, hands intertwined, and I start to speak.

I don't know exactly how prayer works. I don't know why the Lord chooses one person to live while another one dies. Why one family is spared while another is torn apart. I don't know why I was given this ability, this inexplicable gift.

But what I do know is this: I'm going to pray for this woman. I'm going to stay here and pray beside her as earnestly as I know how, and I really hope He hears me tonight.

Author's Note

This is another oddity in the Jack Kardiac canon, much like *The Last Laugh* was in *Squint* and the standalone single, *Limited Time Only*. I don't exactly remember how this story idea came about, but it's possible it was inspired by my own Grandmother, who was an impressive 102 years old when I wrote this.

102. I can't even imagine living to be that old, but I'm incredibly grateful that I have her genes and blood flowing through me. On the other hand, I'm not sure if I honestly *want* to live until I'm that old. A lot of things can go sideways in that time.

At any rate, I really do love how this story came together. I've never heard of anyone named **Sephanie** in my life, but when I was talking to myself about the story specifics and wondered what I should call her, the name Sephanie popped up and I went with it. I didn't know what her backstory was, but the more I focused on the idea of what she could do, the clearer it became. Her love of photography just made sense! It was great.

I really, really enjoy creating characters with abilities that are unique to their situations, and I hope we'll get to see Sephanie again in the future.

Peaches

JACK KARDIAC

peaches

I'M NOT ashamed to admit it: crafting scenes with intense conflict has got to be one of the trickier tasks I've had to tackle over my writing career. Granted, I've only been a writer for three weeks, but still, it's not easy. Switching gears from managing Dee-N-Cee's Mini Mart full-time to filling my time "noodlin' with novelin'," as Dee likes to say... well, it's not for the faint of heart.

No, it's not like you'll be seeing ol' Cecil Wheeler on Oprah for her book club anytime soon. But I'll be honest with you — I wouldn't say no if she asked. She's one fine-lookin' woman, right there.

Or am I thinkin' of that Ellen chick? Is she still around?

Whatever. I'm kinda fuzzy when it comes to those talk show hosts, get 'em confused all the time. Dee watches 'em religiously. She's probably snip a fit if she knew I was as clueless as I'm tellin' you now. But between you an' me? She don't gotta know.

Now where was I?

Oh yeah, *conflict*.

Conflict is the lifeblood of every good story, at least that's what I read in some writing how-to book last week. Or a blog. In a video on the YouTube, maybe? Whatever. All I know is, if a tale's not ripe with conflict, a writer doesn't have a story to stand on. Don't matter how vibrant or vivid a character may be, how quickly you establish the setting, their voice, dialogue, internal monologue, what have you. If there's no conflict in a story, the fact of the matter is you don't *got* no story.

Instead, you got people sitting around gabbing to each other pretty as you please, all tender and delicate with one another like they're stuck in a Brady Bunch episode or something. Hold on. Come to think of it... there was actually an awful lot of conflict in that show, usually involving that one chick.

Maddie? Marsha?

Yeah. It was always about Marsha.

Point being, conflict's just not easy for me to write. I naturally get along with everyone in town, so when I first started coming to The Perky Peach every day to write, I found I got stuck about a week into it when I had to jot down my first fight scene.

And it wasn't just *any* fight scene, mind you. No sir, this was a fight scene where two guys go at one another like wolves, only one's obviously the alpha and the other's some zesty pup about to get his tush tanned a ripe red.

There I was, needing to write a lop-sided action scene, chock full of character conflict, but I was choking on on it. Hard.

That is, until the day Brady Brasket nearly died.

(Ya'll should probably take a seat before I begin.)

Like I mentioned earlier, I've been whittling away at it every evening here at The Perky Peach going on about three weeks now. Dee was thrilled to not have to cook at nights, and frankly I think the both of us were happy to spend some time apart at the end of each day. I've come to believe it's a very real possibility that the two of us severely underestimated the amount of "quality time" we'd be spending with each other when I retired. And no, I'm not using the phrase "quality time" as a euphemism like we used to do when we first got married, mind you.

Nope, at our age a marriage can only take so much quality time around each other, lemme just tell you that right now. Still crazy in love, but if you don't got some space to breathe we'd just be plumb crazy.

Anyhow, some writers hide in Starbucks and some attend fancy cabin writer retreats in Colorado or Maine or wherever. For me I always knew it was going to be The Perky Peach, and it's not just because I love peaches (although I'm not ashamed to admit that I do).

Specialty is peaches, if you didn't deduce that yet. Every kind of menu item you can imagine is up for the offering. Breakfast, Brunch, Lunch, Dinner, Appetizers, Afternoon snacks, Weddings and Bar Mitzvah's, Proms and Parades and Funerals. If there's an occasion where people are gonna gather, they're gonna want to eat something sweet or succulent or savory, mark my words. The Perky Peach is always ready and willing to cater to your every peach-related fantasy, desire and whim.

Their color palette's not a bad thing, either. Granted,

you'd think peach married with red checkers might seem like a somewhat aggressive choice for a table cloth, and you'd be right. Thankfully they toned down the walls a few years ago. A guy could only stand to be stared at by gigantic, googly-eyed, grinning cartoon peaches for so long before he got to feeling downright creeped out. I know *I* was.

So I was first to voice my appreciation when they decided to strip off the wallpaper and go with a plain ol' textured peach — complete with a thin layer of velvety fuzz. I daresay it improved the décor a hundred thousand percent.

But no, it ain't the color or the food that keeps me coming back. Nor is it the owners and operators, Bud and Clara Crestler, although they are two of the kindest, hardest-working souls I've ever had the pleasure of meeting.

Nope. I come back for the aroma.

You heard that right. I write here because there's just something about the crisp, tangy scent of a succulent, sun-kissed peach that seems to ignite something good inside me. Something special. It's like a swift punch to the gut and a simultaneous, sneaky kiss on the cheek, an' I love it.

Some people do drugs to get high in life.

Others need a cup of coffee to start up.

Me? Well, all's I need is the smell of a perky peach.

But that's beside the point.

The day before yesterday I was sitting in the corner of the diner, stumped on Chapter 2 where my two hombres are gearing up to show down. I close my laptop to take a break, sipping on my peach milkshake and eyeing the last lone bite of cobbler on my plate. You'd think I'd be sick of it by now, ordering the same blessed thing day in and day out, but you'd be wrong.

I'm sitting there, looking around the diner for inspiration. Even though it's almost twilight and smack dab in the middle of what would normally be a dinner rush, the diner's almost empty on account of the high school football game going on across town.

I watch Clara walk back to the kitchen as the young woman she was talking to pays her bill and exits shortly thereafter. There's a young couple who're obviously on their first date, sitting to my left in a back corner booth. Might even been a blind date, they were so quiet. Or maybe they were breaking up, I honestly don't know.

Then down at the clear other end of the diner's counter, sitting on a stool, is this stranger. That is, I'd seen him around here every couple of weeks, so I wondered if he was a trucker or something. All I know is, he was strange, kind of creepy.

Wearing all black. Black jeans, black T-shirt and a black cap — the works. Except for a pair of bright white tennis shoes, which I thought was an odd choice of attire. You'd think he was an advertising salesman for a funeral parlor or something.

I'm not really paying him much attention, except that I notice he's eyeing the young girl leaving. Soon as she steps out, he puts a bill down on the counter and steps up to leave.

I watch him closely, preparing to pack up and follow him if he heads after her, but thank heaven for all of us he doesn't. Instead he exits the diner, turns and walks the opposite direction. Didn't know who he was or what his business was around here, but I was definitely going to be keeping my eye on him next time I saw him.

As I watch him walk away, my eye catches sight of one of the most colossal men I've ever seen in my life. He stands outside the entrance, his attention firmly fixed on the sign overhead. Sporting a red and black checkered shirt, a thick black beard and muscles that appear as if they've been inflated with pure testosterone, the guy's a shrunken version of Paul Bunyan. All that's missing is an ax slung over his shoulder. As if to further complete the image, a short, squat gentleman wearing an indigo blue jacket soon appears on the other side of him, engaging him in conversation.

I'm captivated by their interaction. The blue jacket guy talks animatedly, using his arms to gesture up at the sign and back, while Mr. Universe clenches his fists open and closed the entire time. He takes a moment from eyeballing the sign to scan the inside of the restaurant. I deliberately avert my eyes just as his are about to fall across me, then casually look back up a few seconds later to see what's happening.

He just stands there, rooted to the ground, frozen in place. Finally Blue steps forward and opens the front door, coaxing him to go in. They both look equally grim at the idea, but finally Bunyan ducks through the doorway and stands just inside the entrance. He looks like he's about to vomit, while I can't look away.

Clara suddenly materializes from around the corner and greets them with a sunshine smile. "Welcome to The Perky Peach, gentlemen! Booth or table this evening?"

The big guy's eyes flash over to her and dart away. He tries to force a smile. Blue returns Clara's smile with his own.

"Howdy, ma'am!" he says. "Ah... we'll take a booth by the window, if you don't mind."

"Well, considering all of our booths are by windows, that won't be a problem." She winks at him as she retrieves two menus from the counter. "Follow me."

I quickly refocus my attention to my laptop screen as they walk in my direction, careful to appear as disinterested as possible. As a people person I can't help but constantly observe those around me. You know, make notes for future characters and all. But I'm not one to stare, either.

She seats them in the booth next to mine, the giant facing my direction with the little guy's back to me. They pick up the menus and start to browse, Bunyan's sculpted scowl growing more severe with every passing second.

"My name is Clara and I'll be your waitress today," Clara rattles off without batting an eye. "If you love peaches, you're gonna love eating here at The Perky Peach because when it comes to perfect peaches, we've got you covered.

"Everything you could ever want — peach pancakes, peach salsa, peach milkshakes, peach cheesecake and, of course, no dinner at The Perky Peach would be complete without our award-winning Peach Perfection Cobbler." She grins at them. "*A la mode*, of course."

I catch the entire scene, and I swear each and every time she utters the word "peach," the big guy's eye twitches. He flinches, as if the word itself is somehow getting under his skin. Looking back to my laptop, I quickly find and open the Character folder in my writing program. I don't want to miss a thing with this guy. He's definitely one to watch.

"Wow, that's... quite the menu," Blue responds, giving an appreciative nod. He shifts his gaze to the anything-but-jolly giant, realizing he needs to keep the conversation moving. "You got any specials today?"

"Sure do! Today's special is our award-winning peach-glazed pulled pork sandwich. Comes with French fries and a side of coleslaw."

"Wait, your cobbler *and* your pulled pork are *both* award-winning?" Blue says, looking up at her and raising a skeptical eyebrow. "*Really?*"

"If I'm lyin' I'm dyin'." She bounces her eyebrows. "Three years in a row at Indiana County Fair. An' I reckon come next week it's gonna be four."

"That good, huh?"

"Honey, if they don't make you smack your lips and wanna slap your Momma, I'll mark 'em half off."

The guy laughs at that and hands her the menu. "You sold me, Clara. I'm officially sold. Can't wait."

"You won't regret it," she says as she jots in her notepad. Finally she looks over at the Mountain. "And for you, Sugar?"

At this point Bunyan's already put the menu down on the table. The guy looks visibly ill. His face is growing redder, and even from where I sit I can tell his breathing is pretty labored.

Something is really, *really* wrong with this guy.

"Just a burger and fries, please," he says, lifting one of his gorilla hands to pinch the bridge of his nose.

"Medium-well alright?"

"Sure."

"Want cheese with that?"

His lips draw tighter. "Please."

"Maybe a couple of aspirin? On the house."

He doesn't respond, but simply folds his arms across his chest and nods his head, eyes shut tight.

No question. Something is definitely not right with him.

"Yes," his buddy interjects. "Aspirin would be fantastic. Thank you so much."

She looks over at Blue, then back to Bunyan and shrugs.

"Be out with some waters in a few minutes. Less you want something else—"

"Water's perfect. Thanks."

Clara gives the big guy one last look before she shrugs, walks up the aisle and disappears into the kitchen just as Brady Brasket walks in through the front door.

Well, stumbles is a better description, I guess.

Staggers? Shambles. Sure, shambles is a pretty good alternative.

So Brady shambles in, and he's drunk.

Not so drunk he can't eyeball the stools across the aisle from us, mind you, but still pretty sauced. Seems like he gets pretty liquored up at least once or twice a week. Brady's not a bad kid, if you ask me. Good heart, to be honest. The guy just has a serious problem staying sober and holding down a job.

He offers up a shamed glance when he sees me, nodding his head a little too much. "Mr. Wheeler," he mumbles as he walks past.

"Evening, Brady." I return the nod.

He reaches across the counter, pulls himself up and sits down on the stool. Crossing his arms in front of him, he drops his head down on them and lets out an exaggerated moan. I'm unsure if he passes out cold or if he's just resting his eyes when Clara returns to the table with their waters.

She sets the glasses and a set of straws down, then walks over to where Brady's plunked down on the counter.

"Brady, how you doing tonight, Honey?" she asks, resting a hand on his shoulder. "You doing alright?"

He lifts his head slowly, manages a nod. "M'okay, Ms. Clara. I promise..."

"You're not gonna puke all over my clean counter, now, are you?"

His head flops from side to side, a weak smile on his face. "No, ma'am."

"Can I get you a cup of coffee, maybe? You look like you could use one."

He nods his head up and down again, shaking it so much it looks like it's going to pop off his neck and roll across the floor like a freshly-picked pomegranate.

"Okay, I'll be right back, then. Why don't you rest your head a bit, okay?" Clara places a hand on the back of his neck and gently guides his head down to his arms again. He quickly falls silent, breathing deeply.

"You gonna be okay, Jerry?"

It's Mr. Blue, the short guy in the other booth. If they even notice Brady, they don't appear to show it.

The lumberjack giant guy — Jerry, I guess — breathes deeply and nods his head. "Nate, this was a mistake," he whispers. "We shouldn't have come here."

"Hey, it's gonna be okay. Just a few more minutes and we're done and back on the road, alright? Easy peasy."

"You *know* this was a bad idea, Nate, don't you?"

"I know..."

"Of all the places to get stuck, I can't believe we had to end up..." Jerry's words trail off as he glances around the room, his eyes wild and feral. "*Here.*"

I don't know if this guy is hopped up on crack or meth or if it's just plain ol', pure adrenaline coursing through his veins, but he is clearly agitated. White-knuckled and keyed up about something.

"If we had any other options, we'd have taken 'em," Nate

says. "But this was the only place with a decent menu option. Every other place was a coffee shop or a bakery. You saw—"

"It'd have been better to drink or eat that crap than..." He pauses to catch his breath again. "This."

I can't tell if the tone of his voice is disgust or disapproval (or some other dis-word... displeasure? No, that's not it...), but he is not happy. My thesaurus will help me figure it out later. They say every writer needs a good thesaurus. And a good editor.

I don't know how Bud does it in his kitchen, but the guy whips up their dinners incredibly fast. It's like he can read people's minds and knows what they're going to order as soon as they step through the door.

I'm easy, though. I get the same stuff every night.

Peachy Pecan Chicken Salad Sandwich.

(With fries, of course. Gravy on the side.)

Small bowl of peaches in light syrup.

Peach milkshake.

And to top it all off, The Perky Peach Deluxe Peach Cobbler. Carefully crafted with thinly sliced, carefully proportioned peaches, sautéed in cinnamon, sugar and butter with just a pinch of cayenne pepper. Gives each bite just enough kick to wake up my taste buds, night after night.

I apologize. You'd think I'm some kind of Perky Peach salesman, the way I'm rambling on and on about it.

Where was I?

Oh yeah, so Clara arrives with their food and puts it on the table in front of them while I pretend I'm busy writing.

"Here ya go, guys."

"Thank you so much," Nate gushes, eyeing his plate.

"And here's that aspirin I promised," she says, placing a handful of pills on the table by Jerry. He nods silently.

"Now, before I disappear let me just share with you some of our dessert selections that are sure to tempt your tastebuds." Clara plucks a laminated brochure from behind her apron, complete with full color, high-quality photos of their many offerings.

Jerry looks away from her and stares out the window. It looks to me like he's just about ready to shatter it.

"We've got Slow Cooker Amaretto-Poached Peaches, a Peach Parfait with Salted Graham Cracker Crumble, a Ginger-Vanilla Fro Yo with Peach Compote, and finally we have an Iron Skillet Peach Crisp that's simply to die for. Plus, there's—"

Nate holds up a hand. "I'm sorry, but you have to stop."

She looks down at him, her smile faltering for just a second before it reasserts itself. "I'm sorry?"

"You need to stop talking about..." He looks over at Jerry. "*Peaches,*" he whispers.

Now, Clara gets the most crazy look on her face, like he'd just slapped her with a sticky salmon. She puts a hand on her hip, shifts her weight to her other leg and frowns. "Excuse me?" she asks. The tone of annoyance in her voice is pretty evident.

"You need to stop talking about... that fruit," Nate repeats. He shrugs. "Please," he adds.

She continues to stare at him, her face unchanging, like she's trying to determine whether the two of them are on drugs or something.

"Are you two on drugs or something?" she asks quietly.

Nate shakes his head. "No, it's just..." he looks over at Jerry, who's now grown pale as he stares at his plate, not moving. His breathing is slow and rhythmic, shoulders practically doubling in size each time he inhales. It's mesmerizing. Terrifying.

"Look, I'm not going to go into detail about it all, but my friend here had what you'd call a... traumatic experience with... *that fruit...* when he was younger."

"He had a what now?"

"It's... really not worth getting into. He just... well... how do I say this?" He looks back at Jerry and then back at Clara. "He hates peaches."

Jerry winces at the word.

"And everything that has to do with them," Nate continues. "Ever."

Clara's scowl grows deeper, and then she smiles. "Are ya'll messin' with me? You are, aren't you?! Ya'll are just messing with me! Am I on hidden camera or something?" She looks out through the windows trying to spot someone recording them from outside.

"I'm sorry, but I'm being absolutely serious right now. I am one hundred percent *not* messing with you, ma'am."

Her eyes fall back on him again, and I swear she's close to hauling off and punching him in the sternum right then and there. Instead she sighs — a deeply disappointed, motherly sigh, you know the one — and looks over at me, staring like a goofus at the three of them.

"Cecil, Bud's almost got your cobbler all fixed up," she says. "Ready for your check?"

I blush, suddenly feeling foolish for having been caught

so blatantly eavesdropping. "Yes, please," I stammer, nodding my head and looking back at my screen again. I start loudly tapping a bunch of gibberish on the keys.

Clara turns back to them. "I'll get your check too," she says brusquely, then turns and walks away.

I glance over my glasses to see Jerry take a deep breath and pick up his cheeseburger. It looks more like a slider snack, dwarfed inside his mammoth mitts. He's just about to take a bite when he stops. His thick neck cranes his huge head to the side, and he looks directly over at Brady Brasket, who's suddenly sober and staring directly at him.

(Okay, when I say "sober" I mean he was more serious and conscious of his surroundings. He was still wasted out of his gourd, no question.)

Brady has apparently swiveled around on his stool and is sitting there, hunched over and scowling at them with wild, angry eyes like they'd just killed his favorite country cat.

Jerry slowly lowers the burger back to the plate and stares back at him, frowning. Somewhere inside my head a warning siren starts to wail in the distance.

"What'd you fellas just say?" Brady slurs, shaking his head.

Nate looks up from his sandwich. He glances back at Jerry and then over to Brady. "Excuse me?" he asks.

"Said," Brady mutters, precariously leaning forward a few inches. "What the *hell* did you just say?"

Nate looks around their booth and then back to Brady. "We... weren't talking."

Brady raises his arms up and waves them in front of him dramatically. "Naw, naw, naw... I'm not talkin' not just *now*!" he whines. "I mean... a few minutes ago! What was it you fellas said about..." He looks over at Jerry and frowns. "*Peaches*," he spits out, grossly emphasizing the P.

Jerry's shirt seems to shrink a few sizes as his muscles tense beneath it, but I don't think Nate even notices. His eyes are locked on Brady, wondering just like I am what they're about to get into.

"It was nothing," Nate says, shaking his head. "Don't worry about it."

"Weren't *nothin'*!" Brady snaps, sneering at him. "You said it, an' I wanna hear you say it *again*."

"We should leave," Jerry whispers harshly under his breath to Nate.

Nate holds up a hand and shakes his head. He has no intention of leaving. He's probably thinking he can handle this situation himself before things get out of control. I'm not so sure.

"Look, we simply said we didn't really care for peaches."

Brady shakes his head from side to side. "Nuh-uh," he said. "No you din't. You know 'xactly what you said, an' I wanna hear you say it again."

"Let's go." Despite the swollen size of his biceps, Jerry somehow reaches behind him and retrieves his wallet from a back pocket. He starts counting out bills.

"How about you just turn around and pretend none of this happened. Okay, friend?" Nate asks.

"How about *you* shut up an' answer my *question?!?*"

Nate sighs. He turns his head and looks directly at Brady.

"Fine. We said we hate peaches. Happy now?"

Brady nods his head up and down. "That's *right*! That's what I *thought* you said..." He looks away and shakes his head in disgust. Beyond him I see Clara has processed our orders and is loading a tray with my dessert on it. She starts to walk up the aisle, and I wonder if she'll be able to talk Brady down before he goes off and gets himself hurt.

If I were a betting man, my money would be on *not*.

"My Daddy was a peach farmer!" Brady yells, pointing a bony finger at Jerry. "So if ya'll got a problem with *peaches*?" He reaches over and rolls up one of the sleeves on his shirt. "Then ya'll got a problem with *me!*"

"I'm leaving," Jerry announces to Nate, throwing down the money and shifting out toward the end of the booth.

Now, Clara sees what's happening as she's walking up, and I honestly think she means to try to cool things down by stepping between them. Unfortunately, she walks into the gap right as Brady continues his rage-fueled rant, oblivious of her arrival. His left arm swings up wildly, slapping the tray smack dab in the center... and out of her hands.

I watch it all happen, and it's just like in those Hollywood movies, with all the action unfolding as if it were in slow motion.

The two receipts fly off the tray and slowly flutter to the ground, one disappearing beneath a vacant stool. The tray jolts upright and falls away just as the platter tips, flips and abruptly settles on Jerry's head. What remains of my Perky Peach Deluxe Peach Cobbler starts crumbling down his face and shirt like a hot, sloppy peach-fueled avalanche.

The *a la mode* lands on the floor with a soft *splat*, followed by the platter shattering to pieces at Jerry's feet.

Clara swears under her breath and pushes a shocked and visibly concerned Brady back down on his stool. He stares up at the giant now standing above him, blinking furiously as if he's just now grasping the gravity of his actions.

Now, I'm not sure if it's the temperature of the cobbler or the touch of cayenne or just the condensed peach essence itself, but that man's face quickly flushes into a shade of red I've never before seen in my life.

Nate grabs his plate and glass of water, casually stands up in the booth and deftly steps over the back, lowering himself across from me. We lock eyes and he shakes his head, obviously resigned to what's about to happen. He takes a large bite out of his sandwich and chews slowly, savoring the flavor.

Clara backs away from the aisle, making a thousand apologies. She's about to stoop down and begin cleaning up the mess when I calmly reach over and clasp her hand, lowering her down into the relative safety of the booth beside me where we sit and watch.

We watch Nate eat his dinner.

We watch Brady try to slink away.

And we watch Jerry as he reaches out one of those humongous hands and vents his pent up frustration.

I'll be honest with you. I've lived a very long time, and I've seen things in my lifetime that would make you think twice about someone's pain threshold. But in all my years, I've never, *ever* heard someone shriek as high or as loud as Brady Brasket did that night.

Now, I'm well aware some of you reading this are undoubtedly disappointed that I'm not going into graphic detail about what, exactly, Jerry did to that boy. I'm sorry to disappoint, but I shall not be describing it here.

Why not?

Why, because I want you to buy my book, of course.

But I will tell you this much: even though Jerry twisted Brady up like some kind of puking pretzel, he had enough mercy and sense to leave the guy alive. No, Brady won't be typing up any Great American Novels anytime soon, 'least not with those fingers and certainly not with a standard keyboard, but he won't be sipping soup through a straw for the next month, neither.

I walked into The Perky Peach that evening grappling with anxiety about how I was going to write the most intense, action-packed conflict scene of my life. Turns out all I had to do was sit back and wait for Brady Brasket to show up and start acting like a hot-headed idiot.

Life can be funny like that.

Author's Note

This story idea came about while I was visiting my parents in **Tulsa, Oklahoma** one summer. They took my family out for the afternoon to a restaurant diner called **The Peach House**, located in **Broken Arrow**. It was everything **The Perky Peach** is and so much more. Peaches and peach-themed items galore! Now, I'm a fan of peaches to begin with. Love the flavor, the texture, the aroma — it's all good. But as I sat there enjoying my refreshingly tart peach ice cream cone, I couldn't help but wonder... who *wouldn't* love this experience? I mean, how could someone ever hate ***peaches***, right?

A few minutes later my mind supplied the answer, and the basic plot for *Peaches* was born.

Personally, I thoroughly enjoyed the idea of *not* showing the fight scene in the end. I usually gravitate to violent action scenes (as you've seen thus far), so the idea of *not* writing it this time was so original and interesting, I kind of just *had* to go with it.

Don't worry, though... Brady Brasket's story isn't over just yet...

Note: Since writing this story, **The Peach House** has closed its doors. However, there's a similarly-themed destination, **The Peach Barn**, in **Porter, Oklahoma**. So if you're ever in Northeast Oklahoma, be sure to take a trip down to Porter and pay **The Peach Barn** a visit. You'll be glad you did! (Unless your name is Jerry, I suppose...)

Some featured menu items at **The Peach Barn**: *Porter Peach Jam, Porter Peach Salsa, Porter Peach Butter, and Porter Peach BBQ Sauce.*

Pink Slip

JACK KARDIAC

pink slip

"RUSSIA'S A SLEEPING BEAR."

John Jacobs looked up from his computer monitor at Stafford and frowned. "What? What's that supposed to mean?"

"Russia!" Stafford repeated, shaking his head in disbelief. He entered John's office and sat his tall, lanky frame in the chair across from him. "You didn't hear about their little skirmish with Ukraine last night?"

"Naw, I was watching the game..."

"Pfft. And you call yourself an agent..." Stafford shook his head in mock disgust. Before John had a chance to interject, he continued his rant. "Anyway, people think Russia's all dead and gone after we won the Cold War, but Pete's convinced they're gearing up to make a comeback someday. Swears Russia's a sleeping bear."

"Sleeping bear, my butt." John frowned, returning his gaze to the computer screen.

"Your *butt* is a sleeping bear! Hairy thing like that! When was the last time you wiped it?"

"I dunno. When was the last time you puckered up?" Jacobs retorted, smirking.

Stafford smiled and nodded his head. "Touché, John. Touché..." He looked out the door and paused to admire the assets of a female coworker as she bent down to retrieve a dropped paperclip. "So," he mused absently, "You still throwing your BBQ party this weekend?"

"Does a bald eagle poop stars and stripes?"

"Uh, *no*, it definitely does not. But I'm gonna take that as a Yes."

"Yes. I'm still having the party. You comin'?"

"Hell, yeah! Wouldn't miss one of your parties for the free world. You gettin' that expensive, catered brisket again?"

"Wouldn't be a John Jacobs BBQ if I didn't."

"Awesome. Then I'm in. See you there." Stafford held out his fist, outstretched.

John hesitated, but reluctantly leaned across the desk and bumped it lightly.

"Better look out," Stafford crooned quietly as he stood up, "Bossman Pete's on the prowl..." He stood up just as a short, balding man approached the office. "Good morning, sir," he said, nodding.

"Stafford," the man acknowledged. "Let them know I'll be a few minutes late to the Monday meeting, would you?"

"Sure thing, boss." Stafford nodded and rushed through the door.

Pete walked up to John's cubicle and knocked on one of the panels. "Good morning, John. Do you have a few minutes?"

John looked at Pete over his monitor and shrugged. "I

suppose so. But what about the Monday meeting? Don't you want to wait until—"

"No, this is more important, I think." He stared back at John, lips pulled tight.

Was it a strained expression? Stressed or nervous? John couldn't really say, but it looked weird. Disconcerting.

"Okay," John said. "Gimme a sec to log off and I'll be right there." He moved the mouse around the desktop and clicked to log off.

Pete didn't respond, remaining perfectly motionless. He simply stood there, staring at him, carefully watching John's every move.

John found it creepy. Well, creepier than usual, but it wasn't as if the two of them were ever anything more than cordial with each other. As far as supervisors go, John often told himself that he could have ended up with someone even *more* uptight than Pete, but he honestly had a hard time envisioning how, exactly.

John rose and started to exit the cubicle, he suddenly stopped. "Whoops," he said, turning around, "Almost forgot something." He reached back into his desk and retrieved a small, wrapped package and a bottle of water from a side drawer.

He watched as the rest of the agents in the office shuffled down to the meeting room. Everyone but he and Pete and some new guy in a black suit. The stranger's eyes locked onto John and the man winked, giving him an enthusiastic thumbs up before sauntering away.

What was that about?

John frowned and watched him disappear down the hall, then glanced back up the corridor, his eyes narrowing.

Something was very strange about the situation.

Every other agent in the entire office was headed to the Monday morning meeting.

Every agent... except for him, that is.

This was either going to turn out to be something really good...

...or really, really bad.

John mentally prepared for the worst.

Once in the office, Pete closed the door behind them and drew the blinds. John pretended not to notice, preoccupied with the bright red, squishy stress ball resting on Pete's desk.

"May I?" John asked, pointing to the ball.

"Might as well," Pete said, settling into his chair and sighing.

John squeezed the ball, trying to feign confidence rather than nervousness.

"John..." Pete began, folding his hands together and leaning forward.

"Hey," John interrupted. "I got you this the other week." He held out the wrapped package. "You should open it."

Pete stared down at the gift and back up at John. He looked like he had swallowed a bug, but reached over and took it, setting it down on his desk.

"No, seriously," John insisted. "Go ahead and open it."

"John..."

"Please?" John asked, pleading with his eyes.

Pete looked down at his desk and sighed. "Fine," he said, reaching over and pulling the wrapping off the box. Inside was a bright red, metallic container. The words GOURMET and YUMMI GUMMI emblazoned on every side.

"John," Pete sighed, shaking his head.

"It *is* the correct brand, right? The one you love?"

Pete frowned. "Yes, it is, but—"

"And don't worry, I double-checked the ingredients with the manufacturer themselves to make sure it was absolutely, 100% peanut-free."

"Thank you."

"And cruelty-free, of course."

"Um... okay, then..."

"So go ahead. Open it and have one!" John said enthusiastically. "Please? I've always wanted to try one myself."

Pete stopped and sat upright. "You mean to tell me you've never had one of these?"

"Not yet."

"Ever?"

John shook his head.

His supervisor slowly nodded his head, then removed the cellophane and opened the tin. The candies looked and smelled absolutely heavenly, which was going to make the next few minutes that much more difficult. He offered the box to John.

"Can I have a red one?" John asked.

"Sure. Knock yourself out."

"You too?"

"Excuse me?"

"Let's both eat a red one. We can compare how it tastes."

Pete sighed. "Okay, John. Whatever." He reached down and removed a red one, holding it delicately between his fingers. Setting the box down, he sat back in his chair and stared across the table.

John popped the candy in his mouth and started to chew on it, loudly smacking his lips. "Oh, wow. Now *that* is some good stuff! *WOW!*"

"Uh-huh. Look, John," Pete continued, turning the piece of candy over between his fingers. "I wish you hadn't done all this, because I'm afraid I've got bad news."

"What? Problems at home with the missus and kids?" John flashed him a grin.

"No," Pete said, slightly annoyed. "Not bad news for me, John. I mean I have bad news for *you*."

John stopped chewing and gulped the candy down. "Oh," he said, confusion flashing across his face. "Okayyy..."

"John," Pete said. "I'm firing you."

John froze. He stared across the table at Pete, waiting patiently, his face refusing to betray any internal emotion.

"You probably want to know why," Pete continued. "And let me be frank with you. The list kept getting longer and longer."

John's gaze shifted downward, fixating on the surface of the desk. He swallowed, but the sweet, salty aftertaste of the candy was quickly souring in his mouth with an unpleasant, metallic tang.

Pete raised his hand, ticking off points on his fingers. "The three-hour lunches. Arriving to work late. Leaving work early. Hitting on the director's *secretary*, of all people. Not to mention the blatant ineptitude and gross incompetence when it comes to handling cases."

John didn't look up, the silence hanging heavily in the room like freshly gutted seafood.

Pete shook his head, continuing. "Simply put, the Agency feels they've wasted more than enough of the public's time and expense trying to train someone who, to be quite honest, appears to be untrainable. Outright *resistant* to it, actually. It's almost as if you're hostile to the very idea of it, submitting to authority."

Pete looked down and realized he was still holding the gummi candy between his thumb and forefinger. He popped it into his mouth, licked his fingers and wiped them off on his slacks.

John suddenly perked up, as if remembering something. He looked up at Pete and smiled.

Pete shook his head in disappointment. "Don't you have *anything* to say for yourself?" he asked. "You know I'm right about all of this, don't you? You know I should've fired your incompetent ass years ago, right? I mean, come *on*! Name *one* thing, John! Just *one thing* that you're good at. One thing... that..."

Pete cleared his throat, a look of confusion spreading across his face. "That..." He coughed again, louder and more pronounced.

John extended his bottle of water to him. "Water?"

Pete snatched it out of his hand, wrenching the cap off and started taking desperate swigs between labored breaths.

John glanced briefly to the door before returning to Pete. Standing up, he strode over to it and scanned the empty office. Locking it, he returned to Pete's desk and stood beside it, watching Pete's face start to redden and swell.

"I have to disagree with you, Pete," he said. "There is one thing I'm good at. One thing I'm really, *really* good at." He leaned closer to him and smiled.

"Working for the motherland," he whispered, using his native Russian accent.

Pete's eyes grew wide as panic erupted inside him. He scrambled for his top desk drawer, and John reached across to open it for him. Retrieved the EpiPen inside it, he held it up between his finger and thumb.

"Looking for this?" John said, a sinister smile forming on his lips. He casually slipped it into his inside jacket pocket and shrugged. "Too bad I'm so inept, huh? Probably could've helped you out. You know, if I was smart like you."

As Pete continued to stiffen in his chair, wheezing, John reached a hand deep into his own mouth. There was a soft *snap!* as he removed his two back teeth. Pulling his hand out, he wiped off his saliva, revealing the micro USB port embedded into their underside.

Inserting the flash drive into Pete's PC, he quickly typed a series of commands and hit ENTER.

"Rule Number One about sleeping bears, Pete," he said as he waited for the program to execute. "You *really* shouldn't poke them."

When it was finished he pulled the flash drive out and gingerly inserted it into his mouth, snapping it back into place.

At this point Pete had stopped breathing completely and was starting to turn a dark shade of purple. A second later he limply slid off the chair onto the floor with a quiet thud. John walked over to the front door and unlocked it, swinging it open wide before returning to the desk and gazing down at his former supervisor.

Reaching across the desk, John picked up the phone and dialed the front desk. In the most panicked voice he could muster, he shouted at the receptionist to call 911 immediately, followed with "Pete Johnson is having some kind of seizure!"

John gently placed the phone back on the receiver and shifted his gaze back at Pete, now resembling an angry grape with buggy, insane eyes.

"Now comes the fun part." John grinned, threading the fingers of his hands together. "Pete!" he yelled, kneeling beside him. "Pete, can you hear me!?" He brought his fists down hard on the man's chest.

"Pete!!!" he shrieked louder, pounding him again. "Hey! Hey, somebody help me here! Get help!" John leaned in and applied pressure to Pete's chest, like he was trying to inflate a stubborn air mattress. He wasn't sure if he'd successfully broken a rib or two, but he was pretty confident he had effectively stopped Pete's heart.

As coworkers started to stream into the office, John stepped back, summoning faux tears as he shook his head in mock disbelief. John watched in feigned horror and secret glee as they tried to revive Pete over the next few minutes. Internally, he began to compose the comprehensive report he would need to draft about Pete's sudden death for his Agency superiors over the next few days...

...as well as an abrupt one to send back home:

Captain America is dead.
Wake the Bear.

Author's Note

I have a few friends who work in human resources and various government institutions, and they've all shared numerous accounts about how it's surprisingly difficult for some employees to be fired from a job. Sometimes they have to severely screw up in a very publicly visible way before they're finally dismissed.

It's just bizarre.

In *any* other corporate setting, incompetence would be penalized or eliminated accordingly, but in the government? Sometimes it can result in a commendation or promotion, just so the people left behind don't have to deal with a loser anymore.

I'm by no means an acronym fanatic when it comes to my preferred flavors of fiction entertainment. I typically shy away from novels with blurbs that have any mention of CIA, FBI, KGB, NSA, McD or KFC in the description because I'm just *not* interested in spy stories. I'm not. But when I came up with one of my own, I have to say, I *really* liked it!

I'm sure I'll get a few letters about how unfeasible this kind of a scenario is, but hopefully those readers who were able to suspend their disbelief and change out of their twisted, tighty whitey undies enjoyed the escapism.

(Do communists even read weird short stories? Asking for a friend...)

Jail Bait

JACK KARDIAC

jail bait

IF YOU ASKED ANY LIVING, breathing, hot-blooded man in the lower half of Indiana, they would unanimously agree without hesitation that Belinda Beecham was one fine-looking woman. In the beginning God had given her the kind of curves that reduced every high school boy into a simmering puddle of hormones, and a magnetic charm that further fueled the fire in their hearts. Fun-loving and carefree, she would readily laugh at their numerous and constant attempts at humor. The melody of her laughter alone became a veritable aural amphetamine to them. Time after time, boys would vie for the chance to spend even a minute in her company.

Belinda's Scottish heritage had been generous to her, bestowing her with green eyes that could pierce the hardest hearts, along with thick hair that was such a striking shade of red, a representative from Revlon actually contacted her one day to ask if they could patent it. Belinda didn't know the logistics of whether such a thing was even possible, but was open to the idea. Nothing ever really came of it, but she found it flattering, nonetheless.

Yet despite her stunning looks, winning personality and a heart brimming with enough love and compassion that Snow White herself would shrivel up with jealousy, Belinda Beecham lived a lonely life. What's more, she hadn't gone on a date in over three years, and she knew *exactly* why.

Because Belinda Beecham was a cop.

And as much as a man will insist in public that he doesn't care about a woman's profession or her status, the majority of the guys she'd even remotely considered dating simply couldn't reconcile Belinda the Bombshell with Belinda the badge-flashing ball buster.

Supermodel looks and the skills to cuff and stuff a perp with the best of them. It added up to a lethal combination when it came to dating. For the past few years Belinda had quietly conceded herself to the idea that she just might have to spend a few more years in solitude before she'd find a man who was not only attracted to her body, but could actually appreciate her mind and strength of character as well.

She didn't have to be the hero in a relationship. Honestly, she would readily welcome the idea of letting a strong man lead her in life. But she just didn't want to have to apologize for her love of being in law enforcement, which was as much a part of her as her external allure.

Belinda took another sip of her coffee and looked up at the clock. It was almost seven. Going on fourteen hours, she'd been working since five in the morning and was feeling the drain. Usually her shift didn't start until ten, but Doherty had asked if she'd be willing to cover his desk duty so he could catch his son playing in the high school football game across town. Belinda was happy to help, encouraging him to take some good photos or videos for her to enjoy when he returned.

So when she saw Doherty walking up the steps outside the precinct, a mere forty-five minutes after he left, Belinda was confused. Then dismayed.

What happened? And who's he escorting in here?

A door chime rang somewhere in the back of the office as Doherty walked in, gripping the arm of a skinny, sandy-haired man who'd clearly seen better days. The guy had been brutally beaten. Both his right eye and ear were both swollen, a stitched-up split lip and a bloody, broken nose, one nostril stuffed full of cotton.

"Is that Brady Brasket?" Belinda asked, rising to her feet.

"It is," Doherty answered in disgust, helping the man limp across the lobby to the check-in desk.

"Well, what'd he do? Decide to wrestle a bull over on Yonker's farm?"

"Close to it," he said, lowering Brady onto the chair. "The Perky Peach."

"The Perky—" Belinda stopped and shot Brady a confused look. "That Mom and Pop diner over on 8th street? How'd he manage that?"

"Brady here decided it was a good idea to pick a fight with a stranger passing through. A real Goliath kinda guy."

"By the looks of it."

"You'll never guess what it was about," he said.

"His family?"

"Nope." Doherty shook his head. "Peaches."

"Peaches?!" Belinda's face wrinkled in surprise as she laughed. "Brady, is this true?"

"Hi, Belinda," Brady muttered, avoiding her eyes.

"Hi, Brady. Answer my question. Is what Deputy Doherty's saying true? Did you really get in a fight with someone over peaches?"

Brady looked up at her and shrugged, tears forming in his eyes. "Couldn't help myself," he said, his voice on the verge of cracking. "Guy said he hated peaches."

Belinda opened her palms. "And?"

"And... well... my daddy was a peach farmer, you know..."

"I know that, Brady," Belinda said, growing increasingly annoyed. "*And...?*"

"Well... so when he said he hated peaches, I..." Brady shrugged. "I kinda felt like he was sayin' he hated my daddy."

"Ah." Belinda nodded at Doherty. "And there it is. I knew we'd get to the root issue if we only dug deep enough."

Doherty glared at Brady and shook his head. "Dinkus here made me miss half my kid's game! Had to leave right after he threw his second touchdown." He reached over and lightly backhanded Brady on the shoulder.

"Ow!" Brady reacted as if he'd been hit with a hammer.

"Oh, stow it, Brasket!"

"Gentlemen, please," Belinda sighed, holding up her hands. She was having flashbacks to when she'd have to break up fights between the two of them in the high school courtyard. Brady always had a crush on her, while Doherty played the role of protective big brother figure to them both, looking out for her while simultaneously itching to beat the snot out of him. And there they stood once again, the three of them having an impromptu class reunion, now seasoned with a generous dash of alcohol.

"Go on back to the game," she told Doherty. "Might still catch the last quarter if you hurry."

"You sure?" he asked. "I can stay and help you process this turd if you'd like. They stitched him up quick at the hospital, but there's no room for him to stay overnight..."

"...so Brady gets the pleasure of sobering up here, does he?" She looked over and gave him a wan smile. "Won't be the first time, will it, Brady?"

"No, ma'am," he said, lowering his head.

"Won't be the last, either," Doherty said, staring at him.

"No, sir," Brady agreed quietly. "Likely not."

Doherty looked at Belinda and sighed. "Well, if you're sure about—"

"I'm sure. You go on now. Get outta here. We'll be fine."

"Belinda, you're the best."

"Hush your sweet talk, you're a married man!"

"And happily so."

"Give Sheryl my love, and get with the goin' already."

"Thanks again," Doherty said. He turned away and exited the precinct.

Belinda remained silent, taking her seat behind the desk and retrieving the necessary form to process Brady's incarceration. After writing in silence for the first five minutes, she heard Brady clear his throat.

"Permission to speak?" he asked in a hushed tone.

Belinda laughed.

"Brady," she chided. "This isn't detention and I'm not a judge. You don't have to raise your hand or ask permission to speak around here."

"I just... I didn't want to disrupt you while you were writing is all."

She looked up at him and smiled. "Well, that's awful kind of you."

"Thank you."

Brady fell silent again. Belinda stared at him. "What's on your mind, Brady?"

"I just..." he started, his eyes looking around the room as if searching for the right words, "I just wanted to say I'm sorry is all."

"Well, it ain't me you should apologize to, sounds like."

He looked over at her and frowned, not understanding.

"Doherty?" she said, leaning forward and raising her eyebrows. "*He's* the guy who got his night ruined. Not me."

Brady nodded, "Yes, ma'am. I'd guess you're right."

"Brady Brasket. I'm twenty-seven years old, only a year older than you, for Pete's sake. You don't gotta be 'ma'am'in' me."

"I know, I just... it's a habit, I guess."

"Because I'm in uniform?"

"Yes, ma'..." He stopped himself and looked down at the floor. "Yes," he repeated, nodding.

"Well, I appreciate it anyway. I might as well take what little respect I can get in life, right?"

At this Brady stood erect and lifted his head, his eyes suddenly intense. "Is someone here disrespecting you, Belinda?"

"No, I meant..."

"Because I swear to God, if I ever heard of someone comin' in who isn't treatin' you the way you oughta be treated... well... I'd like to have words with him, I would!"

Belinda held her hands up. "Whoa, there. Down boy."

"I'm serious!"

"And so am I," she said, grinning at him. Then she pointed at his chair. "Take a seat, please."

He obeyed, but his eyes were still on edge, fired up.

"Look," Belinda said quietly. "Don't you worry about me. I promise you, Brady, I can handle myself — in or *out* of my uniform."

Brady stared at her, his face suddenly flushing a bright red as he valiantly fought the urge to stare at her chest.

Belinda suddenly recognized her poor choice of words. "Now, now, I didn't mean…"

"It's okay, Belinda," he said, stifling a smile. "I understood what you meant."

"Oh, Lordy," she muttered, her own face glowing brighter. She fought to resist the smile that was trying to form across her lips.

Belinda returned to her paper again and pretended to double-check her work. Inside, her heart had begun fluttering, her mind plaguing her with an endless array of questions.

What was happening to her?

Why was her heart beating so fast?

Was she so desperate for a man that she'd suddenly found Brady Brasket, of all people, charming and funny?

Sure, he'd been a good enough kid back when they hung out in high school, but ever since he'd gotten booted out of law school Brady hadn't exactly been much of a model citizen around town. Typically little more than public drunkenness and that one count of indecency when his pants got stuck in the dryer at the laundromat.

So why in the world was she wrestling with these feelings *now*? It didn't make any sense. In fact, it downright disturbed her.

Conjuring up her most serious face, Belinda looked back at Brady. Lord, but his eye was gonna swell up good over the night. If she'd had a slab of steak she'd have slapped it on him, right then and there.

"Brady, what've you been drinking tonight?"

Brady looked down and grew a deeper shade of red, chuckling to himself.

"I say something funny?"

He shook his head. "No, you didn't."

"Then why're you laughing, Brady?"

He looked up at her and frowned, eyes pleading. "Do I gotta tell you?"

She shook her head. "No, I suppose you don't. I'm just asking, is all."

He nodded his head and looked down at the floor, then took a deep breath. "Cough syrup," he muttered, then started to chuckle.

Belinda leaned closer, not believing what she'd heard. "Cough syrup?" she repeated.

"Yeah," he said, shrugging. "Cherry flavor."

Belinda leaned back and burst into laughter. She shook her head and glanced at him, their laughter harmonizing for a solid minute. When their fit was finally finished, she jotted on his admission form and handed it to him along with a pen.

"Brady Brasket," she said, shaking her head. "You truly are something else, you know that?" She pointed to a dotted line at the bottom of the page. "Sign here, please."

He reached over and gingerly took the pen from her. "I

gotta do it with my left hand, I'm afraid. Big ox broke a few fingers on my good one." He held up his right forearm, wrapped tightly with gauze, his middle and index finger stiffened straight.

When he was finished she turned the paper around and signed her own name, then dated it and slipped the form on top of a growing pile collecting on the corner of the desk.

"Well, I was going to offer you an aspirin," she said, grinning. "But it sounds like you've got plenty of painkillers coursing through you already."

"Plus the ones the doc gave me at the hospital," Brady added, nodding his head to the side.

"Of course."

"But maybe I can have an antacid?"

Belinda picked up a nearby phone book and started thumbing through the pages.

"I said I could really use an ant—"

"Heard you the first time, honey," she said, nodding her head. "I'll see if I can't find you one later on. Now, arc you in the mood for Chinese? Or Italian?"

Brady looked at her and blinked twice.

"Dinner," Belinda said. "I haven't eaten yet and I'm starving."

"You... you're gonna have dinner with me?" he stammered, blushing again. "Like... a date?"

Belinda's face flushed. "Hell, no, this ain't a date!" she snapped. "*You're in jail!* I'm your *jailer*, Brady! No, it's not... a..." She shook her head defensively.

How dare he even think that?

How could he even say such a thing?

Oh, how he was making her blood churn.

Belinda closed her eyes and breathed in deeply. Then she opened them and locked onto Brady's one open eye. "Let me be absolutely clear: this is not a date, Brady Brasket. I'm simply offering to share some of my food with you, is all."

"Like those two dogs eatin' spaghetti?"

"Excuse me?"

"You know, in that one Disney cartoon? *Lady and the Tramp?*"

She looked at him, blinking.

"Never mind," he said, looking away.

Belinda's mind suddenly recalled the movie and the moment he was describing. Two dogs eating spaghetti and ending up selecting the same strand of pasta, culminating in their kissing. Her imagination suddenly conjured up the uninvited image of her and Brady sharing a strand of spaghetti in the center of a dirty downtown alley.

Belinda felt herself growing hotter, but this time she wasn't sure if it was out of sheer fury or... something else.

"Chinese or Italian?" she repeated louder.

"I'd rather you pick, if you don't—"

"Fine. We're getting pizza."

"Meat Lover's?" Brady asked, perking up again.

Belinda looked at him and fought hard to keep from smiling at him.

She failed miserably.

"Yes, Brady," she sighed, a warm smile forming across her lips, "We'll get a Meat Lover's."

After Belinda placed the order, the two of them walked down the steps into the basement where the jail cells were set up. The air carried a distinct blend of dust and dampness, evoking Brady's childhood memories of his grandparents' cellar. It also reminded him of the night he had spent down here two months ago when he'd been arrested for causing a public disturbance.

All three cells were empty, with the doors open wide. Belinda walked to the back corner cell and swung out her arm. "Here you go. All made up with fresh linens and everything."

"Service with a smile?" Brady asked as he walked past her.

"You wish." She placed a hand on his back and gently pushed him into the cell.

Brady walked to the cot and sat down, suppressing a smile. He wasn't sure if it was the lingering remnants of the cough syrup or the pain meds that made him feel light-headed and warm, but he wanted to believe it was neither. He looked at Belinda and sighed. "Thank you, Belinda," he said. "For everything."

She shut the cell door and locked it, sadness washing over her. "You know, Brady," Belinda said quietly, "these bars just might be the best thing to ever happen to you."

He sat on his cot and stared down at the floor, nodding his head in pensive agreement. She was right, of course. He knew she was right, and *she* knew she was right. He needed to grow up, to stop screwing around and actually do something *good* with his life for once.

Tonight could be that night. Tonight could be the night everything changed for good ol' Brady Brasket.

He watched Belinda walk away. She was worth it. She was worth changing for. He could prove to her he didn't have to be the screw-up he'd become. For Belinda Beecham? He'd never touch another drop of cough syrup ever again.

Unless he was really and truly, honest-to-God sick.

(But even then, only with her blessing.)

"Hey, Belinda?" Brady asked, suddenly standing to his feet.

She stopped walking and turned around. "Yes?"

"I just..." He shifted nervously from one leg to the other. "I just wanna say that even though I'm not particularly happy with the circumstances that brought me here right now, spending the night in jail and all..."

Brady looked up at her, focusing on her face with his unswollen eye. "I'm real glad that I'm here with you."

Belinda felt her face flush again, and hoped the lighting was too dim and his eye too swollen for him to see her blushing from across the room. She turned back and nodded, resting a hand on the bannister leading back up to the lobby.

"You get some rest, now, Brady." She started walking up the metal steps. "I'll be back down when the pizza's here."

He watched her disappear upstairs and continued to stand, staring up at the door. After a few seconds he sat back down, sighed deeply and shook his head.

Why did he keep doing this?

Why did he keep screwing up his life, making bad decisions left and right, as if it were a hobby?

He knew why.

He knew *exactly* why.

He had *always* known why... and she just left the room.

Again.

Brady didn't want to admit it, but as the question continued to skitter about inside his head, he knew exactly why he had decided to become the town screw-up.

Belinda Beecham.

Even now as a so-called "adult," Brady was too intimidated to just ask her out on a date. He spent too many years in Doherty's shadow throughout high school and beyond, afraid she'd still see him as that gawky kid who always had a crush on her.

So he'd chosen the path of least resistance. He may have lacked the guts to go up and ask her out directly, but he was a virtual genius when it came to orchestrating ways to see her on a regular basis here at the precinct.

Granted, he hadn't considered how his delinquency wouldn't exactly be the attractive factor Belinda might have been seeking in a man, but he honestly hadn't thought it through that much. He just knew he loved spending time with her, so if he could manufacture ways to make it happen more often? He would.

But... not like this.

Not anymore.

It was high time for a change in Brady Brasket's life.

Brady reclined on the cot and frowned.

This wasn't who he wanted to be. And this sure as spit wasn't the kind of man Belinda could ever respect... not in the sorry state he was stumbling into her life every other week.

Tonight hadn't been his fault, though! If it wasn't for that moronic ape at The Perky Peach, he wouldn't even be *in* this mess! Who'd ever heard of someone hating peaches? They're *peaches*, for cryin' out loud!

He shook his head in disgust, then realized he was more disgusted with himself for even starting the fight than he was with the stranger for finishing it.

Brady had made more than his share of mistakes in his lifetime. It was time to make the hard choice and be the kind of man Belinda deserved. Someone who'd stand by her side through thick and thin, who she'd not only be unashamed to be seen with, but maybe someone who she might actually be *proud* of!

Brady's eyes lit up. The sudden image of the two of them as a couple floated across his mind. She smiled and leaned forward, those emerald eyes melting him from the inside out. "I'm so proud of you, Brady," she whispered, blowing him a kiss.

Brady melted into the mattress, grinning as he stretched himself out across the cot, letting the reverie lull him to sleep. As his eyes started fluttering shut, he prayed one final prayer to a God he had ignored for longer than he cared to admit.

God? Are you there? It's me, Brady.

Just one more chance, Lord. One more chance.

Lemme have one more chance to make things right and prove to Belinda that I'm just the kind of man she needs.

One more chance, and I'll never ask you for anything else the rest of my life.

He forced his bandaged hand up to his chest and crossed his heart before quickly drifting off to sleep.

The sound of shattering glass jolted Brady from his sweet dreams. He bolted up instantly, his head throbbing from the swift movement. Instinctively he reached up to massage his temple, forgetting about his stiff, wrapped fingers. Poking himself hard in the temple, he moaned as the sharp pain shot through his fingers, radiating up his hand and arm.

He groaned, then looked around him and frowned.

Where *was* he? In jail?

What the heck was he doing in jail? *Again?!?*

Brady looked around the basement, eyes stopping when they reached the body lying on the cot in the far corneer cell. A man reclined on the mattress, hands laced behind his head and legs crossed, just relaxing. He was dressed in all black, and when he noticed Brady looking at him he lifted his chin.

"S'up," the man said, smiling.

Brady stared at him, lost in confusion. He looked down at his throbbing hand, saw the bloodstains on his shirt and suddenly he remembered it all.

The Perky Peach...

The peach-hating gorilla...

Belinda.

Belinda!

Brady heard shouting from upstairs, followed by two gunshots. Then a third. He ran to the edge of his cell and grabbed the bars with his good hand.

"Belinda!" he yelled. "What's goin' on up there? You okay?!?"

The door swung open at the top of the steps and Brady watched as a teenager with a *Pete's Pizza Pies* shirt stepped through the door frame. He was carrying a pizza box and looked absolutely terrified.

Brady frowned.

Why the heck was Belinda shooting at a delivery boy? That didn't make any sense.

The boy started to run down the steps just as Brady frantically waved his arm through the bars.

"Hey!" he yelled. "What's going on up there?!?"

The kid turned his head to glance at him, his balance wavering. One leg slipped between the last two steel steps, and Brady winced as he heard a sharp *crack*, followed by the boy falling face-first onto the concrete floor. The pizza box skittering across the distance, coming to rest just outside Brady's cell.

"Hey, you okay man?" he asked as he lowered himself down and reached for the box. His fingers brushed the edge of it, but couldn't take hold. "What's happening out there?"

The kid didn't respond. Brady grimaced as a pool of blood began to form beneath the head.

Well, that can't be good...

Two more shots from upstairs and suddenly Belinda appeared in the doorway. She cautiously descended the steps while fumbling to reload her gun.

Brady rose to his feet. Although couldn't see beyond her into the lobby, the expression on Belinda's face was enough to convince him they were all in some serious trouble.

"Look out!" he shouted, but it was too late.

Belinda stepped back on the kid's trapped leg and fell backwards, further mashing his face into the floor. Her gun flew out of her hand and skittered across the floor, bouncing off the bars before coming to a spinning stop in front of Brady's cell.

Brady knelt down, reached out his good hand and grabbed it.

"Brady!" Belinda hissed, scrambling back to her feet.

"What?!?" He looked over and caught her expression — a concerning mixture of panic and terror.

Then he saw it.

In the doorway at the top of the steps stood... an ant.

A *gigantic* ant.

Brady's eyes grew wide and he fought the urge to swear, somehow remembering Belinda was still in the room and within earshot. She backed away from the steps and ran toward Brady's cell, fumbling with the keys on her belt.

The ant resembled a fire ant, but its sheer size was mind-boggling, easily as big as a medium dog. It stood rigid on the top step, only the head and antennae twisting to better survey the room. Spotting Belinda below, it scurried down after her, stopping when it reached the delivery boy's lifeless body.

"Hurry," Brady whispered to her as she flipped through her keys. He pointed the gun ahead of him aiming it at the ant, but he had serious doubts he could A) fire it effectively, B) ever hit it from across the room or C) even pierce its outer shell.

Belinda found the key and was twisting it in the lock when a second ant appeared at the top of the steps.

Accompanied by a third.

And a fourth.

"Belinda..." Brady moaned quietly.

"Shhhhh..." she whispered, pushing the door open and

slipping inside. The cell had just clicked shut when Brady groaned again.

"What's wrong? Are you hurt?" She looked him up and down, frowning.

"The pizza's still out there..." he said, gesturing with his wrapped hand.

Belinda looked over at the pizza box outside the cell, then back at Brady. Her eyes narrowed. "Tell me you're kidding," she growled.

Brady looked at her and froze. He gulped. "I'm... kidding. Totally kidding." He glanced behind him and grabbed her by the arm. "Follow me," he said.

Leading her to the corner of the cell, he pulled the mattress off the cot and propped it up on its side in front of her. He lowered himself beside her, leaning the stained shield upright to hide them from the insects' direct line of sight.

A repulsive ripping sound filled the air as three of the ants descended upon the delivery boy, starting to brutally sever him limb from limb. Despite all the years Brady had observed ants on sidewalks as a kid, all the endless hours he'd binged on nature programs, he'd never in his life seen ants behave like this.

Two more ants ran about the room, pressing themselves against the metal bars, their hardened armor clanging loudly. At first Brady was terrified they'd soon slip between the bars, but their heads alone were simply too large to make it in. Even if they *could* somehow manage to push their head through, he doubted their bodies could follow.

Another ant broke away from the delivery boy and darted to the corner where it studied the pizza box. It picked it up with its pincers and lifted it. The perfect Meat Lover's pizza slipped out and fell face down on the floor with a wet splat. The ant studied it for a moment before losing interest and turning away.

Brady closed his eyes and sighed, trying not to focus on how insanely hungry he was. He felt Belinda's hand grab ahold of his, giving it a light squeeze.

"It's okay," she whispered into his ear. The sweet smell of her perfume wafted into his lone nostril unstuffed with cotton. "We'll order another one tomorrow. I promise."

In that instant, Brady's world was swiftly transformed. The looming threat of being trapped in a jail surrounded by monstrous, man-eating ants faded from his mind entirely. In fact, he couldn't have cared less about the ants, the pizza, or even the fact that he was in jail.

No, at that moment only three things resonated inside his head.

Belinda had said the word "we."

...closely followed by the word "tomorrow."

...and concluded with a personal promise. To *him*.

So even as the room started filling with over a half dozen ants surrounded by a weird foggy mist, and despite the fact that he heard the distant screams of people outside, none of it was enough to disturb his newfound peace of mind. Today, Brady Brasket was holding hands with Belinda Beecham, finally offering the woman he loved the comfort and protection she had always deserved.

As far as Brady was concerned, this was a picture-perfect ending to an absolutely terrible and terrifying day.

Author's Note

This story originated with a single slice of dialogue:

"These bars might end up being the best thing to ever happen to you."

I had been thinking about how God tends to orchestrate our lives in amazing, incredibly complex ways. So many times when we go through trials and endure some seriously painful circumstances, we rant and rail and shake our fists at God, accusing Him of not being fair, or loving, or whatever it might be we think His character is lacking at the moment.

Yet if we *honestly* believe that He is good at all times and that He loves us, then we can trust that He knows what He's doing — in *any* given moment of our lives.

Wait, this is becoming some kind of devotional. My apologies.

But you see my point, don't you?

Sometimes the very thing that comes into our lives, the thing we believe is the Worst. Thing. EVER....

...is actually preparing us for the future.

(I was about to say "just a blessing in disguise," but it sounded so cliché that I couldn't. Aren't you glad? Yay us.)

And who knows? Maybe we'll hear about Brady and Belinda again sometime in the future. (Assuming ants can't figure out how to chew through steel bars any time soon... ahem...)

Extermination
JACK KARDIAC

extermination

Jerry grabbed a nearby broom and dust pan and stared down at the three bloody fingers on the floor. The amount of blood seeping out of each individual digit both impressed and disgusted him. It looked as if somebody had taken a jar of spoiled jam and scooped globs onto the floor in three separate sections, decorating each with strips of strudel.

As he grimaced as he swept them with his broom, leaving long, bloody streaks in their wake. Jerry resolved to ask his wife to not make strudel for a long, long time. At least a few weeks.

Chemical Hank was unquestionably one sandwich short of a picnic, but Jerry couldn't help wondering what kind of toxic, drug-fueled concoction was floating around in the blood splattered on his formerly flawless tile floor.

He walked to the nearest trashcan and unceremoniously dumped the fingers inside, then walked toward the back office, searching for the mop and a mop bucket.

"Hey Tyler," he called out. "You know where the mop bucket is?"

"Back here with me," a voice called from around the corner. "I'm using it in the bathroom. Remember?"

Jerry frowned. Apparently the toilet was a bigger problem than Tyler had admitted earlier. He walked around the counter and saw his son pushing the mop around the base of the toilet down the hall.

"You *did* turn the water off, didn't you?" he asked, his brows furrowing in concern.

Tyler looked up and smiled. "I did," he said. "...eventually."

Jerry smiled. "Good enough. When you're done, we need to mop up that idiot's blood on the floor." He hiked a thumb over his shoulder toward the mess.

"On the dance floor?"

"Uh... what?"

"You know, that Michael Jackson song? Blood on the Dance Floor?"

Jerry looked at him blankly, not even knowing where to begin. "Um..."

"Don't worry about it," Tyler said, giving him a thumbs up. "I'll take care of it." He started humming to himself.

Jerry shook his head and laughed. He walked back around the counter into the office and was about to sit down when a bright flash lit up the room. He winced, then looked up at the corner of the room on the video monitor where the light had come from. Standing closer to the monitor, Jerry studied the video footage at the front of the store. He had yet to hear any thunder or even rainfall, but there was definitely something happening outside that looked an awful lot like lightning.

On the screen, two shadowed figures scrambled up to the door. Jerry frowned. Tyler must have forgotten to lock the front doors after letting Chester out. Were Hank and his buddy back so soon, thirsty for revenge?

No, these guys looked different, although it was hard to identify them from the poor resolution and the growing darkness outside the storefront. He watched as they pulled the front door open and ran inside. Jerry walked out of the back office toward the center of the store.

"Hello?" he called out. "Who's there? Can I help you?"

"Mr. Jerry?" a voice responded behind an aisle. "Is that you?"

Jerry smiled. There was only one person who called him "Mr. Jerry," and that was Mr. Wo, the guy who ran the eccentric Asian collectible shop up the street. He could never convince him to just call him plain old "Jerry," but that was fine, because Jerry never actually called him "Wo" either.

"Yeah, it's me. Follow my voice." He walked around the aisle and saw them huddled in the entrance area, by the front cash register. Beside Mr. Wo stood Lance — or "Lancelot" as Mr. Wo referred to him — the blind guy usually hanging out by the steps at the apartment up the street.

"You guys," Jerry said as he approached them, "You know this isn't really a good time. We just had an attempted robbery and..."

"You didn't see what happened outside?" Lance interrupted. His voice was incredulous, genuinely surprised.

"The lightning?" Jerry asked. "Sure, I saw it just now back in the office on the video monitor, but it doesn't look like it's raining, so–"

"No," Mr. Wo said, "Is not just lightning. Worse. Much worse."

Jerry noticed he was clenching a black satin satchel, his face riddles with anxiety and worry.

"Well," he said. "It doesn't look like it's raining now, so maybe the storm has passed? You guys are more than welcome to hang out here for a few minutes while Tyler and

I finish cleaning up, but then we're locking up in a few minutes, all right?"

Tyler walked around the corner of the aisle, mop in hand. "Hey Dad, where was the blood you wanted me to mop up?" He stopped when he noticed Mr. Wo and Lance standing by the counter. "Oh," he said, "Hey guys. What are you doing here?"

"They're just here to get out of the storm for a few minutes, until it clears up."

"There's a storm?" Tyler asked, eyebrows raising.

"We can't go," Mr. Wo says quietly. "Not yet."

Lance shook his head in agreement. "No way."

"Why not?" Jerry asked. "What happened out there? You two seem awfully spooked."

"We should stay here," Wo said. "Not go out. Not yet."

Jerry's frown deepened and he crossed his arms over his chest. "Okay. I hear what you're saying, Wo, but you're not telling me *why*. What's going on out there? What happened?"

Mr. Wo looked down at his hands, reaffirming his grip on the bag, shaking his head. "There is... evil... outside," he murmured quietly.

Jerry almost laughed, but caught himself. "Well," he began, "I'm sorry to tell you this, but there's evil in here too. Remember, I just told you about the two idiots who tried to rob us? So if you're trying to—"

"Dad."

Jerry looked over at Tyler. "What?"

"Wh-what the hell is that?" Tyler whispered, pointing over their shoulders toward the front of the store.

Jerry and Wo turned in unison to look up the aisle leading to the checkout counter. Lance spun in the opposite direction and faced the wall.

"What is it?" he said in a hushed tone. "Tell me what you see! I'm *blind*, remember! I can only see what you tell me!"

Jerry stared at the store window in disbelief, studying the impossibly large monster stationed outside in the center of the street. He instantly understood what his eyes were seeing, but his mind couldn't register it, couldn't make any sense out of it.

What he was seeing was... impossible.

"It's... it's an..." he stammered.

Mr. Wo swore something in another language. He didn't offer to translate it, but it sounded emphatic. Exclamatory. Possibly profane.

"What?!?" Lance said, a little louder. "What is it?!"

"It's a freaking ant," Tyler declared.

Lance balked, turning his head toward him and scowling, his mouth twisting up like someone had shoved a lemon between his lips. "A what? *An ant?!*"

"Both of you," Jerry said quietly, keeping his voice even and calm. "Be quiet."

"It's the size of a Doberman," Tyler continued, eyes transfixed on the window.

"Tyler!" Jerry hissed. He slowly reached over and placed a hand on his shoulder. "Son," he whispered. "I *really* need you to shut your mouth. Right damn now."

Tyler looked up at him and nodded. He stared back at the window in stunned silence.

The ant was alone, frozen in place, encased in shadow from the overhead streetlight. Tyler wasn't lying. It was enormous, easily the size of a large dog. A very large dog.

It stood there, antennae twitching in different directions, head aloft as if it were sampling the air, savoring it. Its entire body was a shade of reddish-brown, except for the abdomen, which gleamed a dark black. The pinchers opened and closed repeatedly, rhythmically, and even from across the street Jerry could hear the clicking as they collided into each other.

In any other circumstance it would've been considered beautiful to look at, an unparalleled and amazing specimen, if it wasn't so impossibly gigantic. Despite its curiosity, it didn't appear as if it were even aware of their presence.

Everyone in the pawn shop stood absolutely still, absolutely silent...

...until a bright flash appeared from behind them, followed by the soft sound of a camera shutter.

Jerry's eyes widened. He turned to the side slowly to find Tyler holding up his smartphone.

Realizing his mistake, Tyler lowered the phone and shook his head. "Sorry," he whispered loudly, "I didn't know the flash was on..."

Jerry said nothing. He craned his neck and stared back out the window.

The monster ant had now shifted its full focus on them.

Just as the creature started to advance toward them, an SUV careened down the street and plowed into it. The creature's massive head became wedged under the wheel well, the abdomen rolling over onto its side until it was firmly lodged beneath the vehicle's front axle.

There was a flurry of movement inside of the SUV cab, and suddenly all four doors opened as a group of people swarmed out of it, yelling loudly.

Jerry didn't see any other ants outside, but he knew it was only a matter of time, especially when one of their own had been injured. Didn't they give off some kind of a secretion? A potent "Help me, I'm injured!" aroma? A silent, telepathic scream?

He ran to the front door and opened it wide. "Hey!" he hissed at them. "Shut up and get in here! Now!"

All five people stared at him for a moment, unmoving. A second later, they bolted for the open door in unison. It was a strange group, Jerry thought: two guys wearing baseball hats, another in a suit and tie, a girl wearing jeans, a jacket and a backpack, a policewoman and a skinny redheaded guy with bandages around his hands and face, with... a pizza box tucked under one arm?

Who *were* these people?

One after the other they filed into the store, stopping just past Mr. Wo, Tyler, and Lance.

"Who the hell taught you how to drive?" the guy in the suit yelled.

"I did, actually," the larger man in a baseball cap said. "You got a problem with it?"

"Hell yes!" Wall Street barked back. "Because of him we just lost our ride!"

The man took a step closer, gesturing to Jerry and the crowd. "Because of him, we just saved these people's lives!"

The policewoman, blowing a strand of bright red hair out

of her face, stepped forward and stood between them, arms raised. "Can we all just calm down and shut up, please?"

"Yeah," the bandaged guy beside her echoed. "Just shut up already."

"That includes you, Brady," she reprimanded, glaring at him.

Brady nodded sheepishly. He continued to frown at the guy in the suit.

Seconds later, Jerry turned toward Tyler and held out his hand.

Taylor looked at it and frowned. He shrugged, mouthing the word *what?*

"Phone, please," Jerry whispered.

Tyler's shoulders sagged, and he reached behind him and pulled it out of his back pocket, handing it over. Jerry stuffed it inside his own pocket and looked back outside.

The ant was struggling to get loose from the front of the vehicle, the SUV visibly lifting up and down with all of its efforts. Jerry wasn't positive, but it actually looked like it had grown bigger than it was before it was hit. Swelling until it was almost the size of a small horse.

A moment later two other ants of equal size arrived and encircled the first, antennae twitching as if evaluating the situation. They approached it, studying it, then turned to each other and exchanged a silent message between themselves.

One locked onto the front tire with its pincers while the other fastened itself to the stuck ant's torso. In unison, they both pulled in different directions. The tire hardly budged, and their friend was still stuck, tightly trapped beneath the truck, despite its frantic wriggling to free itself.

Both ants released their grip and stepped back, reassessing the situation. Making a second attempt, they both seized the stuck ant just below the neck. With three sharp tugs, the body finally came loose and plummeted to the ground, twitching in its final moments.

The head remained wedged in the wheel well of the SUV. It had stopped twitching.

"Holy crap…" Brady whispered. "Belinda, did you see—?"

"Shhhh!" Belinda held her hand up to shush him.

"What's happening?" Lance asked.

Jerry raised his arms to silence them all, and everyone stopped talking. They watched as the two ants examined their handiwork.

The creatures scrutinized the freshly freed body, attention shifting between the head and the torso. Without a moment's hesitation, they both picked up the body and scurried away, leaving the head and a trail of clear goo in their wake.

The lifeless ant's gaze remained fixed on the pawn shop, cold, unblinking eyes glaring at the lot of them, as if blaming them for its sudden demise.

"All right," Jerry said, turning around to look at the rest of them. "If you don't mind, I think we should go ahead and move to the back of the store. Probably less chance of…" He looked over at Tyler and smiled. "Being seen by any other of those things."

"Seen by what?" Lance pressed. "What did ya'll see?"

"Nothing much," Mr. Suit and Tie muttered. "Just a little ant-on-ant treachery, death and decapitation. You know, the usual National Geographic stuff."

Lance fell silent and swallowed. He shook his head, trying to shake the images out of his mind.

They started to shuffle after Jerry toward the back office, exchanging concerned glances with one another. Tyler accompanied the baseball pair, Mitch and Mikey, while Mr. Wo placed Lance's hand on his shoulder and led him along slowly. He didn't notice the executive staring at him, eyes lingering on the bag Wo clutched tightly his hand.

Belinda and Brady followed, with the twenty-something girl walking behind them, studying all of them from a distance.

As they walked past the back counter, Mr. City Slicker motioned toward the floor where the blood splatters had almost dried. "What the hell happened here?"

Jerry looked back and shrugged. "Some people tried to rob me earlier tonight," he said. "It didn't end well for them."

The man continued to stare at the blood, his face betraying no emotion, as the others carefully walked around the puddles, following Jerry through the door into the back room.

There weren't enough seats to go around, but Jerry offered the two chairs to Belinda and the girl. The girl accepted, while Belinda chose to remain standing, arms crossed over her chest, her face a mixture of confusion and determination.

"My name is Jerry Crane," he began, "And this is my son, Tyler. Over in the corner is Mr. Wo and Lance. This is my shop, Mr. Wo works just up the street, while Lance..."

"Lancelot," Lance corrected him, grinning.

Jerry paused. "Fine. Lancelot, how would you describe what you do these days?"

"I'm a freelance financial planner," Lance said, beaming. "Currently accepting new clients."

Jerry snickered, exchanging glances with Mr. Wo, who almost managed a smile.

"What?" Office Guy asked, snickering. "We supposed to all go and introduce ourselves now? Like it's some kind of a party?"

Jerry frowned at him. "No, but considering we're probably going to be together in the immediate future as we sort things out, I'd rather call people by their actual names, rather than 'Hey you,' or 'Hey asshole.'" He paused, locking eyes with the man.

John laughed at him. "Fine. I'll start. My name is Agent John Jacobs, or 'Special Agent Asshole,' if you prefer. I work for the government."

"The government?" Tyler asked. "NSA? CIA? FBI?"

"Something like that," Jacobs answered, smirking. He didn't say anything else, but just smiled at him coldly.

"Well," the redhead woman began, "My name is Belinda Beecham, and I'm a cop, obviously." She gestured at her uniform, then nodded toward Brady. "This here is Brady Brasket—"

"Hey, Brady," Tyler blurted out.

"Hey, Tyler."

Jerry looked over at Tyler. "You two know each other?"

"Yeah," Tyler continued. "We went to grade school together. What's with the pizza box?"

Brady looked under his arm, having completely forgotten

he was carrying it. "Uhh… we ordered it for dinner… before things went wonky…"

"Those things do that to you?" It was the kid with the baseball cap.

Brady shook his head. "Naw," he said. "This happened a few hours ago, by a big, stupid gorilla over at The Perky Peach."

The older man with the baseball cap choked. "Holy—! There's gorillas out there, too?!?"

"What? No, I mean—"

"Brady," Belinda interjected, shooting him a stern look. She turned to the others. "He means a big guy. There aren't gorillas running around town, at least not that we're aware of."

"You two a thing?" Jacobs asked, pointing from one to the other.

"Excuse me?" Belinda shot back.

"Simple question," he continued. "You two got something going on? 'Cause it kinda feels like—"

"Brady is currently in my custody and under my care," she snapped. "That's all you need to know."

"Is he dangerous?" Jerry asked.

Belinda looked at him, mouth agape, as if struggling to speak. "Does he *look* dangerous to you?"

In unison they all turned to look at Brady, who held up his bandaged hands and frowned.

"Brady? You think you pose a danger to anyone here?" Belinda asked him.

"No, ma'am," he sighed, shaking his head. "Not me. Not tonight."

She looked back at Jerry. "Satisfied?"

He nodded.

"Well, now that that's settled," the older guy in the baseball hat said. "My name is Mitch, and this is my son, Mickey. We were on our way outta town when all this stuff hit the fan, and happened to run across everyone else along the way."

"Not to mention the freakin' ant in the road," Jacobs muttered under his breath.

"Do you got a problem, man?" Mitch yelled, standing to his feet. "'Cause I don't care if you have a badge or not, I will—"

"Sephanie!" the girl in the corner blurted out.

The two men broke their standoff stares and turned to look at her, along with everyone else.

"My name is Sephanie," she repeated.

"So...." Tyler said slowly. "Like Stephanie..."

She nodded. "But without the 'T'. Yeah. And... I'm a blogger and travel photographer, I guess. Still sort of trying to figure out what I want to be when I grow up."

"You mean *if* you grow up," Jacobs said, shrugging. "What with all the monster ants and all."

"What is your deal, man?" Mickey asked. "You've had a bug up your butt from the moment you hopped in the truck!"

"Yeah? I guess I have! Maybe running for my life in a city full of giant insects will do that to a guy! Did you ever think of that?!?"

"Look," Belinda said, holding her hands up between them to calm them down. "We're all pretty stressed out right now. We get it. But we're going to need to try to get along if we're going to survive this, alright?" She inadvertently glanced over at Brady. "And I don't know about you guys, but I'm pretty damn determined to live through the night."

There was a quiet murmur among them as Belinda lowered her arms, glaring at Jacobs. He smirked back at her, shook his head and looked away.

"And what about you," Jerry said, motioning to the corner of the room. "What's your name?"

They all turned their heads and were startled to see a man standing beside them, just on the outskirts of their misshapen circle. He was young, mid-20's, and had black hair cut in a professional, Wall Street kind of look. He wore an impeccable black suit, formal white shirt and a matching black tie. Hands in his pockets, he slowly looked up and smiled at them.

"Hi there," he said. "You can call me Joe."

There was a moment of stunned silence in the room, where nobody uttered a word. Belinda wasn't sure, but she thought she noticed a few of them bristle when they looked at him. She'd never seen him before in her life, but her instincts told her he was bad news, a thorn just like Jacobs had become.

"And what is it you do?" she asked.

His grin shrank for a second, his lips stretched thin as he paused to come up with a response. "I suppose you could say I'm a... collector, of sorts."

"That makes sense," Jerry said. "I saw you in here earlier, didn't I? Just before those bozos tried to rob me?"

"You did."

"You're not mixed up with them, are you?"

He shook his head. "I know them by reputation," he said. "But no, I'm not *with* them, if that's what you're asking."

"Good enough," Jerry said.

The man turned toward Sephanie, took a hand out of his pocket and waved casually at her. "Hey, Sephanie."

She frowned. "Hello…" She paused, rolling her eyes. "Joe."

"Long time no see."

"Uh-huh."

"Wait, you know this guy?" Jacobs said, jerking a thumb toward him.

She was about to respond when Joe interrupted. "You could say we run in the same circles." He flashed her a grin.

"Sure," Sephanie said. "Let's go with that."

"Well, not to break up your reunion," Belinda said. "But we really need to come up with a plan. Do any of you have an idea of what's going on? Of how those things got here?"

"Whoa, whoa, whoa," Jacobs protested, shaking his head. "Who put you in charge here? Lady, I work for the federal government! And last I checked, federal law enforcement outranks locals when it comes to decision-making. So you can just—"

"Fine," Belinda said, crossing her arms. "You're right, technically." She looked around the room. "Who wants this guy to be in charge?"

The room fell silent.

"Nobody?"

No one said a word, while a few visibly shook their heads. Belinda looked over at Jacobs and raised an eyebrow. She made a half-hearted attempt to suppress her smile.

"Screw this," Jacobs said, standing to his feet and storming out of the room.

"Alright, then," she continued, watching him leave. "Now that that's out of the way..." She looked over at Jerry, then pointed to the video monitor in the corner of the room. "Is there a way to get a live TV feed on that thing?"

"Sure," Jerry said. "Give me just a second..." He walked over and reached around back, plugging a cable into it before turning one of the knobs on the front. An image of a TV newsroom flashed on the screen. He turned up the volume.

"...repeat, if you haven't found shelter you need to do so immediately! The National Guard is on the way, but local police and emergency services are overrun at this point. Everyone is in danger, everyone is fending for themselves right now. Calling 911 will not help! So if you're watching this and you're not in a safe place, stop what you're doing and get to one immediately!" The anchorman paused, looking off screen and nodding.

"I've just received word that we're getting a live feed from downtown, so we'll cut to that now, and then..." There was a pause as the image on screen changed to a view of a downtown street. It was swarming with huge, red ants. There was no newscaster in view, only the single camera shot. Offscreen, the anchorman's voice changed pitch.

"Is that...? Oh, no... no, no no..."

There was the sound of a microphone scraping against fabric, and then frantic footsteps fading into the distance, followed by a loud banging somewhere. The studio sounds were in stark contrast to the video feed of the street, but it was clear the town had been completely and utterly overrun.

"How... how is this even possible?" Brady asked, shaking his head. "I mean, they're freaking *ants*!"

"I don't know," Jerry said. turning the TV volume down. "I just don't know."

"I know a guy with a bunker," Tyler blurted out.

"What?" Mitch asked. "What do you mean?"

"A bunker," Tyler repeated. "My friend has an underground bunker. Made it in case there was ever an apocalypse situation. Like this."

"Is it close?" Mickey asked. "Can we get to it on foot?"

Tyler's shoulders sank. "No. It's all the way across town, now that I think about it. Sorry."

The room fell silent again, processing their dilemma as a group, searching for answers and solutions.

Lance spoke. "Collector Man. What is it you collect?"

Joe shrugged. "Oh, a little bit of this, a little bit of that..."

"And you said your name was 'Joe'?"

"Yeah. Sure. I'm gonna go with Joe for now."

"Rather than Joseph?"

"Oh, hell no. I'm *definitely* not a Joseph," Joe said. "Trust me."

Mitch sighed. "So, does anyone have any idea what those things are, exactly?"

"I thought you said they were ants," Lance said. "Which, if I'm going to be perfectly honest with you, doesn't really make a lot of sense..."

"Big ants," Tyler replied. "Like, super-sized."

"They swarmed and overran the precinct," Belinda said. She bit her lower lip, staring down at the floor. "Brady and I barely got away. I... I can't imagine what it's like at the football game across town."

"Me neither," said Joe. He tried not to smile, staring at the floor while trying to appear as grim and mournful as possible.

"But as far as we know," Jerry said, "they're just ants, right? As in, there aren't any other gigantic insects or animals out there, are there?"

"We didn't see any," Mitch said, shaking his head.

"But that doesn't mean there aren't any," Mickey chimed in.

"Aren't monster-sized ants bad enough?" Lance asked.

Mr. Wo was silent the entire time, eyes fixed on the black bag in his hands. He wondered if there was any connection between what happened to him earlier that night and what was happening now. He glanced up to see Sephanie looking directly at him.

She stared at him for a few more seconds, not looking away. "I think it's safe for us to assume that those things are going to come back, likely finding a way inside," she said. "So it would probably be good if we were able to somehow defend ourselves when that happens." She looked over at Jerry. "I don't suppose you have any weapons around this place?"

"Weapons?"

She nodded.

"I assume you mean guns?"

Sephanie shrugged. "Guns, knives, whatever you think will do the job."

"Insect repellant..." Mickey said, smiling.

"That we have," Jerry said, nodding his head. "At least a few cans, for whatever good that'll do us." He shook his head.

"But all of the guns in the store are under a time lock, unfortunately."

"I'm sorry. A time lock?" Mitch asked. "How does that work?"

"Gun safe automatically locks every night at nine. Doesn't open until eight o'clock the next morning."

"Why would you ever—"

"Discourages would be thieves wanting to plan a heist when we're closed."

Mickey snickered. "Did you just say 'heist'?"

Jerry ignored him.

"I thought you said you guys had been robbed earlier tonight," Belinda said.

"*Attempted* robbery, yes," Jerry said. "But they weren't able to get away with anything valuable. Unless you count their lives, minus a few fingers and part of an ear."

Tyler laughed out loud at that, covering his mouth when he realized everyone was staring at him.

"Well, great. That's just great," Brady said, shaking his head. "So aside from Belinda here and that John Jacobs Jackhole outside, are you saying we have no guns?"

"Sorry," Jerry shrugged, shaking his head.

"That's all right," Lance said, "I probably would've shot one of y'all in the ass anyway."

"Dude," Mickey said.

"On accident, of course."

"If it's any comfort to anyone," Jerry continued, motioning to his son. "Tyler here is an excellent marksman. He's taken first prize in sharpshooting past four years running at the Indiana State Fair."

"That's pretty impressive," Belinda commented.

"Thank you!" Tyler exclaimed, his eyes inadvertently dropping down to her hip, then her holster.

Belinda smiled. "But you're not getting my gun, honey."

Tyler blushes and looks away, embarrassed.

"How about a golf club?" Lance asked. "If these things are as big as you guys say they are, maybe I could conk one or two of them in the kisser. I got a pretty mean swing, you know."

Jerry nodded. "I think we could make that happen."

"You have any balls?" Mitch asked.

Jerry glared at him. "Excuse me?"

"You know, *balls*," he repeated. "Baseballs, billiard balls, golf balls..."

"Oh, yeah!" Tyler exclaimed. "We've got a ton of balls! Follow me!"

Mitch and Mickey trailed after him while Brady and Belinda accompanied Jerry. Sephanie exchanged a glance with Joe before heading towards the exit..

Joe smiled at her. "Hey, hold on a second, Scphanic," he said walking behind her. "Can we chat? Just you and me?"

With a deep breath and sigh, she looked back at him. "Sure, why not? Let's get it over with already."

"Awesome," he said and followed her out the door.

There was silence for a few seconds and then Lance coughed loudly. "Well," he said, turning his head in Wo's direction. "Looks like it's just you and me, honeybunch."

Wo laughed, despite himself. "You wish," he said. "I'll go find you a golf club or something."

"I'll take a crossbow," Lance chuckles. "I'm not too picky, you know. And I promise I won't shoot you in the ass. Not on purpose, at least."

Mr. Wo laughed again as he walked out into the other part of the store.

"Don't mind me," Lance said to himself, settling back into his chair. "Imma just sit here while ya'll go fight off some big-ass ants…"

Sephanie strolled into the hardware aisle, casually perusing the assortment of tools and assorted items while Joe kept a discreet distance, feigning interest in the displays. She selected a crowbar, hefting it to gauge its weight, then simulated an overhead swing in the air. Turning toward Joe, she slapped it against her palm a few times, savoring its heft.

"So," she said. "What do you want?"

"Sephanie," Joe grinned at her. "We never talk anymore."

"And you wonder why that is?"

"Come on! What did I ever do to you?"

Sephanie shook her head. "Do you even have to ask?"

"Okay, Okay," he said, raising his hands in protest. "Aside from taking your parents and brother, that is."

Sephanie fell silent. The grip on the crowbar tightened, her knuckles whitening beneath the tension.

"Fine, fine," Joe said, taking a step back. "Look, I'm sorry, okay? Is that what you want to hear? I'm sorry. For *everything*."

"Save it," she snapped, "I don't want to hear it anymore." For a moment Sephanie felt a tightness in her chest, a flicker of worry for Bud and Clara over at The Perky Peach. Did they find safety? Were they safe from these insane insects outside?

Then she relaxed, remembering what she'd seen in them months before. No matter how bad things were going to get tonight, how hopeless the situation might seem from the outside, she knew they would make it. She was sure of it.

"Look, I get it," Joe continued. "You don't like me much. That's fine. But honestly, I just... I can't help but wondering..." Joe raised a hand behind his head, rubbing his neck nervously. "How are you doing?"

"How am I *doing*?" she repeated.

"Yeah." He nodded. "I mean, how are you? Really, I mean. How are you these days? Are you doing okay?"

Sephanie laughed. "Wow. You really do suck at making small talk, don't you?"

His smile faltered. "Can you blame me? Nobody really wants to talk to me when I show up, as you can imagine. And if I could be perfectly honest with you? I've had a pretty crappy week so far, so maybe you could give me a bit of a break, huh?"

"Oh really? Am I hurting your feelings, Joseph?"

His lips drew tight. "A little," he said. "Yes. And maybe that surprises you..."

"Oh no, I know you can feel things... I just didn't think remorse or sadness was one of them."

"What? You think my life is a continuous, non-stop party? Like I feel nothing but giddiness and glee? Like I'm up all the time?"

Sephanie shrugged, staring at him.

"Well, I'm not. And you know what else? I'll have you know, a lady shoved my hand down a garbage disposal yesterday! Then turned it *on*! Hurt like hell!"

"You would know..."

"Yes! *Exactly!* I *would* know! Thank you very much! Then I—"

"Why are you *here?*" Sephanie said, glaring at him.

"What do you mean?"

"You know exactly what I mean. *Joe.*"

"Sephanie..." he said softly, shaking his head. "Why are you playing games with me? You *know* why I'm here. In fact, you know who I'm here *for.*" He stood back, crossing his arms. "Don't you?" It wasn't a question.

Sephanie drew silent.

"Who's it going to be?" Joe asked. "The blind guy? That grouchy owner, the one with the corn cob up his butt? Please say it's him. Or maybe his kid? Oh! I know! It's the lovebirds, isn't it?"

"I'm not telling you," Sephanie muttered.

"Is it the baseball guy and his kid? I'll bet it is. Funny thing, he came up on my calendar the other year, and ever since he's kind of sidestepped me a few times already. Now *that* would be pretty satisfying, if I could be honest."

"You're sick."

"It's him, isn't it?" he rubbed his hands together. "Oh, man, am I looking forward to this."

"It's not him," she said, shaking her head.

Joe laughed. "Uh-huh. Okay, then. You know, you should really try playing more poker someday. Just saying."

Sephanie looked away from him, shaking her head.

"Or maybe..." he said, looking at her more closely and raising his eyebrows. "It's you."

She remained silent, the look in her eye faltering for a moment.

He walked around her in the aisle and turned to face her,

still keeping his distance. "Tell me the truth. Can you even *see* your own number? Is that a thing? I bet there's a mirror around here somewhere, if you give me a minute…

"What about you?"

"Excuse me?" he said, confused. "What about me?"

"You ever considered that maybe it's you this time?" Sephanie asked.

"'Maybe it's me?'"

She nodded. "Why not? Would it bother you if it was?"

Joe hesitated for a second, frowning. He began chuckling nervously. "What… what are you even talking about? Of *course* it's not me! It *can't* be me! I mean… I'm *me*." He forced a smile on his face. "And there's only one *me*."

Sephanie laughed loudly. "Are you sure of that?"

Joe's frown returned, growing deeper. "That's not funny. Why are you laughing? Are you saying you've seen someone else? Another…" he lowered his voice, glancing back over his shoulder. "Me?"

She covered her mouth for a moment, then lowered her hand. "You honestly believe that, don't you?"

"Believe what?"

"That you're the only one. That you're… what? Indispensable? You're irreplaceable?"

Joe's lips pulled tight across his mouth, his eyes widening.

Sephanie thought she saw his skin lose a bit of color, becoming even paler in the fluorescent lighting.

"Wh… what are you saying?" Joe demanded, stepping closer to her. "Are you telling me there's someone else? Is that what you're saying? That I'm not…" he shook his head. "Not…"

Joe's face darkened. He stepped toward her, his face a mixture of confusion and frustration.

Sephanie held the crowbar up behind her, preparing to swing.

"Is everything okay here?"

Sephanie turned around to see Belinda and Brady at the end of the aisle. Belinda's hand casually rested on her holster, while Brady held what looked like a samurai sword between his bandaged hands, leaning the blade against his shoulder.

Sephanie smiled and nodded. "Yes," she said looking back at Joe. "We were just having a long overdue conversation. Maybe more of a *revelation*, you could say." She gave him a smirk and took a few steps back in the aisle toward Belinda.

"Brady," Belinda said curtly, "would you please see this gentleman back to the office? We're going to have a little bit of girl time here, if you don't mind."

Brady nodded, taking a step toward Joe. He lowered the sword a little bit onto his shoulder. "Hey," he said as he approached Joe. "Check it out! I got myself a sword, man! You want one? I think they had another in the other aisle. 'Course, it's not as nice as this one, but I think you might like it."

Joe stared at him. He glanced back at Sephanie, frowned, and turned to face Brady. "No, I don't need a freaking sword," he growled. "I have all the swords I could ever want back home." He stomped past Brady, headed toward the back office.

As soon as they left the aisle, Sephanie turned around and smiled at Belinda. "Thank you."

"Not a problem," Belinda said. "So, is he an old boyfriend or—"

"No!" Sephanie protested, a little too loudly. "No, no, no... he is *not*. Never was. Never *will* be."

Belinda held up her hands in defense. "Alright. Fine. I just thought maybe..."

"No," Sephanie repeated, shaking her head. "There is absolutely *nothing* romantic about my relationship with that guy, whatsoever."

"With Joe."

Sephanie laughed. "Sure. If that's what he's going by these days, we'll just stick with that."

"That's not his real name?" Belinda asked.

Sephanie sighed. "Joe. Damien. Forsyth. The guy changes names as often as some guys change their underwear, so really doesn't matter what he goes by."

"I don't know about you, but most guys I know don't change their underwear as often as you think they do."

Sephanie smiled. "Point taken."

"You're saying he's bad news? That maybe I need to keep an eye on him?"

Sephanie took a deep breath and looked away for a few seconds before locking eyes with Belinda. Her features softened as she focused her peripheral vision on the numbers above Belinda's head. "No," she said, smiling, "you won't. Joe's not going to pose a problem for you tonight. I promise."

Mitch and Mickey walked around the corner of the aisle ahead of them, both carrying large buckets and sporting matching grins. Mickey looked at them and his smile widened. "Ladies," he said proudly, "we have balls."

Belinda groaned. "Oh, Lordy."

Mitch frowned and shook his head. "I'd just like to take a moment and apologize for my son..."

"Thank you," Sephanie said.

"...what he *meant* to say was, 'Ladies, we have BIG balls.'" Mitch raised his bucket and removed out a sizable softball. "And lots of them."

Belinda looked over at Sephanie and rolled her eyes. "Apple doesn't fall far from the tree with these two, does it?"

"What can I say?" Mitch said, walking past them. "Kid has a knack for wind up and delivery."

"Please tell me that's not a euphemism," Sephanie said.

"Only for baseball, madame," Mitch said, grinning at her. "Only for baseball."

As the four of them gingerly stepped around the three bloody puddles on the floor, Belinda glanced at the counter and caught sight of the silver gun on it. She looked over at Jerry, standing behind the counter. "I thought you said you didn't have any guns."

He frowned at her, and then glanced down at the counter. "You mean this thing?"

She nodded.

"Oh, you don't want anything to do with this," he said, shaking his head. "This thing has been bad news from the moment it came in here. Trust me."

"If you say so." Belinda walked past him toward the office. "Just keep it away from the kids, alright?"

"Absolutely."

John Jacobs was approaching the office from the back of the store when he stopped, turned left, and looked down the aisle. Mr. Wo was walking in his direction, holding his satchel in one hand and a golf club in the other. When Wo saw Jacobs he stopped walking, the two men frowning at each other. They continued to stare for a full five seconds, John Jacobs studying the other man's face and attire. When his eyes fell down to the satchel, he raised his eyebrows, perplexed.

"Who the hell are you?" Jacobs asked.

Mr. Wo remained still and silent. He stared back at him, his eyes cold, revealing little.

Jacobs glanced down at the bag again and then back up at Wo. "You going to answer that or not?" he asked, jutting his chin toward the bag.

Wo looked at him and frowned, his eyes narrowing. "Whatever it is you think you hear," he said, "you do not." He shook his head. "You need to turn back, walk away now."

Jacobs bristled at being ordered around. He took a step closer. "Who *the hell* are you?" he repeated, growing angrier. "And why in the *hell* is the President of the United States calling *you!*?"

Wo blinked. "Excuse me?"

Jacobs thrusts a finger toward the satchel. "There it is again!" he yelled. "It's still ringing! I know you can hear it, old man! And I *also* know what the President's emergency phone sounds like, okay? I *told* you, I work for the *government*! So whoever you are, you need to give that phone to me right now and let me take care of this, okay? Stop messing around already!"

Mr. Wo took a step back, pulling the bag behind his back. "No," he whispered quietly, "not again."

"You think I'm kidding, buddy? I am not. I am most definitely *not* kidding," Jacobs said, stepping closer. "Now hand it over!"

Wo raised the golf club, preparing to swing.

Jacobs took a step back and laughed. "Whatever, guy," he said, reaching behind him. "Didn't anyone ever tell you? You don't bring a golf club to a gunfight."

"This is not a fight you can win," Mr. Wo said. He shook his head sadly. "You do not know what this is. You don't—"

"Are you kidding me right now? Mister, I'm the *only* one here who knows *exactly* what that is *and* what it means! That phone is our ticket out of here!"

"No!" Wo yelled. "It is not what you think! You do not want this. Please, *listen to me!*"

"Shut it," Jacobs said, unholstering his gun and whipping it in front of him. "Now hand it over!"

"No!"

"I *will* shoot you, buddy. Don't think that I won't!"

"Hey! What's going on here?" Jerry stood in the office door, trying to assess the situation.

Jacobs looked back at him and sneered. "Nothing! It's none of your concern, old man! Get back inside." He turned back around to confront Wo, but the man is gone.

"Dammit!"

Running down the aisle, Jacobs had decided against turning to the left, reasoning Wo would probably predict that Jacobs would predict he'd try to hide in the back of the store.

Instead he turned a quick right, ducking just as a golf club whistled through the air where his head had been. Jacobs swore and lashed out with his free fist, punching Wo hard in the gut.

The older man stumbled backward, losing his grip on the golf club as it clattered to the floor. He wrapped both hands tightly around the neck of the satchel. After regaining his balance, he stood up straighter, glaring back at Jacobs.

"Hey!" Jerry yelled again coming around the counter to confront Jacobs. "What the hell are you doing? I thought you said you were an agent!"

Jacobs moved closer to Wo. "I am! And this is official special agent business, so back off!"

"Hell if I will! This is my shop, and if you think you can..." Jerry's voice trailed off, growing quieter. "...if you think..."

There was a long pause.

"Oh crap," he whispered.

Jacobs glanced back at Jerry, realizing the man had shifted his focus off of him. Instead the older man's gaze was fixated on the front of the store, captured by the large window behind Mr. Wo.

A gigantic ant — easily twice the size of the one they had previously encountered — now observed them through the window pane.

Surrounded by a half a dozen smaller ants, each the size of a toy poodle, all entranced by what was happening on the other side of the glass.

"Oh crap," Jacobs whispered.

"Wo!" someone shouted from the office. "Run!"

A small, white blur flew through the air, smashing into Jacobs's gun hand. It went off with a bright flash, the loud report punctuated by the silence surrounding it.

Jacobs swore as the baseball fell to the floor. Instinctively he stepped forward and kicked it, then watched regretfully as it ricocheted off a few panels across the room, finally rolling to a stop against the front door's lower window pane.

A dozen insect eyes turn in unison, staring at the ball.

Mr. Wo ran.

Mr. Wo darted away from the store's front just as the glass door erupted into fragments behind him. He caught the sound of something scraping against the door frame, instinctively looking back as an ant the size of a moose struggled to force its way inside.

Up ahead of him, Mitch and Mickey had positioned themselves behind the counter, pitching balls of all sizes past Wo as he ran down the aisle toward them. The balls bombarded the encroaching ant, each projectile hitting it squarely in the head, one of them lodging into one of the insect's eyes.

The ant reeled back, attempting to retreat but getting pinned as another ant tried to squeeze through the frame behind it. As they both squirmed in the entrance, Wo saw the shadows of countless other ants approaching from the street, curious antennae tapping against the plate glass window pane.

A third ant appeared behind the others and charged forward, shattering the glass upon impact.

"Oh crap," Mitch exclaimed, continuing to throw balls at the onslaught of ants. "Oh crap, oh crap, oh crap..."

"Dad..." Mikey said, a note of concern saturating his voice. Both of his arms continued flinging baseballs as quickly as they could swing. "*Dad...*"

"I know, I know..." he said, starting to back away from the counter.

Mr. Wo turned to run, stopping when he felt his arm jerk backward beside him. He looked back, prepared to kick at an ant, but instead saw John Jacobs backing away from him, one hand pointing the gun at him.

The other holding the satchel.

"I'll take this, thank you very much," Jacobs said. He turned and ran down the aisle, away from Wo and the onslaught of ants.

"No!" Wo exclaimed, but it was too late.

It was too late for all of them.

"We must go!" Wo yelled at Mitch and Mickey as he ran toward them, waving his arms frantically. "Go now! Or we all die!"

"We're goin', we're goin'!" Mitch yelled. He and Mickey dumped the rest of their balls over the counter into the aisle in the hopes of slowing down the red, glowing, growing horde rushing toward them.

The three of them scrambled toward the back office as the sound of chaos and destruction grew louder behind them. They had no idea why the creatures were giving off an eerie glow, but the reddish-orange light from behind cast their shadows on the walls ahead of them, like ghostly figures pointing the way to safety.

The sound of gunfire erupted in the store, and Belinda appeared at the end of the aisle along with Jerry and Brady, backing toward the office. Behind them, a frantic ant scrambled about on the floor in pain, struggling to remove the samurai sword buried in its upper torso.

As the three of them scrambled around the counter, they noticed Joe ahead of them at the open door. He had a gleeful grin, holding an arm to the side as if ushering them into the room. As soon as they poured through the doorway, he stepped into the doorframe and leaned into the room.

"See you real soon," he said, bouncing his eyebrows in excitement. Then he stepped back and shut the door, leaving them all bewildered.

"What the..." Jerry stuttered. "What does that idiot think he's doing?"

"What?" Lance said from the back corner. "What's happening? Someone tell me what's—"

"Gigantic ants are attacking the store!" Tyler yelled. "An' that guy — Joe — just shut us in here!"

"And he's still out there?"

"Yeah!" Mickey says.

"With those things? Those ants?" Lance asked, confused.

"*YES!*" Jerry said.

More gunfire erupted from outside, followed by another window shattering in the distance.

Lance frowned. "So... he's like a rootin' tootin' cowboy or something? A hero?"

Sephanie coughed. "Uh, no. He's most definitely *not* a hero. Trust me."

"But why else would he...?"

"I have no idea, but whatever his reasoning? It's all about him and *only* about him."

"Shut up!" someone yelled.

Everyone stopped talking and looked over at Mr. Wo, shaking and on the brink of tears. "Shut up! Shut up!! You must listen to me or you all die!"

"Excuse me?" Brady said, "You can't talk to Belinda like—"

"SHUT UP!" Wo screamed. "OR EVERYONE DIE!"

Everyone stopped talking, staring at him.

"That man... Jacob! He took bag. Very bad bag! Evil inside! When he open..." Wo paused, looking at his hands, shaking. He remembered what had happened to those kids outside his store a few minutes ago, out in the street, how they had all died horrible, painful deaths.

"The only way to live is cover eyes, like this..." He placed his hands over his eyes, pressing them against his face firmly. "Understand?"

They all stared at him, unmoving.

"Ummm...." Mickey said, looking around the room. "I don't think playing peek-a-boo will—"

"Listen to him," Sephanie interrupted, stepping up beside Wo. "He's telling the truth."

Mitch frowned. "And how would you know if...?"

"I just... I just know, okay? And if you guys would just listen to him and do exactly what he says..." She paused to glance around the room at each person's invisible, individual number hovering above their heads. "You'll all survive tonight. I promise."

Jerry coughed. "So, Wo," he said. "You're saying we have to keep our eyes covered? For how long? What if—"

"Until I say it clear," Wo said. "Until then..." He covered his eyes with his hands again. "You keep eyes shut."

Jerry nodded. "Alright then. Tyler?"

"Yeah?"

"Would you please come stand by me, son?"

Tyler frowned, then walked across the room. Jerry reached over to the counter and grabbed a nearby rag. He folded it over quickly and lifted it up, placing it over Tyler's eyes. "Hold this here, please."

Tyler held it against his head, trying to keep from laughing. Jerry opened a drawer, retrieved a roll of duct tape and started wrapping, moving Tyler's hands aside as he encircled his head.

"Dad! What—"

"Sorry, son," Jerry said as he finished, pressing the tape firmly into place against Tyler's head. "I'm not taking a chance. Not tonight."

"Brady," Belinda said, reaching past Jerry and retrieving the roll of tape.

"Yeah?" Brady said, looking over at her.

"Hands over your eyes, please."

Joe strolled leisurely through the store, indifferent to the swarm of ants surrounding him. They disregarded him as well, scurrying through the aisles in search of elusive prey. He admired their relentless tenacity, appreciated their formidable size. Like the others, he had no idea how they grew to such large proportions, and he didn't care.

He loved what they were doing, their contribution to the cause. How they came to be was irrelevant. The numbers didn't lie. It was a great day to take a life.

The echo of another gunshot resonated from the back corner of the store, prompting Joe to change his direction as he slowly sauntered toward it.

John Jacobs in a bad place, fending off a small, tenacious ant with a deep red, limp pool noodle. He had long ago thrown his gun away and was now trying to beat it off with the flimsy pool toy, to little effect. The creature grabbed hold of the noodle and yanked, almost causing Jacobs to lose his balance. He yelped, fighting to regain his balance and caught sight of Joe watching him across the room, arms crossed.

"Help me!" Jacobs screamed. "Do something!!"

Joe shrugged. Then he reached into his pocket and pulled out the gun that had been sitting on the counter. He smiled as he tossed it into the air where Jacobs deftly caught it with one hand.

Jacobs stared down at the gun. It was clearly old, and didn't look like it would be effective against these terrors whatsoever, but he didn't care. He was desperate, and an old gun was better than no gun at all.

"I wouldn't do that if I were you," Joe called out. *Here comes the boom.*

John Jacobs lowered the gun toward the nearest ant, leveling the sight at its head and pulled the trigger.

Nothing happened.

He swore, pulling the trigger again. A bright flash erupted from the end of the muzzle, the ant recoiling away from him for a moment, a small, neat hole having formed on the left side of its head, now leaking a luminescent, glowing substance.

Joe raised his eyebrows, surprised. "Well, that was a bit unexpected," he said to himself.

Jacobs aimed at the ant as it pushed forward, ignoring the wound. He pulled the trigger. A second flash discharged from the rear of the gun, sending an errant bullet directly through the crook of his elbow.

Screaming, Jacobs dropped the gun and used his good arm to scramble on top of a nearby display case, careful not to drop the satchel. The holey ant had scurried aways, and for a few fleeting moments, he felt safe.

Jacobs placed the satchel between his knees and frantically began pulling on the cord around the top of it with his one good hand.

"Cue the fireworks!" Joe yelled gleefully from across the room. "Siss! Boom! Bah!"

Jacobs ignored him. He swore in frustration, unable to undo the knot with his one hand. Holding the satchel up to his mouth, he clenched his teeth tightly over the rope and yanked as hard as he could. The cord unspooled and fell limply to the floor, the bag's opening falling loose.

He grabbed the bag at its base and dumped it over at his feet, searching for the phone that he knew was somewhere inside of it, the call that would save his life.

The satchel was empty.

"What the... that's impossible!" Jacobs yelled. He picked up the bag, studied it and turned it over again, shaking it harder. He slammed it down on the top of the display case repeatedly, swearing loudly as absolutely nothing fell out.

Then he froze, hearing it once again.

The distant ringing.

It was still inside the bag.

Jacobs was about to look into the mouth of the bag when something shot out of it, crashing through the ceiling above him.

He swore and stumbled back, steadying himself as he teetered close to the edge of the display. Overhead he heard a deafening roar in the sky, echoing across the city. The building began to tremble, as if caught in an earthquake. He cast a quick glance at the bag and noticed the thick smoke billowing out of the opening, caressing his skin. Panic surged inside him and he hurled it away, chucking it into the center of the store where it continued to fill the aisle in a dense, gray haze.

The room reverberated with growling, the air becoming thick with the spreading smoke. John looked up at the hole in the ceiling overhead. He thought he detected movement, a fleeting impression in the darkness, and then he spotted them —two massive, luminous eyes peering back at him through the mist.

John didn't hesitate. He vaulted from the display case, but it was too late. The dragon emerged from the opening in a swift, fluid motion, like a snake strike, seizing him midair.

John's scream was abruptly cut short as the creature stretched its neck upright, swallowing the man whole.

Joe laughed. "Impressive."

The dragon ignored him, coiling its expansive body into

the back corner of the store and scanning the room with its glowing eyes, as if assessing the unfolding situation.

Its keen eyes zeroed in on Joe, who nonchalantly offered a wave in its direction. The dragon grunted in contempt, expelling a fresh plume of smoke from its nostrils. Amidst the dense haze, it detected the frenzied glimmers of glowing embers in motion, homing in on the sound, the movement.

A tight, strained smile spread across the creature's lips, and then it began.

It lowered its head to the floor, focused on a pair of dog-sized ants tentatively approaching it. It snapped out at them at lightning speed and retracted back to the corner, reassessing the frenetic activity of the ant army spreading throughout the store. Deep within itself, it listened to the anguished screams of John as he encountered the stomach's new additions. The dragon's eyes pulsated in delight.

Moments later, a brilliant radiance emanated from the dragon's belly, swiftly coursing through its entire body. It was full of energy. Full of new life. It had never felt more alive, more invigorated. The crimson glow briefly subsided, the dragon calculating its next action.

It was eternally hungry. Insatiable. These creatures had provided it with the greatest form of sustenance and satisfaction it had experienced in a thousand lifetimes. They belonged to it, *inside* it.

As the ants launched their assault upon the dragon, overwhelming it with their relentless bites, pinches and stings from every angle, an earth-shaking roar escaped the monster's mighty jaws. Undeterred, the ants persisted in their onslaught, signaling the swarm to continue. Bending down, the dragon seized the largest among them, clamping its formidable jaws together repeatedly, rending the massive creature into mush.

Ant innards fell from its jaws and splattered on the floor, luminescent blood oozing down the dragon's neck like an overflow of glowing lava. The dragon's eyes flared with resurrected bloodlust, and its body shook with anticipation.

Sweeping through the store from wall to wall, it consumed every ant in its path, each one proving to be even more gratifying than the previous morsel.

When the store had been cleared, it hovered briefly, scouring the area for anything that may have escaped its attention.

Joe stepped out into the middle of the aisle. The dragon, its eyes aglow with a bright orange radiance, turned its head toward him, fixating on him. He began a slow applause as he chuckled to himself, strolling across the room toward the colossal creature. It had expanded to three times its initial size, its immense form straining to contain itself within the cramped confines of the store.

"Wow," Joe remarked, his tone laced with awe. "I mean... just... *wow*."

He pivoted, extending his arms as he surveyed the store. "That's truly impressive," he continued. "Seriously, I've never seen anything quite like it. Ever! Not even joking!"

The dragon's breath was soft, labored, heavy inhalations and exhalations as it keenly observed Joe's every movement. Its lips curled back, baring its formidable teeth.

"Whoa, whoa... easy there, big guy," he said, raising his hands in surrender. "Sun's gettin' real low, okay?"

The dragon stared down at him, transfixed.

"You understand me, right? You understand THE

WORDS THAT ARE COMING OUT OF MY MOUTH?"

"Of course you do," Joe said dismissively, waving a hand. "You're not some dumb beast, right?" He leaned in toward the dragon conspiratorially. "Look, you and me, we speak the same language. And I gotta say, I'm *really* diggin' your style. Seriously, if I were a dragon? An all-you-can-eat ant buffet would be my idea of heaven. You may think I'm lying, but no joke, I would *love* it."

Joe leaned back and shrugged, feigning boredom as he lifted a hand to inspect his nails.

"But you wanna know what's even better than scarfing down a handful of apocalyptic ants?" he asked, pointing at the monster. "I'll tell ya what... a city FULL of 'em!"

The dragon's lip curled, a rumbling growl forming in its throat. Joe didn't seem to notice.

"Does the big dwagon want some nom noms?" Joe cooed mockingly. "A little yum-yum chow for my friend? Yeah? Come on, then. Follow me."

Joe walked down the aisle toward the front of the store when suddenly he lurched forward, pushed from behind.

Joe frowned. What just happened? Did that thing just nudge him? Did that stinking lizard just push him with its snotty, oversized snout? Gross!

He whirled around and stared back at the dragon, which had enclosed the distance between them to a few feet. The creature's jaws moved leisurely, a steady rhythm as if chewing on something.

Joe's eyes narrowed. Was that a strip of black cloth hanging off its lip? It looked slick, almost shiny, kind of like...

...his suit.

Joe craned his neck, glancing over his shoulder at his butt, or what was left of it. One entire cheek was now missing, blood beginning to stain his suit. The gaping wound didn't hurt whatsoever, which shocked him. Why didn't he feel anything?

Then the tingling began, a gradual numbness that began to spread.

Joe stared at his butt, fascinated. So *that* was how it felt when he touched someone else! He managed a brief smile before the rising fury consumed him.

"*What. The hell*," he growled. "Why'd you go and do that for? I'm on your side, you big idiot!"

The dragon continued to chew, staring at him in boredom. It suddenly stopped, turning its head to the side, as if sensing something new, something it had missed.

It locked eyes on the office door in the back of the room.

Joe forgot all about his indignity, and ran across the store until he positioned himself between the dragon and the door. "What are you doing?" he yelled, shaking his head. "I just told you where you can fill up! Outside! All you can eat!"

The creature stopped a few feet from him, raising its head and inhaling deeply, mouth agape as it savored the invisible scent.

"Cut it out," Joe snapped, his anger escalating. "This is insane. Go outside already! Get out of here! *Bad dragon!*"

Ignoring him, it advanced toward the office.

Joe lunged forward and punched it in the snout.

The dragon jerked back in shock. It shook its head from side to side, trying to eliminate the tingling spreading across its face, a numbness unlike anything it had ever experienced. It lowered its head and locked eyes with his, growling deeply.

"Look, I get it," Joe said, staring it down. "And any other day I'd say have it, kill 'em all, but..." He looked over his shoulder at the office, picturing the occupants inside. Joe sighed, and turned back to face the dragon, his face firm and resolute.

"I'm only going to say this once," he said, shaking his head slowly. Tears welled up in his eyes, and despite his efforts to hold them back, two droplets collided and traced a line down his cheek.

"You can't have her." Joe lifted a hand and wiped his cheek clean. "*Ever.*"

The dragon hovered in front of him and snorted, a muted chuckle escaping its throat.

"You know you're smarter than this. Back off. *Now.* Or I promise you, this night won't end well for you. I guarantee—"

It suddenly surged forward, jaws wide, engulfing him completely. Joe shrieked in shock, and even when the mouth closed his stream of muffled profanities continued as he slid down the gigantic gullet.

The monster retreated to the center of the room, coiling around itself. It glanced back at the office and then away, a pained look in its eyes.

Its glow intensified once again as its body refueled with a renewed sense of power. Its horned head bumped against the ceiling tiles as its body expanded, forcing its bulk toward the only escape at front of the store. With a forceful burst, the creature shattered the remaining window structure ahead and spilled out onto the street. Within seconds it had disappeared around the corner and vanished into the fog-filled night in search of more food.

Wo didn't move.

Even after the echoes of screams had faded into the distance, carrying with them the distinct tremors caused by the creature, he remained rooted in place, hunched over on the floor, his hands firmly covering his eyes.

They were safe inside the room, just as Wo had said they would be, as Sephanie had promised them. But was it truly over? Was it safe to see?

Wo stayed silent, breathing deliberately as he gradually rose to a kneeling posture. He strained his ears to catch any sounds beyond the door. Aside from the distant wail of car alarms, he heard nothing.

No dragon.

No ants.

Shifting one of his fingers aside, Wo cautiously observed through the gap. Everyone in the room had their hands over their eyes. Even Brady and Tyler had remained silent during the ordeal, despite the obvious discomfort of having their hands taped to their heads. It had been a wise choice, Wo thought. Better to safeguard a loved one than risk losing them to the beast.

A low growl emanated from somewhere across the room, and Wo shuddered, closing his eye again, covering his face. Was it back? Had it somehow returned to the store, breaching the room, like an unseen spirit?

"Hey. Wo."

It was Lance, sitting in the corner. Even though he'd been blind for the greater part of his life, he had also elected to cover his eyes, just to be safe. "Wo," he repeated, a little louder.

"Hush," Wo hissed.

Lance shut his mouth.

The growling resumed, accompanied by the distinct sound of air being displaced, and the distinct sound of scurrying feet.

"Wo," Lance said again, putting his hands down at his sides. "That thing? The dragon thing growling?"

"Hush!" Wo whispered.

"It ain't in here," Lance continued. "It's coming from the TV. Through the speakers."

"He's right," Jerry said, lowering his hands and staring at the monitor across from him. "Look!"

The screen displayed the abandoned TV news feed, the camera having toppled onto its side. The image consisted of the gigantic ants, no longer acting in synchronized movement or purpose. Instead, they scattered in all directions, a chaotic frenzy as they scrambled to evade the tenacious demon descending upon them from the sky.

"Holy... crap..." Mitch said, tapping Mickey on the shoulder. "That's... that's..."

"Yes," Wo said quietly. "The dragon."

"Wait, what's going on?" Tyler said, turning his head and hands to face the monitor.

"Yeah!" Brady yelled. "I can't see nothin', here!"

"Welcome to my world, sonny," Lance said.

"Hold still, Brady," Belinda chided through gritted teeth

as she removed her knife from her belt. "I don't want to accidentally cut you."

Within seconds they all gathered around the screen, watching the scene unfold, transfixed. The ants were being swiftly sucked into the dragon's massive jaws as it darted across the city streets. Even though confined to such a small monitor, it was clear to everyone watching that three things were happening.

First, the dragon's glow became brighter with each and every ant it ate.

Second, it continued to grow, its length easily equivalent to a twenty-car train and its girth at an estimated thickness of a small tunnel.

And third… it really, *really* liked eating ants.

"What's happening?" Lance asked.

Sephanie reached over and grabbed one of his hands, holding it in both of hers. "So, there's a gigantic glowing dragon, and it looks like it's eating all the ants…"

"Eating ants!" Brady exclaimed. "That thing is practically a Giant Ant Hoover! Thing's sucking them down like they're hot wings dipped in my mama's buffalo sauce!"

Belinda glanced at him and was about to say something, but stopped herself. She smiled, nodding at him, realizing his description was more accurate than anything she could have come up with in the moment.

Within seconds all the ants had vanished from their viewpoint, yet the dragon continued to flash across the camera, darting between buildings in search of additional prey.

"Oh, no..." Wo whispered.

"What?" Tyler asked. "What is it?"

"I think..." Wo said slowly. "It is coming back."

A wave of fear pulsed through the room, but then Jerry held a hand up to keep them quiet. "Hold on," he said. "I don't think so..." He pointed at the screen.

The dragon teetered on the fringes of the screen, lingering above the downtown area. It no longer moved about the city, but hovered in the sky, almost frozen in place.

Belinda narrowed her eyes and moved closer to the screen. "Is it me, or is that thing..."

"Shaking?" Mitch said. "Yeah, I'd say it is."

The massive creature hung suspended in the air. It began to twitch and jerk, as if it were having a seizure every time its internal glow pulsated.

"I know that look," Brady said, shaking his head. "That thing's gonna blow chunks."

"Oh yeah," Tyler said, nodding in agreement. "He's gonna hurl any second now."

It didn't.

Instead, it suddenly swelled up, doubling to twice its size...

...and popped.

Exploded, actually.

The TV screen erupted in a blinding white flash, and the room was suddenly engulfed in a deafening boom from outside. The impact was immediate; the entire space shuddered and shook as if caught in the throes of an earthquake. Sephanie's scream cut through the chaos, and she clung tightly to Lance, her nails inadvertently digging into his arm.

Gradually the violent tremors coursing through the building subsided, the room's reverberations fading away. Everyone uncovered their ears and exchanged glances with each other, unsure what to do next.

"I want y'all to be honest with me, now," Lance said. "Did we just die?"

"No," Jerry said, laughing. "We are most certainly not dead, Lance."

After they had gathered their courage and cautiously emerged out of the confines of the office, they took in the utter chaos around them. The once orderly displays now resembled a battlefield, strewn with debris. Amidst the wreckage, a gaping hole marred the ceiling near the back corner of the store.

Wo, undeterred by the disorder, separated himself from the group, carefully navigating through the scattered remnants as he made his way toward the back of the store.

"Wo?" Jerry's voice cut through the silence. "Where you going?"

Wo held a hand up but said nothing, absorbed in his task. With deliberate movements, he cleared obstacles from his way until he stood beneath the hole in the ceiling, his gaze fixed upon it with a furrowed brow.

He searched his surroundings, moving aside displaced clutter until he located it.

The satchel.

Approaching it carefully, he lowered his foot down on the velvety surface, the softness yielding beneath his weight. He stomped on it twice in a deliberate, almost cathartic gesture of sadness and regret. Stepping back, he breathed deeply and braced himself, waiting for any sign of a response.

Silence.

A brief moment passed, then Wo's hands moved with practiced precision, securing the attached cord around the satchel's mouth. With deft movements, he twisted and knotted the cord repeatedly, cinching the opening shut as tightly as he could.

A fleeting sense of relief washed over him, like a cool breeze after a severe storm. The weight of the night's events seemed to lift from him, replaced by a peace and sense of purpose. All was not lost. They could rebuild, reclaim their neighborhood, their city, even in the wake of such demonic devastation.

The corners of his mouth turned upward, a tentative smile breaking through the exhaustion and tension. It was over. The nightmare was finally over.

He turned to return to the others, but stopped himself when he felt the satchel's weight increase, almost imperceptibly. It was subtle, but he has felt the shift inside both it and himself.

The smile on Wo's face faltered, replaced by a growing unease as he heard it, the low, ominous growl resonating from within.

This was not The End.

Author's Note

I'm a short story writer at heart, but you already know this. Truth is, I've written a handful of novels as well. One was a suspense thriller that closely resembled parts of *Die Hard*. Another was about a mud monster terrorizing a remote village in **Papua, Indonesia**. Then there are the half-baked ones, the missionary thriller, the teen spy caper, and one other I can't recall at the moment.

Point is, you haven't heard of my novels because I don't like working on them. My attention span is a rare commodity, and spending endless hours editing a novel makes me not like that novel very much. The more I play with it, the less fun it becomes.

Will they ever see the light of day? Eh... maybe? But not anytime soon. I'm having too much fun writing short stories! Which brings me to *Extermination*.

Extermination, much like *Predators* in Snapdragon and *Collision Course* in Squint, is a comprehensive culmination of the stories that preceded it, and at a little over 12,000 words, it's technically a novelette. (Not to be confused with the cooler-sounding *novella*, which is between 20,000 and 60,000 words...)

Was it easier to write than a novel? Sure. More satisfying? Absolutely. Being able to weave those characters together into one setting and come up with a decent resolution? Most rewarding. But it also took 3 full days of editing to get it in shape. (For you budding writers out there, dictation is a fast way to get your story thoughts out on the page. It's also a great way to make a mess that you have to go through and polish up later...)

Still, like the other stories in the mix, I liked how it came out and tied up this satchel of sweet and savory stories in the end. But I'm biased, so if you enjoyed *Death & Peaches*, would you please consider leaving a review for it online? Please? Your kind words go a long way to bumping up the algorithm, and rewards me with fuzzy feelings that make me want to write and publish more short stories, more often.

Again, thanks for your patience all these years. Hopefully you felt it paid off. :)

- Jack

Final Note: This *is* The End.

<h1 align="right">acknowledgments</h1>

I don't do these things by myself, you know. I have many, many accomplices who helped, and I'd like to call them out here.

My Beta Readers. You were exposed to my rough drafts, plodded through the muck and gave me suggestions on how I might shape those Play-Doh monstrosities into something beautiful (or at least, a bit less misshapen). My appreciation and respect for your time and attention is boundless, and I am in your debt.

I'm talking to you, John Prentice, Steve Richards, Lou Boothe, Betsy Love, Alissa Holyoak, Breanna Cypers, Aria Gray, Emily Walker, Doc Marvel, Petticoat Betty / Persephone, Rachel Smith / Entrada Publishing and Amandear. Thank you all!

My Advance Readers. I might've thought I'd ironed out all the rough spots in these tales, but your laser eyes helped me see the errors in my ways. I can't thank you enough for your help!

Thanks be to Chase Claussen, Laura Hodgson, Steve Richards (*pulling double duty*) and Alina & Josiah Harris.

My Esteemed Editors. Everybody needs an editor, especially me. I love editing, as most of you know. But you know what I also love? People who are equally dedicated to the craft and aren't shy about slicing and dicing my words to make them bleed (and shine). As always, any and all mistakes, errors and logic are a result of my pigheadedness and NOT a reflection on your shiny skill set.

Let's give it up for Cindy Draughon, Sharayu Marracino, Madison Lawson and Laura Hughes at Stag Beetle Books. These stories wouldn't be what they are without you.

My Readers. You've made it to The End. Again, you had a lot of other things you could have (and probably *should* have) been doing instead of reading this book. So please know that you are my greatest fan, and I look forward to connecting with you in the future on the next collection. It'll be worth the wait! (And I promise, the wait won't be as long next time...)

Oh, and your reviews and kind words go a long, long way is helping these stories get noticed on certain online platforms. (Hint, hint...) So if you've made it this far and you're still grinning from your dopamine boost, please consider leaving a review where you purchased said book? I'd really, really appreciate it!

about the author

Jack Kardiac was born in **Siloam Springs, Arkansas** and grew up in **Tulsa, Oklahoma**. He was raised on a steady diet of comic books, **Twilight Zone** episodes, and **Alfred Hitchcock** paperbacks. He sometimes  watches *Die Hard* every Christmas and *Peter Jackson's King Kong* every summer. Almost.

When he's not writing, he's reading books he wished he'd written or comic books he collected as a kid, watching too much *Futurama*, and gorging on instrumental swagger rock, funk and indie pop, with a dash of EDM and post-rock.

Jack recently returned from the remote jungles of Indonesia where he taught **Creative Writing** to young, impressionable minds, and currently lives in the place of his birth once again.

And yes, he still has a twin brother.

why stop now?
(Even More Short Stories Written Just for You!)

Using a deft mix of **humor**, **horror** and **humanity**, the 11 original stories in *Squint* feature some of the standard **Jack Kardiac** themes fans have come to love: **creatures, super-powered people** and swift **justice** for all! Without question, *Squint* is guaranteed to give you some surprises you won't soon forget! (*Complete with original covers, illustrations and author's notes for each story.*)

In ***Squint: And 10 More Surprising Short Stories***, you'll experience:

> *...an angry teen shooter who makes a fatal mistake.*

> *...a carjacking victim who comes up with a permanent solution.*

...a guy discovers it's never a good idea to steal a girl's Taco Bell.

...a soldier waking up to confusion and terror in a strange land.

...a con-man who receives a life-changing message from God.

...a little girl defending her family the only way she can.

...one tribe's sizable savior that soon becomes an even bigger problem.

...a mugging gone horribly wrong (Hint: it pays to know the right people).

...an angry father, a heartbroken daughter and an unexpected gift.

...a rich and powerful businessman

who finally finds his place in the world.

...the end of the world (slightly more fun with a friend).

Have a taste for the *unexpected*?

Craving stories that are short and sweet, yet nicely spiced?

Snapdragon will feed your need.

In 7 original stories ranging from creepy creatures to unlikely assassins and a few sudden surprises, **Snapdragon** brings you...

• A desperate man who's asked to do the impossible in *End of the Rainbow*...

• An assassination attempt that has unexpected consequences in *Assassin's Suicide*...• A hike in the woods that spins out of control when a tall stranger comes out to play in *Kicking Around*...

• A prehistoric predator that finds its proper place among the food chain in *A Light Snack*...

• A hired goon who has more than one reason to hate Florida in *Orange, Black & Blue*...

• A friendly neighbor watching his friend's cat gets more than he bargained for in *Model Pet*...

• A kidnapping that's suddenly cut short when a girl's secret friend comes to her aid in *Snapdragon*...

Written for fans of **Alfred Hitchcock**, **Richard Matheson** and **The Twilight Zone**, **Snapdragon** will satisfy you with stories to sink your teeth into. But let the reader beware: some of these tales just might bite back...

just desserts
a la mode

There were so many extra graphics to go along with the book, but we just didn't have enough room for it all!

Thankfully, they're easily-uploaded to the internet. So grab your phone or tablet, flip the page and scan the QR code to go get your goods. (Or visit www.jackardiac. com/DeathAndPeaches/ExtraArt directly)

- Jack

Original Death & Peaches Art from Lexi Linton

Art by Eden Pittman

Okay, NOW you've reached The End. 😀

For reals.

Which also means it's a fantastic time to take 3 minutes out of your schedule and jot a quick, pithy review. Even if you just give it a few stars, it counts. Seriously. Every bit helps.

Much thanks!

- Jack